L'ATLANTIDE

ADVENTURE LIBRARY
VOLUME 5

Pierre Benoit

(aka *Atlantida*—or—*The Queen of Atlantis)*

Translated by Mary C. Tongue and Mary Ross

With a foreword by David Hatcher Childress

With an introduction by Doug Ellis

2013
Normal, IL

PUBLICATION HISTORY AND COPYRIGHT INFORMATION

Copyright © 1920 Ridgway Company. From ADVENTURE, August 18, September 3, 1920.

ISBN 978-1-884449-35-2

"Foreword" copyright © 2013 David Hatcher Childress.

"Editor's Introduction" copyright © 2013 Doug Ellis.

Cover photographs © Nejron | Dreamstime.com and © Icon72 | Dreamstime.com.
Cover design by Tom Roberts.

Black Dog Books, 1115 Pine Meadows Ct., Normal, IL 61761-5432.
www.blackdogbooks.net / info@blackdogbooks.net

This is a work of fiction. All names, characters, places and scenes portrayed are products of the author's imagination. Any resemblance to actual persons, living or dead, is purely coincidental.

Publisher's note: This story is a reflection of the time period and accepted ideals of the era in which it was written. This book may contain language and opinions that some readers may find objectionable.

Contents

Foreword: The Lure of Atlantis

As we look back at the early days of human civilization I like to think that it goes many tens of thousands of years into the past. The idea that there was a human civilization some 10,000 years ago or more is considered to be fiction by most historians of today. But those of us who are interested in the topic would say that such a civilization—or civilizations—must have existed before the last Ice Age. The general name for such a pre-Ice Age civilization comes from the Greek philosopher and historian Plato who said it was *Atlantis*. In French it is *Atlantide*.

Atlantis is but one of many ancient sagas to be regarded by academia as a legend. The city of Troy, whose war against the Greeks was chronicled by the ancient poet Homer in *The Iliad,* was long held to be a myth until pioneering German archaeologist Heinrich Schliemaan uncovered its ruins in 1870s.

Many tales found in *The Bible* were considered as nothing more than stories or parables. But in recent decades archeology has proven to be one of *The Bible's* closest allies. "A wave of archaeological discoveries is altering old ideas about the roots of Christianity and Judaism . . . and affirming that the Bible is more historically accurate than many scholars thought," stated *U.S. News & World Report.*[1]

With the finding of a half-mile stone causeway, resting twenty feet under the surface off the north shore of North Bimini Island in 1968, media attention again focused on the possibility of proving Plato's story of the lost civilization. Quickly dubbed the Bimini Road, the causeway's discovery gave credence to psychic Edgar Cayce's 1936 prediction that the "Lost Continent of Atlantis" would be found in the Bahamas. Many documentaries about Atlantis are now filmed in the waters off Bimini and feature the massive submerged stonework that comprises the Bimini Road. Having scuba dived over the Bimini Road, I can tell you it is a wonder to behold.

Famed oceanographic explorer Jacques-Yves Cousteau, aboard the research vessel, *Calypso,* led a highly-publicized thirteen-month expedition throughout the Mediterranean, seeking evidence of Atlantis. Cousteau's team of researchers

---

1   J. Mann "New Finds Cast Fresh Light on the Bible" *U.S. News & World Report,* August 24, 1981, p.34

and divers ended its search of the Aegean in 1976, looking for traces of the ancient civilization around the Greek island of Santorini. The caldera comprising Santorini proves it to be the site of one of the largest volcanic eruptions in recorded history and a possible candidate as the location for Atlantis. Cousteau's findings were presented in the documentary *Calypso's Search for Atlantis* (1978).

Other underwater "ruins" near Cyprus, Malta, Morocco, the Azores, and the Canary Islands have been sighted as evidence for Atlantis. Indeed, wherever megalithic ruins—above water or below it—are found, there is often some association with Atlantis, especially if some evidence of an island catastrophe can be found. It is said that more books have been written about Atlantis than any other subject—except the Bible. And that book also has stories of a pre-flood civilization that today we would give the name "Atlantis."

L'Atlantide, the award-winning and great adventure novel by Pierre Benoit, puts an interesting new turn onto the Atlantis story. Benoit set his ancient civilization in an inland sea. As this sea dries up due to climatic changes, Atlantis, instead of being swallowed up by the ocean in the traditional telling, is swallowed up by the arid shifting sands of the North African desert.

Each new archeological or geological discovery sparks further interest and study in the ongoing search for Atlantis—the discovery of new megalith sites; a bronze statue uncovered here, an newly translated ancient text or perhaps a mosaic tile floor newly excavated—harkens back to the lost splendors told of the advanced culture of the ancient Atlanteans.

With so many ancient writings and legends now being proven accurate by modern archaeology, who is to say that Atlantis won't yet be discovered?

David Hatcher Childress
Desert Redoubt, January 2013

David Hatcher Childress is an explorer, author, publisher and world traveler. Called the real life "Indiana Jones," his writings focus on alternative history and historical revisionism and include topics on ancient archaeological sites, technology of the gods, lost cities, ancient astronauts, the Knights Templar and Nikola Tesla. Among his many books are *Lost Cities of Atlantis, Ancient Europe & The Mediterranean* (Adventures Unlimited Press, 1995) and *Atlantis and the Power System of the Gods* (Adventures Unlimited Press, 2002), co-authored with Bill Clendenon.

Featured in the History Channel's series "Ancient Aliens," Childress has also appeared on A&E, Discovery Channel, Travel Channel, NBC and the Fox Network.

Visit David's website at www.DavidHatcherChildress.com.

Editor's Introduction

Few novels that appeared in the pulp magazines can lay claim to having won a major literary award, having been translated into 15 languages, having sold over two million copies and having been filmed at least eight times. Pierre Bénoit's classic tale of Atlantis, *L'Atlantide,* is one of those few.

To be fair, *L'Atlantide* (which was serialized in the pulp magazine *Adventure* in two installments, August 18, 1920 and September 3, 1920) did not first appear in a pulp. Its original publication—in Bénoit's native French—was in book form in France in February 1919, but its appearance in *Adventure* marked its first English language publication. Bénoit's second novel, *L'Atlantide* was a rousing success, winning the Grand Prize of the French Academy in 1919. Bénoit wrote several novels during the next decade, and was admitted into the Academy in 1931. He remained a prolific novelist throughout his life, with over 40 novels published.

The silent *L'Atlantide* (1921), starring French actress Stacia Napierkowska in the title role of Antinéa.

The first of the film adaptations of *L'Atlantide* was filmed the same year as its appearance in *Adventure,* although it wasn't released until 1921. Directed by French-Belgian film maker Jacques Feyder, *L'Atlantide* was a silent movie shot in North Africa, the same location as the setting for the novel. It was enormously popular in France, and is perhaps the best of the film adaptations of the book. The next version to be filmed, *L'Atlantide* (1932, also known as *The Mistress of Atlantis),* directed by Georg Wilhelm Pabst and starring Brigette Helm (of *Metropolis* fame) as Antinea, was also shot in North Africa. It too is well done and remains fairly faithful to the novel. Subsequent films are of lesser interest, although many have their moments.

Bénoit's father was a military officer

L'Atlantide (1932), starring Brigette Helm.

in the French army, stationed in French North Africa. It was there that Bénoit (1886-1962) grew up, living in the French colony for 15 years, from 1892 to 1907. When Bénoit writes of the region in L'Atlantide, it is from the vantage point of one who spent his formative years there and is very familiar with the region, its people, and their customs and legends, as well as the activities of the French military in the area. This authentic depiction of an exotic backdrop, against which Bénoit sets his fantastic lost race tale, perhaps contributed to its enthusiastic reception.

Following L'Atlantide's translation into English, it was sold to Adventure, the leading general fiction pulp of the day. Its editor, Arthur Sullivant Hoffman, felt the story read better as a complete novel and intended to run it as such in the August 18, 1920 issue. However, after that issue had been typeset and was ready to go to press, Bénoit's agent contacted Hoffman, requesting that the novel be serialized in Adventure. Publication complete in one issue would, the agent felt, harm the potential for a book sale. Hoffman reluctantly agreed, hastily moving "The Rest Cure" by Farnham Bishop forward from its intended appearance in the September 3, 1920 issue and splitting L'Atlantide in two, with about 80% of it appearing in the first installment.

Hardcover book publication in the U.S. did follow later in 1920, as the novel was published by Duffield and Company under the title Atlantida. The translation used was the same one that had run in Adventure, with minor changes due to differing editorial policies between the two publishers. The translation as it appeared in Adventure is reprinted here for the first time in book form. Although the translators were not credited in Adventure, Mary C. Tongue and

10

Mary Ross were given their proper credit in the book edition. Concerning this translation, in a letter to "The Camp-Fire" *(Adventure's* letter column) published in the January 10, 1922 issue of *Adventure,* Arthur Gilchrist Brodeur (then Professor of English at University of California, Berkeley and a regular contributor as an author to the magazine), wrote the following:

> Recently I met Professor Gilbert Chinard, of Johns Hopkins, who was at the University of California until last year. I mentioned to him that bully story of Pierre Bénoit's—*L'Atlantide.* I said that the English style was so admirable that I was sure the author himself made the translation for *Adventure;* for I couldn't conceive of so splendid a translation being done by any but a stylist who knew English as well as French, and to whom French was native. But Professor Chinard told me that the translation was made by a girl in this country, who had been sharply and unjustly criticized, in reviews of the story, for the quality of her translation. He urged me to tell you my opinion of her work, in order that something might be done to counteract the wrongheaded criticism that had been heaped upon her.
>
> I know something about translation, having put in the best part of four years on such a job myself, and having studied very carefully the technique of translation before I felt ready to get at it. Translation as it is usually done is rotten hack work; but at its best it is a fine art. Sometimes it is much harder than the original composition. I regard the English translation of *L'Atlantide,* as it appeared in *Adventure,* as the best specimen of the translator's art that I ever saw.

The work that Brodeur alludes to having translated was *The Prose Edda* by Snorri Sturlson. His translation was published by The American-Scandinavian Foundation in 1916 and remains in print to this day. As does Pierre Bénoit's timeless classic of lost Atlantis and its beautiful but terrible Queen, Antinea— *L'Atlantide.*

Doug Ellis
Chicago, Illinois

A practicing attorney, Doug Ellis is one of the foremost researchers and collectors of pulp magazines in the world. A 1996 recipient of the Lamont Award, he is the founder of Tattered Pages Press, a small publishing house devoted to the study and reprint of pulp-era material; and is the publisher of *Pulp Vault,* a scholarly journal devoted to the all-fiction magazines.

Doug is also the author of *Uncovered: The Hidden Art of the Girlie Pulps* (Adventure House, 2004), the first in-depth study of the girlie magazines, and co-author of *The Adventure House Guide to the Pulps.* For Black Dog Books he has edited *In the Grip of the Minotaur* by Farnham Bishop and Arthur Gilchrist Brodeur, *King Corrigan's Treasure* by H. D. Couzens, *The Black Death* by Marion Polk Angellotti and the acclaimed *Best of Adventure* series.

Introductory Letter

Hassi-Inifel, November 8, 1903

If the following pages are ever to see the light of day it will be because they have been stolen from me. The delay that I exact before they shall be disclosed assures me of that.

As to this disclosure, let no one distrust my aim when I prepare for it, when I insist upon it. You may believe me when I maintain that no pride of authorship binds me to these pages. Already I am too far removed from all such things. Only it is useless that others should enter upon the path from which I shall not return.

Four o'clock in the morning. Soon the sun will kindle the *hamada* with its pink fire. All about me the *bordj* is asleep. Through the half-open door of his room I hear André de Saint-Avit breathing quietly, very quietly.

In two days we shall start, he and I. We shall leave the *bordj*. We shall penetrate far down there to the South. The official orders came this morning.

Now, even if I wished to withdraw, it is too late. André and I asked for this mission. The authorization that I sought, together with him, has at this moment become an order. The hierarchic channels cleared, the pressure brought to bear at the Ministry—and then to be afraid, to recoil before this adventure!

To be afraid, I said. I know that I am not afraid. One night in the Gurara, when I found two of my sentinels slaughtered, with the shameful cross cut of the Berbers slashed across their stomachs—then I was afraid. I know what fear is. Just so now, when I gazed into the black depth whence suddenly all at once the great red sun will rise, I know that it is not with fear that I tremble. I feel surging within me the sacred horror of this mystery and its irresistible attraction.

Delirious dreams, perhaps. The mad imaginings of a brain surcharged and an eye distraught by mirages. The day will come, doubtless, when I shall reread these pages with an indulgent smile, as a man of fifty is accustomed to smile when he rereads old letters.

Delirious dreams. Mad imaginings. But these dreams, these imaginings, are dear to me.

"Captain de Saint-Avit and Lieutenant Ferrières," reads the official dispatch, "will proceed to Tasili to determine the statigraphic relation of Albien sandstone and carboniferous limestone. They will, in addition, profit by any opportunities of determining the possible change of attitude of the Axdiers towards our penetration," etc.

If the journey should indeed have to do only with such poor things I think

13

that I should never undertake it.

So I am longing for what I dread. I shall be dejected if I do not find myself in the presence of what makes me strangely fearful.

In the depths of the valley of Wadi Mia a jackal is barking. Now and again when a beam of moonlight breaks in a silver patch through the hollows of the heat-swollen clouds, making him think he sees the young sun, a turtle-dove moans among the palm trees.

I hear a step outside. I lean out of the window. A shade clad in luminous black stuff glides over the hard-packed earth of the terrace of the fortification. A light shines in the electric blackness. A man has just lighted a cigarettete. He crouches, facing southwards. He is smoking.

It is Cegheir-ben-Cheikh, our Targa guide, the man who in three days is to lead us across the unknown plateaus of the mysterious Imoschaoch, across the *hamadas* of black stones, the great dried oases, the stretches of silver salt, the tawny hillocks, the flat gold dunes that are crested over, when the *alizé* blows, with a shimmering haze of pale sand.

Cegheir-ben-Cheikh. He is the man. There recurs to my mind Duveyrier's tragic phrase—

"At the very moment the Colonel was putting his foot in the stirrup he was felled by a saber blow."[1]

Cegheir-ben-Cheikh! There he is, peacefully smoking his cigarettete, a cigarettete from the package that I gave him. May the Lord forgive me for it.

The lamp casts a yellow light on the paper. Strange fate, I never knew why, decided one day when I was a lad of sixteen that I should prepare myself for Saint-Cyr, and gave me there André de Saint-Avit as classmate. I might have studied law or medicine. Then I should be today a respectable inhabitant of a town with a church and running water, instead of this cotton-clad phantom, brooding with an unspeakable anxiety over this desert which is about to swallow me.

A great insect has flown in through the window. It buzzes, strikes against the rough cast, rebounds against the globe of the lamp, and then, helpless, its wings singed by the still burning candle, drops on the white paper.

It is an African May-bug, big, black, with spots of livid gray.

I think of the others, its brothers in France, the golden-brown May-bugs, which I have seen on stormy summer evenings projecting themselves like little particles of the soil of my native countryside. It was there that as a child I spent my vacations and, later on, my leaves. On my last leave, through those same meadows, there wandered beside me a slight form, wearing a thin scarf because of the evening air, so cool back there.

But now this memory stirs me so slightly that I scarcely raise my eyes to that dark corner of my room where the light is dimly reflected by the glass of an indistinct portrait. I realize of how little consequence has become what had seemed at one time capable of filling all my life. This plaintive mystery is of no more interest to me. If the strolling singers of Rolla came to murmur their

---

[1] H. Duveyrier, "The Disaster of the Flatters Mission." Bull. Geol. Soc., 1881.

famous nostalgic airs under the window of this *bordj* I know that I should not listen to them and, if they became insistent, I should send them on their way.

What has been capable of causing this metamorphosis in me? A story, a legend perhaps, told at any rate by one on whom rests the direst of suspicions.

Cegheir-ben-Cheikh has finished his cigarettete. I hear him returning with slow steps to his mat in barrack B to the left of the guard post.

Our departure being scheduled for the tenth of November, the manuscript attached to this letter was begun on Sunday, the first, and finished on Thursday, the fifth of November, 1903.

Olivier Ferrières
Lieutenant
3rd Spahis

This letter together with the manuscript which accompanies it, the latter in a separate sealed envelope, was entrusted by Lieutenant Ferrières, of the Spahis, the day of the departure of that officer for the Tasili of the Tuareg (Central Sahara), to Sergeant Chatelain. The sergeant was instructed to deliver it, on his next leave, to M. Leroux, honorary counsel at the court of appeals at Riom, and Lieutenant Ferrières' nearest relative. As this magistrate died suddenly before the expiration of the term of ten years set for the publication of the manuscript here presented, difficulties arose which have delayed its publication up to the present date.

Chapter I
A Southern Assignment

SUNDAY, THE SIXTH OF JUNE, 1903, BROKE THE MONOTONY OF THE LIFE THAT WE were leading at the Post of Hassi-Inifel by two events of unequal importance: The arrival of a letter from Mlle. de C—— and the latest numbers of the *Official Journal* of the French Republic.

"I have the Lieutenant's permission?" said Sergeant Chatelain, beginning to glance through the magazines he had just removed from their wrappings.

I acquiesced with a nod, already completely absorbed in reading Mlle. de C——'s letter.

> When this reaches you, mama and I will doubtless have left Paris for the country. If it be a consolation to imagine me as bored here as you possibly can be where you are, make the most of it. The Grand Prix is over. I played the horse you pointed out to me and, naturally, I lost.
>
> Last night we dined with the Martials de la Touche. Elias Chatrian was there—always amazingly young. I am sending you his last book, which has made quite a sensation. It seems that the Martials de la Touche are depicted there without disguise. I will add to it Bourget's last and Loti's and France's and two or three of the latest music hall hits.
>
> In the political world, they say the law about congregations will meet with strenuous opposition. Nothing much in the theatres. I have taken out a summer subscription for *l'Illustration.* Would you care for it? In the country no one knows what to do. Always the same lot of idiots ready for tennis. I shall deserve no credit for writing to you often.
>
> Spare me your reflections concerning young Combemale. I am less than nothing of a feminist, having too much faith in those who tell me that I am pretty—yourself in particular. But indeed I grow wild at the idea that if I permitted myself half the familiarities with one of our lads that you have surely with your Oulèd-Naïls— Enough of that; it is too unpleasant an idea.

I had reached this point in the prose of this advanced young woman when a scandalized exclamation of the Sergeant made me look up.

"Lieutenant!"

16

"Yes?"

"They are up to something at the Ministry. See for yourself."

He handed me the *Official Journal*. I read:

"By a decision of the first of May, 1903, Captain de Saint-Avit (André), unattached, is assigned to the Third Spahis, and appointed Commandant of the post of Hassi-Inifel."

Chatelain's displeasure became fairly exuberant.

"Captain de Saint-Avit, Commandant of the post. A post which has never had a slur upon it. They must take us for a dumping ground."

My surprise was as great as the sergeant's. But just then I saw the evil, weasel-like face of Gourrut, the convict we used as clerk. He had stopped his scrawling and was listening with a sly interest.

"Sergeant, Captain de Saint-Avit is my ranking classmate," I answered dryly.

Chatelain saluted, and left the room. I followed.

"There, there," I said, clapping him on the back, "no hard feelings. Remember that in an hour we are starting for the oasis. Have the cartridges ready. It is of the utmost importance to restock the larder."

I went back to the office and motioned Gourrut to go. Left alone, I finished Mlle. de C——'s letter very quickly, and then reread the decision of the Ministry, which gave the post a new chief.

It was now five months that I had enjoyed that distinction and, on my word, I had accepted the responsibility well enough and been very well pleased with the independence. I can even affirm without taking too much credit for myself that under my command discipline had been better maintained than under Captain Dieulivol, Saint-Avit's predecessor. A brave man, this Captain Dieulivol, a non-commissioned officer under Dodds and Duchesne, but subject to a terrible propensity for strong liquors, and too much inclined, when he had drunk, to confuse his dialects, and to talk to a Hausa in Sakalave.

No one, however, was ever more sparing of the post water-supply. One morning when he was preparing his absinthe in the presence of the sergeant, Chatelain, noticing the captain's glass, saw with amazement that the green liquor was blanched by a far stronger admixture of water than usual. He looked up, aware that something abnormal had just occurred. Rigid, the carafe inverted in his hand, Captain Dieulivol was spilling the water, which was running over on the sugar. He was dead.

For six months since the disappearance of this sympathetic old tippler, the powers had not seemed to interest themselves in finding his successor. I had even hoped at times that a decision might be reached, investing me with the rights that I was in fact exercising. And today this surprising appointment.

Captain de Saint-Avit. He was of my class at Saint-Cyr. I had lost track of him. Then my attention had been attracted to him by his rapid advancement, his decoration, the well-deserved recognition of three particularly daring expeditions of exploration to Tebesti and the Air; and suddenly, the mysterious drama of his fourth expedition—that famous mission undertaken with Captain Morhange, from which only one of the explorers came back. Everything is forgotten quickly in France. That was at least six years ago. I had not heard Saint-Avit mentioned since. I had even supposed that he had left the army. And now, I was to have him as my chief.

"After all, what's the difference," I mused. "He or another! At school he was charming, and we have had only the most pleasant relationships. Besides, I haven't enough yearly income to afford the rank of captain."

And I left the office, whistling as I went.

We were now, Chatelain and I, our guns resting on the already cooling earth, beside the pool that forms the center of the meager oasis, hidden behind a kind of hedge of *alfa*. The setting sun was reddening the stagnant ditches which irrigate the poor garden-plots of the sedentary blacks.

Not a word during the approach. Not a word during the shoot. Chatelain was obviously sulking.

In silence we knocked down, one after the other, several of the miserable doves which came on dragging wings, heavy with the heat of the day, to quench their thirst at the thick green water. When a half-dozen slaughtered little bodies were lined up at our feet I put my hand on the sergeant's shoulder.

"Chatelain!"

He trembled.

"Chatelain, I was rude to you a little while ago. Don't be angry. It was the bad time before the siesta. The bad time of midday."

"The Lieutenant is master here," he answered in a tone that was meant to be gruff, but which was only strained.

"Chatelain, don't be angry. You have something to say to me. You know what I mean."

"I don't know really. No, I don't know."

"Chatelain, Chatelain, why not be sensible? Tell me something about Captain de Saint-Avit."

"I know nothing." He spoke sharply.

"Nothing? Then what were you saying a little while ago?"

"Captain de Saint-Avit is a brave man." He muttered the words with his head still obstinately bent. "He went alone to Bilma, to the Air; quite alone to those places where no one had ever been. He is a brave man."

"He is a brave man, undoubtedly," I answered with great restraint. "But he murdered his companion, Captain Morhange, did he not?"

The old sergeant trembled.

"He is a brave man," he persisted.

"Chatelain, you are a child. Are you afraid that I am going to repeat what you say to your new captain?"

I had touched him to the quick. He drew himself up.

"Sergeant Chatelain is afraid of no one, Lieutenant. He has been at Abomey, against the Amazons, in a country where a black arm started out from every bush to seize your leg, while another cut it off for you with one blow of a cutlass."

"Then what they say, what you yourself—"

"That is talk."

"Talk which is repeated in France, Chatelain—everywhere."

He bent his head still lower without replying.

"Head of a donkey!" I burst out. "Will you speak?"

"Lieutenant, Lieutenant," he fairly pleaded, "I swear that what I know, or nothing—"

"What you know you are going to tell me, and right away. If not, I give you my word of honor that for a month I shall not speak to you except on official business."

Hassi-Inifel: thirty native Arabs and four Europeans—myself, the sergeant, a corporal and Gourrut. The threat was terrible. It had its effect

"All right, then, Lieutenant," he said with a great sigh. "But afterward you must not blame me for having told you things about a superior which should not be told and come only from the talk I overheard at mess."

"Tell away."

"It was in 1899. I was then mess sergeant at Sfax with the Fourth Spahis. I had a good record and besides, as I did not drink, the adjutant had assigned me to the officers' mess. It was a soft berth. The marketing, the accounts, recording the library books which were borrowed—there weren't many—and the key to the wine cupboard—for with that you can't trust orderlies. The colonel was young and dined at mess. One evening he came in late, looking perturbed, and, as soon as he was seated, called for silence:

"'Gentlemen,' he said, 'I have a communication to make to you, and I shall ask for your advice. Here is the question: Tomorrow morning the *City of Naples* lands at Sfax. Aboard her is Captain de Saint-Avit, recently assigned to Feriana, en route to his post.'

"The colonel paused. *Good,* thought I, *tomorrow's menu is about to be considered.*

"For you know the custom, Lieutenant, which has existed ever since there have been any officers' clubs in Africa. When an officer is passing by his comrades go to meet him at the boat and invite him to remain with them for the length of his stay in port. He pays his score in news from home. On such occasions everything is of the best, even for a simple lieutenant. At Sfax an officer on a visit meant one extra course, vintage wine and old liqueurs.

"But this time I imagined from the looks the officers exchanged that perhaps the old stock would stay undisturbed in its cupboard.

"'You have all, I think, heard of Captain de Saint-Avit, gentlemen, and the rumors about him. It is not for us to inquire into them. The promotion he has had, his decoration if you will, permits us to hope that they are without foundation. But between not suspecting an officer of being a criminal, and receiving him at our table as a comrade, there is a gulf that we are not obliged to bridge. That is the matter on which I ask your advice.'

"There was silence. The officers looked at each other, all of them suddenly quite grave, even to the merriest of the second lieutenants. In the corner, where I realized that they had forgotten me, I tried not to make the least sound that might recall my presence.

"'We thank you, Colonel,' one of the majors finally replied, 'for your courtesy in consulting us. All my comrades, I imagine, know to what terrible rumors you refer. If I may venture to say so, in Paris at the Army Geographical Service, where I was before coming here, most of the officers of the highest standing had an opinion on this unfortunate matter which they avoided stating but which cast no glory upon Captain de Saint-Avit.'

"'I was at Bamaku, at the time of the Morhange-Saint-Avit mission,' said a captain. 'The opinion of the officers there, I am sorry to say, differed very little from what the major describes. But I must add that they all admitted that they had nothing but suspicions to go on. And suspicions are certainly not enough, considering the atrocity of the affair.'

"'They are quite enough, gentlemen,' replied the colonel, 'to account for our hesitation. It is not a question of passing judgment, but no man can sit at our table as a matter of right. It is a privilege based on fraternal esteem. The only question is whether it is your decision to accord it to Saint-Avit.'

"So saying, he looked at the officers, as if he were taking a roll-call. One after another they shook their heads.

"'I see that we agree,' he said. 'But our task is unfortunately not yet over. The *City of Naples* will be in port tomorrow morning. The launch which meets the passengers leaves at eight o'clock. It will be necessary, gentlemen, for one of you to go aboard. Captain de Saint-Avit might be expecting to come to us. We certainly have no intention of inflicting upon him the humiliation of refusing him, if he presented himself in expectation of the customary reception. He must be prevented from coming. It will be wisest to make him understand that it is best for him to stay aboard.'

"The Colonel looked at the officers again. They could not but agree. But how uncomfortable each one looked!

"'I cannot hope to find a volunteer among you for this kind of mission, so I am compelled to appoint someone. Captain Grandjean, Captain de Saint-Avit is also a captain. It is fitting that it be an officer of his own rank who carries him our message. Besides, you are the latest-comer here. Therefore it is to you that I entrust this painful interview. I do not need to suggest that you conduct it as diplomatically as possible.'

"Captain Grandjean bowed, while a sigh of relief escaped from all the others. As long as the colonel stayed in the room Grandjean remained apart, without speaking. It was only after the chief had departed that he let fall the words—

"'There are some things that ought to count a good deal toward promotion.'

"The next day at luncheon everyone was impatient for his return.

"'Well?' demanded the colonel, briefly.

"Captain Grandjean did not reply immediately. He sat down at the table where his comrades were mixing their drinks and he, a man notorious for his sobriety, drank, almost at a gulp, without waiting for the sugar to melt, a full glass of absinthe.

"'Well, Captain?' repeated the colonel.

"'Well, Colonel, it's done. You may be at ease. He will not set foot on shore. But, ye gods, what an ordeal!'

"The officers did not dare speak. Only their looks expressed their anxious curiosity.

"Captain Grandjean poured himself a swallow of water.

"'You see, I had got my speech all ready in the launch. But as I went up the ladder I knew that I had forgotten it. Saint-Avit was in the smoking-room with the captain of the boat. It seemed to me that I could never find the strength to tell him, when I saw him all ready to go ashore. He was in full-dress uniform, his saber lay on the bench and he was wearing spurs. No one wears spurs on shipboard. I presented myself and we exchanged several remarks, but I must have seemed somewhat strained, for from the first moment I knew that he sensed something.

"'Under some pretext he left the captain, and led me aft, near the great rudder-wheel. There I dared speak. Colonel, what did I say? How I must have stammered! He did not look at me. Leaning his elbows on the railing he let his eyes wander far off, smiling slightly. Then of a sudden, when I was well tangled up in explanations, he looked at me coolly and said:

"'I must thank you, my dear fellow, for having given yourself so much trouble. But it is quite unnecessary. I am out of sorts and have no intention of going ashore. At least I have the pleasure of having made your acquaintance. Since I cannot profit by your hospitality, you must do me the favor of accepting mine as long as the launch stays by the vessel.'

"'Then we went back to the smoking-room. He himself mixed the cocktails. He talked to me. We discovered that we had mutual acquaintances. Never shall I forget that face, that ironic and distant look, that sad and melodious voice. Ah, Colonel, gentlemen—I don't know what they may say at the Geographic Office, or in the posts of the Sudan. There can be nothing in it but a horrible suspicion. Such a man capable of such a crime— Believe me, it is not possible!'

"That is all, Lieutenant," finished Chatelain, after a silence. "I have never seen a sadder meal than that one. The officers hurried through lunch without a word being spoken, in an atmosphere of depression against which no one tried to struggle. And in this complete silence you could see them always furtively watching the *City of Naples* where she was dancing merrily in the breeze a league from shore.

"She was still there in the evening when they assembled for dinner, and it was not until a blast of the whistle, followed by curls of smoke escaping from the red and black smoke-stack, had announced the departure of the vessel for Gabes, that conversation was resumed, and even then less gaily than usual.

"After that, Lieutenant, at the Officers' Club at Sfax, they avoided like the plague any subject which risked leading the conversation back to Captain de Saint-Avit."

Chatelain had spoken almost in a whisper and the little people of the desert had not heard this singular history. It was an hour since we had fired our last cartridge. Around the pool the turtle-doves, once more reassured, were bathing their feathers. Mysterious great birds were flying under the darkening palm trees. A less warm wind rocked the trembling black palm-branches. We had laid aside our helmets so that our temples could welcome the touch of the feeble breeze.

"Chatelain," I said, "it is time to go back to the *bordj.*"

Slowly we picked up the dead doves. I felt the Sergeant looking at me reproachfully, as if regretting that he had spoken. Yet during all the time that our return trip lasted I could not find the strength to break our desolate silence with a single word.

The night had almost fallen when we arrived. The flag which surmounted the post was still visible, drooping on its standard, but already its colors were indistinguishable. To the west the sun had disappeared behind the dunes gashed against the black violet of the sky.

When we had crossed the gate of the fortifications Chatelain left me.

"I am going to the stables," he said.

I returned alone to that part of the fort where the billets for the Europeans and the stores of ammunition were located. An inexpressible sadness weighed upon me.

I thought of my comrades in French garrisons. At this hour they must be returning home to find awaiting them, spread out upon the bed, their dress uniform, their braided tunic, their sparkling epaulettes.

"Tomorrow," I said to myself, "I shall request a change of station."

The stairway of hard-packed earth was already black. But a few gleams of light still seemed palely prowling in the office when I entered.

A man was sitting at my desk, bending over the files of orders. His back was toward me. He did not hear me enter.

"Really, Gourrut, my lad, I beg you not to disturb yourself. Make yourself completely at home."

The man had risen and I saw him to be quite tall, slender and very pale.

"Lieutenant Ferrières, is it not?"

He advanced, holding out his hand.

"Captain de Saint-Avit. Delighted, my dear fellow."

At the same time Chatelain appeared on the threshold.

"Sergeant," said the newcomer, "I cannot congratulate you on the little I have seen. There is not a camel-saddle which is not in want of buckles and they are rusty enough to suggest that it rains at Hassi-Inifel three hundred days in the year. Furthermore, where were you this afternoon? Among the four Frenchmen who compose the post, I found only on my arrival one convict, opposite a quart of *eau-de-vie*. We will change all that, I hope. At ease."

"Captain," I said, and my voice was colorless, while Chatelain remained frozen at attention, "I must tell you that the sergeant was with me, that it is I who am responsible for his absence from the post, that he is an irreproachable non-commissioned officer from every point of view, and that if we had been warned of your arrival—"

"Evidently," he said, with a coldly ironical smile. "Also, Lieutenant, I have no intention of holding him responsible for the negligences which attach to your office. He is not obliged to know that the officer who abandons a post like Hassi-Inifel, if it is only for two hours, risks not finding much left on his return. The Chaamba brigands, my dear sir, love firearms, and for the sake of the sixty muskets in your racks I am sure they would not scruple to make an officer, whose otherwise excellent record is well known to me, account for his absence to a court-martial. Come with me, if you please. We will finish the little inspection I began too rapidly a little while ago."

He was already on the stairs. I followed in his footsteps. Chatelain closed the order of march. I heard the sergeant murmuring, in a tone which you can imagine—

"Well, we are in for it now."

Chapter II
Captain de Saint-Avit

A FEW DAYS SUFFICED TO CONVINCE US THAT CHATELAIN'S FEARS AS TO OUR OFFICIAL relations with the new chief were vain. Often I have thought that by the severity he showed at our first encounter Saint-Avit wished to create a formal barrier, to show us that he knew how to keep his head high in spite of the weight of his heavy past. Certain it is that the day after his arrival he showed himself in a very different light, even complimenting the sergeant on the upkeep of the post and the instruction of the men. To me he was charming.

"We are of the same class, aren't we?" he said to me. "I don't have to ask you to dispense with formalities; it is your right."

Vain marks of confidence, alas! False witnesses to a freedom of spirit, one in face of the other. What more accessible in appearance than the immense Sahara, open to all those who are willing to be engulfed by it? Yet what is more secret? After six months of companionship, of communion of life such as only a post in the South offers, I ask myself if the most extraordinary of my adventures is not that I am leaving tomorrow toward unsounded solitudes with a man whose real thoughts are as unknown to me as these same solitudes for which he has succeeded in making me long.

The first surprise which was given me by this singular companion was occasioned by the baggage that followed him.

On his inopportune arrival alone from Wargla he had trusted to the *mehari* he rode only what can be carried without harm by such a delicate beast—his arms, saber and revolver, a heavy carbine and a very reduced pack. The rest did not arrive till fifteen days later, with the convoy which supplied the post.

Three cases of respectable dimensions were carried one after another to the captain's room and the grimaces of the porters said enough as to their weight.

I discreetly left Saint-Avit to his unpacking and began opening the mail which the convoy had sent me.

He returned to the office a little later and glanced at the several reviews which I had just received.

"So," he said; "you take these."

He skimmed through, as he spoke, the last number of the Zeitschrift der Gesellschaft für Erdkunde in Berlin.

"Yes," I answered. "These gentlemen are kind enough to interest themselves in my works on the geology of the Wadi Mia and the high Igharghar."

"That may be useful to me," he murmured, continuing to turn over the leaves.

"At your service."

"Thanks. I am afraid I have nothing to offer you in exchange, except Pliny, perhaps. And still—you know what he said of Igharghar, according to King Juba. However, come help me put my traps in place and you will see if anything appeals to you."

I accepted without further urging.

We commenced by unearthing various meteorological and astronomical instruments—the thermometers of Baudin, Salleron, Fastre; an aneroid, a Fortin barometer, chronometers, a sextant, an astronomical spyglass, a compass glass. In short, what Duveyrier names as material that is simplest and easiest to transport on a camel.

As Saint-Avit handed them to me I arranged them on the only table in the room.

"Now," he announced to me, "there is nothing more but books. I will pass them to you. Pile them up in a corner until I can have a book-shelf made."

For two hours altogether I helped him to heap up a real library. And what a library! Such as a post in the South had never before seen. All the texts consecrated, under whatever titles, by antiquity to the regions of the Sahara were reunited between the four rough-cast walls of that little room of the *bordj*. Herodotus and Pliny, naturally, and likewise Strabo and Ptolemy, Pomponius Mela and Ammian Marcellinus. But besides these names, which reassured my ignorance a little, I perceived those of Corippus, of Paulus Orosus, of Eratosthenes, of Photius, of Diodorus of Sicily, of Solon, of Dion Cassius, of Isidor of Seville, of Martin de Tyre, of Ethicus, of Athenais; the *Scriptores Historiae Augusti,* the *Itinerarium Antonini Augusti,* the *Geographi Latini Minores* of Riese, the *Geographi Graeci Minores* of Karl Muller. Since, I have had the occasion to familiarize myself with Agatarchides of Cos and Artemidorus of Ephesus, but I admit that in this instance the presence of their dissertations in the saddle-bags of a captain of cavalry caused me some amazement.

I mention further the *Descrittione dell' Africa* by Leon l'African, the Arabian Histories of Ibn-Khaldûn, of Al-Iaqoub, of El-Bekri, of Ibn-Batuta, of Mahommed El-Tounsi. I remember the names of only two volumes of contemporary French scholars. There were also the laborious theses of Berlioux[2] and of Schirmer.[3]

While I proceeded to make piles of as similar dimensions as possible I kept saying to myself:

"To think that I have been believing all this time that in his mission with Morhange, Saint-Avit was particularly concerned in scientific observations.

---

2   *Doctrina Ptolemaei ab injuria recentiorum vindicata, sive Nilus superior et Niger verus, hodi-ernus Eghiren, ab antiquis explored.* Paris, 8vo, 1874, with two maps. (Note by M. Leroux.)

3   *De nomine et genere popularum qui Berberi vulgo dicuntur.* Paris, 8vo, 1892. (Note by M. Leroux.)

Either my memory deceives me strangely or he is riding a horse of another color. What is sure is that there is nothing for me in the midst of all this chaos."

He must have read on my face the signs of too apparently expressed surprise, for he said in a tone in which I divined a tinge of defiance—

"The choice of these books surprises you a bit?"

"I can't say it surprises me," I replied, "since I don't know the nature of the work for which you have collected them. In any case I dare say, without fear of being contradicted, that never before has an officer of the Arabian office possessed a library in which the humanities were so well represented."

He smiled evasively and that day we pursued the subject no further.

Among Saint-Avit's books I had noticed a voluminous note-book secured by a strong lock. Several times I surprised him in the act of making notations in it. When for any reason he was called out of the room he placed this album carefully in a small cabinet of white wood, provided by the munificence of the administration.

When he was not writing and the office did not require his presence, he had the *mehari* which he had brought with him saddled and a few minutes later, from the terrace of the fortifications, I could see on the horizon the double silhouette disappearing with great strides behind a hummock of red earth.

Each time these trips lasted longer. From each he returned in a kind of exaltation which made me watch him with daily increasing disquietude during meal hours, the only time we passed quite alone together.

"Well," I said to myself one day when his remarks had been more lacking in sequence than usual, "it's no fun being aboard a submarine when the captain takes opium. What drug can this fellow be taking, anyway?"

Next day I looked hurriedly through my comrade's drawers. This inspection, which I believed to be my duty, reassured me momentarily. *All very good,* I thought, *provided he does not carry with him his capsules and his Pravaz syringe.*

I was still in that stage where I could suppose that André's imagination needed artificial stimulants.

Meticulous observation undeceived me. There was nothing suspicious in this respect. Moreover, he rarely drank and almost never smoked.

Nevertheless there was no means of denying the increase of his disquieting feverishness. He returned from his expeditions each time with his eyes more brilliant. He was paler, more animated, more irritable.

One evening he left the post about six o'clock, at the end of the greatest heat of the day. We waited for him all night. My anxiety was all the stronger because quite recently caravans had brought tidings of bands of robbers in the neighborhood of the post.

At dawn he had not returned. It was not until midday that he came and then his camel collapsed under him, rather than knelt.

He realized that he must excuse himself but he waited till we were alone at lunch.

"I am so sorry to have caused you any anxiety, but the dunes were so beautiful under the moon! I let myself be carried farther and farther."

"I have no reproaches to make, dear fellow; you are free and the chief here. Only allow me to recall to you certain warnings concerning the Chaamba brigands, and the misfortunes that might arise from a commandant of a post's absenting himself too long."

He smiled.

"I don't dislike such evidence of a good memory," he said simply.

He was in excellent, too excellent, spirits.

"Don't blame me. I set out for a short ride as usual. Then the moon rose. And then I recognized the country. It is just where, twenty years ago next November, Flatters followed the way to his destiny in an exaltation which the certainty of not returning made keener and more intense."

"Strange state of mind for a chief of an expedition," I murmured.

"Say nothing against Flatters. No man ever loved the desert as he did."

"Palat and Douls, among many others, have loved it as much," I answered. "But they were alone when they exposed themselves to it. Responsible only for their own lives, they were free. Flatters, on the other hand, was responsible for sixty lives. And you cannot deny that he allowed his whole party to be massacred."

The words were hardly out of my lips before I regretted them. I thought of Chatelain's story, of the Officers' Club at Sfax where they avoided like the plague any kind of conversation which might lead their thoughts toward a certain Morhange-Saint-Avit mission.

Happily I observed that my companion was not listening. His brilliant eyes were far away.

"What was your first garrison?" he asked suddenly.

"Auxonne."

He gave an unnatural laugh.

"Auxonne. Province of the Côte d'Or. District of Dijon. Six thousand inhabitants. P.L.M. Railway. Drill school and review. The colonel's wife receives Thursdays, and the adjutant's on Saturdays. Leaves every Sunday—the first of the month to Paris, the three others to Dijon. That explains your judgment of Flatters.

"For my part, my dear fellow, my first garrison was at Boghar. I arrived there one morning in October, a second lieutenant, aged twenty, of the First African Batallion, the white chevron on my black sleeve—sun stripe, as the bagnards say in speaking of their grades.

"Boghar! Two days before, from the bridge of the steamer, I had begun to see the shores of Africa. I pity all those who, when they see those pale cliffs for the first time, do not feel a great thrill in their hearts at the thought that this land prolongs itself thousands and thousands of leagues. I was little more than a child. I had plenty of money. I was ahead of schedule. I could have stopped three or four days at Algiers to amuse myself. Instead I took the train that same evening for Berroughia.

"There, scarcely a hundred kilometers from Algiers, the railway stopped. Going in a straight line you won't find another until you get to the Cape. The diligence travels at night on account of the heat. When we came to the hills I got out and walked beside the carriage, straining for the sensation, in this new atmosphere, of the kiss of the outlying desert.

"About midnight, at the camp of the Zouaves, a humble post on the road embankment overlooking a dry valley whence rose the feverish perfume of oleander, we changed horses. They had there a troop of convicts and impressed laborers on their way, under escort of riflemen and convoys, to the quarries in the South. In part, rogues in uniform from the jails of Algiers and Doucra—without arms, of course; the others civilians—such civilians!—this year's recruits, the young bullies of the Chapelle and the Goutte-d'Or.

"They left before we did. Then the diligence caught up with them. From a distance I saw in a pool of moonlight on the yellow road the black irregular mass of the convoy. Then I heard a weary dirge; the wretches were singing. One gave the stanza in a sad and guttural voice which trailed dismally through the depths of the blue ravines, and the others took up in chorus the horrible refrain—

> "'A la Bastille, à la Bastille,
> On aime bien, on aime bien
>   Nini Peau d'Chien;
> Elle est si belle et si gentille
>   A la Bastille'

"I saw them all in contrast to myself when the diligence passed them. They were terrible. Under the hideous searchlight their eyes shone with a sombre fire in their pale and shaven faces. The burning dust strangled their raucous voices in their throats. A frightful sadness took possession of me.

"When the diligence had left this fearful nightmare behind, I regained my self-control.

"'Further, much further south,' I exclaimed to myself, 'to the places untouched by this miserable bilgewater of civilization.'

"When I am weary, when I have a moment of anguish and longing to turn back on the road that I have chosen, I think of the prisoners of Berroughia, and then I am glad to continue on my way.

"But what a reward, when I am in one of those places where the poor animals never think of fleeing because they have never seen man, where the desert stretches out around me so widely that the old world could crumble and never a single ripple on the dune, a single cloud in the white sky come to warn me."

"It is true," I murmured. "I, too, in the middle of the desert at Tidikelt, once felt that way."

Up to that time I had let him enjoy his exaltations without interruption. I understood too late the error that I had made in pronouncing that unfortunate sentence.

His mocking, nervous laughter began anew.

"Ah! Indeed! At Tidikelt? I beg you, old man, in your own interest, if you don't want to make an ass of yourself avoid that species of reminiscence. Honestly you make me think of Fromentin, or that poor Maupassant, who talked of the desert because he had been to Djelfa—two days' journey from the street of Bab-Azound and the government buildings, four days from the Avenue de l'Opera—and who, because he saw a poor devil of a camel dying near Bou-Saada, believed himself in the heart of the desert, on the old route of the caravans. Tidikelt, the desert!"

"It seems to me, however, that In-Saleh—" I said, a little vexed.

"In-Saleh? Tidikelt! But, my poor friend, the last time that I passed that way there were as many old newspapers and empty sardine boxes as if it had been Sunday in the forest of Vincennes."

Such a determined, such an evident, desire to annoy me made me forget my reserve.

"Evidently," I replied resentfully, "I have never been to—"

I stopped myself, but it was already too late.

He looked at me squarely in the face.

"To where?" he said with good humor.

I did not answer.

"To where?" he repeated.

And, as I remained strangled in my muteness:

"To Wadi Tarhit, do you mean?"

It was on the east bank of Wadi Tarhit, a hundred and twenty kilometers from Timissau, at 25.5 degrees north latitude, according to the official report, that Captain Morhange was buried.

"André," I cried stupidly, "I swear to you—"

"What do you swear to me?"

"That I never meant—"

"To speak of Wadi Tarhit? Why? Why should you not speak to me of Wadi Tarhit?"

In answer to my supplicating silence, he merely shrugged his shoulders.

"Idiot!" was all he said.

And he left me before I could think of even one word to say.

So much humility on my part had, however, not disarmed him. I had the proof of it the next day, and the way he showed his humor was even marked by an exhibition of wretchedly poor taste.

I was just out of bed when he came into my room.

"Can you tell me what the meaning of this is?" he demanded.

He had in his hand one of the official registers. In his crises of nervousness he always began sorting them over in the hope of finding some pretext for making himself militarily insupportable.

This time chance had favored him.

He opened the register. I blushed violently at seeing the poor proof of a photograph that I knew well.

"What is that?" he repeated disdainfully.

Too often I had surprised him in the act of regarding, none too kindly, the portrait of Mlle. de C—— which hung in my room not to be convinced at that moment that he was trying to pick a quarrel with me.

I controlled myself, however, and placed the poor little print in the drawer.

But my calmness did not pacify him.

"Henceforth," he said, "take care, I beg you, not to mix mementoes of your gallantry with the official papers."

He added, with a smile that spoke insult—

"It isn't necessary to furnish objects of excitation to Gourrut."

"André," I said, and I was white, "I demand—"

He stood up to the full height of his stature.

"Well what is it? A gallantry, nothing more. I have authorized you to speak of Wadi Tarhit, haven't I? Then I have the right, I should think—"

"André!"

Now he was looking maliciously at the wall, at the little portrait, the replica of which had just been subjected to this painful scene.

"There, there; I say, you aren't angry, are you? But between ourselves you will admit, will you not, that she is a little thin?"

And before I could find time to answer him he had left, humming the shameful refrain of the previous night:

"A la Bastille, à la Bastille,
On aime bien, on aime bien,
Nini, Peau de Chien."

For three days neither of us spoke to the other. My exasperation was too deep for words. Was I, then, to be held responsible for his avatars? Was it my fault if, between two phrases, there seemed always some allusion—

"The situation is intolerable," I said to myself. "It cannot last longer."

It was to cease very soon.

One week after the scene caused by the photograph the courier arrived. I had scarcely glanced at the index of the Zeitschrift, the German review of which I have already spoken, when I started with uncontrollable amazement. I had just read:

"Reise und Entdeckungen zwei französischer offiziere, Rittmeisters Morhange und Oberleutnants de Saint-Avit, in westlichen Sahara."

At the same time I heard my comrade's voice.

"Anything interesting in this number?"

"No," I answered carelessly.

"Let's see."

I obeyed; what else was there to do?

It seemed to me that he grew paler as he ran over the index. However, his tone was altogether natural when he said—

"You will let me borrow it, of course?"

And he went out, casting me one defiant glance.

The day passed slowly. I did not see him again until evening. He was gay, very gay, and his gaiety hurt me.

When we had finished dinner we went out and leaned on the balustrade of the terrace. From there out swept the desert, which the darkness was already encroaching upon from the east

André broke the silence.

"By the way, I have returned your review to you. You were right; it is not interesting."

His expression was one of supreme amusement.

"What is it? What is the matter with you anyway?"

"Nothing," I answered, my throat aching.

"Nothing? Shall I tell you what is the matter with you?"

I looked at him with an expression of supplication.

"Idiot," he found it necessary to repeat once more.

Night fell quickly. Only the southern slope of Wadi Mia was still yellow. Among the boulders a little jackal was running about, yapping sharply.

"The dib is making a fuss about nothing—bad business," said Saint-Avit.

He continued pitilessly—

"Then you aren't willing to say anything?"

I made a great effort, to produce the following pitiful phrase:

"What an exhausting day! What a night—heavy, heavy— You don't feel like yourself; you don't know any more—"

"Yes," said the voice of Saint-Avit as from a distance, "a heavy, heavy night; as heavy, do you know, as when I killed Captain Morhange."

Chapter III
The Morhange-Saint-Avit Mission

" So I KILLED CAPTAIN MORHANGE," ANDRÉ DE SAINT-AVIT SAID TO ME THE NEXT day at the same time and in the same place, with a calm that took no account of the night, the frightful night I had just been through.

"Why do I tell you this? I don't know in the least. Because of the desert, perhaps. Are you a man capable of enduring the weight of that confidence and further, if necessary, of assuming the consequences it may bring? I don't know that, either. The future will decide. For the present there is only one thing certain: The fact, I tell you again, that I killed Captain Morhange.

"I killed him. And, since you want me to specify the reason, you understand that I am not going to torture my brain to turn it into a romance for you, or commence by recounting, in the naturalistic manner, of what stuff my first trousers were made, or, as the neo-Catholics would have it, how often I went as a child to confession and how much I liked doing it. I have no taste for useless exhibitions. You will find that this recital begins strictly at the time when I met Morhange.

"And first of all, I tell you, however much it has cost my peace of mind and my reputation, that I do not regret having known him. In a word, apart from all question of false friendship, I am convicted of a black ingratitude in having killed him. It is to him, it is to his knowledge of rock inscriptions, that I owe the only thing that has raised my life in interest above the miserable little lives dragged out by my companions at Auxonne, and elsewhere.

"This being understood," said André de Saint-Avit, "I will now continue with the facts."

It was in the Arabian Office at Wargla, when I was a lieutenant, that I first heard the name Morhange. And I must add that it was for me the occasion of an attack of bad humor. We were having difficult times.

The hostility of the Sultan of Morocco was latent. At Tuat, where the assassination of Flatters and of Frescaly had already been concocted, connivance was being given to the plots of our enemies. Tuat was the center of conspiracies, of razzias, of defections, and at the same time the depot of supply for the insatiable nomads.

The Governors of Algeria—Tirman, Cambon, Laferrière—demanded its occupation. The Ministers of War tacitly agreed. But there was Parliament, which did nothing at all because of England, because of Germany, and above all because of a certain Declaration of the Rights of Man and of the Citizen, which prescribed that insurrection is the most sacred of duties, even when the insurgents are savages who cut your head off.

In short, the military authority could only, at its own discretion, increase the southern garrisons and establish new posts: this one, Berresof, Hassi-el-Mia, Fort MacMahon, Fort Lallemand and Fort Miribel. But as Castries puts it, you don't hold the nomads with *bordjs;* you hold them by the belt. The hotbed was the oasis of Tuat. Their honors, the lawyers of Paris, had to be convinced of the necessity of taking possession of the oasis of Tuat. The best way would be to present them with a faithful picture of the plots that were being woven there against us.

The principal authors were, and still are, the Senussi, whose able chief has been forced by our arms to transfer the seat of his confederation several thousand leagues from there, to Schimmedrou—in the Tibesti. They had—I say they through modesty—the idea of ascertaining the traces left by these agitators on their favorite places of concourse—Rhat, Temassinin, the plain of Adjamor, and In-Salah. It was, you see, at least after leaving Temassinin, practically the same itinerary as that followed in 1864 by General Rohlfs.

I had already attracted some attention by two excursions, one to Agades and the other to Bilma, and was considered by the staff officers to be one of the best informed on the Senussi question. I was therefore selected to assume this new task.

I then suggested that it would be of interest to kill two birds with one stone and to get in passing an idea of the northern Ahaggar, so as to make sure whether the Tuaregs of Ahitarhen had continued to have as cordial relations with the Senussi as they had had when they combined to massacre the Flatters' mission. I was immediately accorded the permission.

The change in my plan was as follows: After reaching Ighelaschem, six hundred kilometers south of Temassinin, I would penetrate between the high land of Muydir and Ahaggar and strike off to the southwest as far as Sheikh-Salah. There I would turn northwards again, towards In-Salah, by the road from the Sudan and Agades.

In all, hardly eight kilometers additional in a trip of about seven hundred leagues, with the certainty of making as complete an examination as possible of the roads which our enemies, the Senussi of Tibesti and the Tuareg of the Ahaggar, must follow to arrive at Tuat. On the way, for every explorer has his pet fancy, I was not at all displeased to think that I would have a chance to examine the geological formation of the plateau of Egele, about which Duveyrier and the others are so disappointingly vague.

Everything was ready for my departure from Wargla. Everything; which is to say, very little. Three camels: mine, my companion Bou-Djema's—a faithful Chaamba whom I had had with me in my wanderings through the Air; less of a guide in the country I was familiar with than a machine for saddling and unsaddling camels—then a third to carry provisions and skins of drinking-water—very little, since I had taken pains to locate the stops with reference to the wells.

Some people go equipped for this kind of expedition with a hundred regulars and even cannon. I am for the tradition of Douls and René Callie; I go alone.

I was at that perfect moment when only one thin thread still held me to the civilized world, when an official cable arrived at Wargla. It said briefly—

> Lieutenant de Saint-Avit will delay his departure until the arrival of Captain Morhange, who will accompany him on his expedition of exploration.

I was more than disappointed. I alone had conceived the idea of this expedition. I had had all the difficulty that you can imagine to make the authorities agree to it. And now, when I was rejoicing at the idea of the long hours I would spend alone with myself in the heart of the desert, they sent me a stranger, and, to make matters worse, a superior.

The condolences of my comrades aggravated my bad humor.

The yearly report, consulted on the spot, had given them the following information:

> Morhange (Jean-Marie-Francois), class of 1881. Breveted. Captain, unassigned. (Topographical Service of the Army.)

"There is the explanation for you," said one. "They are sending one of their creatures to pull the chestnuts out of the fire after you have had all the trouble of making it. Breveted! That's a great way. The theories of Ardant du Picq or else nothing, about here."

"I don't altogether agree with you," said the major. "They knew in Parliament, for someone is always indiscreet, the real aim of Saint-Avit's mission: To force their hand for the occupation of Tuat. And this Morhange must be a man serving the interests of the army commission. All these people—secretaries, members of Parliament, governors—keep a close watch on each other. Someone will write an amusing paradoxical history someday of the French colonial expansion, which is made without the knowledge of the powers in office, when it is not actually in spite of them."

"Whatever the reason, the result will be the same," I said bitterly. "We will be two Frenchmen to spy on each other night and day along the roads to the south. An amiable prospect when one has none too much time to foil all the tricks of the natives. When does he arrive?"

"Day after tomorrow, probably. I have news of a convoy coming from Gardaia. It is likely that he will avail himself of it. The indications are that he doesn't know very much about traveling alone."

Captain Morhange did arrive, in fact, two days later by means of the convoy from Gardaia. I was the first person for whom he asked.

When he came to my room, whither I had withdrawn in dignity as soon as the convoy was sighted, I was disagreeably surprised to foresee that I would have great difficulty in preserving my prejudice against him.

He was tall, his face full and ruddy, with laughing blue eyes, a small black moustache, and hair that was already white.

"I have a thousand apologies to make to you, my dear fellow," he said immediately, with a frankness that I have never seen in any other man. "You must be furious with my importunity in upsetting your plans and delaying your departure."

"By no means, Captain," I replied coolly.

"You really have only yourself to blame. It is on account of your knowledge of the southern routes, so highly esteemed at Paris, that I wished to have you to initiate me when the Ministries of Instruction and of Commerce and the Geographical Society combined to charge me with the mission which brings me here. These three honorable institutions have in fact entrusted me with the attempt to re-establish the ancient track of the caravans, which from the ninth century trafficked between Tunis and the Sudan, by Toweur, Wargla, Es-Souk and the bend of the Niger at Bourroum; and to study the possibility of restoring this route to its ancient splendor.

"At the same time, at the Geographic Bureau, I heard of the journey that you are undertaking. From Wargla to Sheikh-Salah our two itineraries are the same, only I must admit to you that it is the first voyage of this kind that I have ever undertaken. I would not be afraid to hold forth for an hour on Arabian literature in the amphitheatre of the School of Oriental Languages, but I know well enough that in the desert I should have to ask for directions whether to turn right or left.

"This is the only chance which could give me such an opportunity and at the same time put me under obligation for this introduction to so charming a companion. You must not blame me if I seized it, if I used all my influence to retard your departure from Wargla until the instant when I could join you.

"I have only one more word to add to what I have said; I am entrusted with a mission which, by its origin, is rendered essentially civilian. You are sent out by the Ministry of War. Up to the moment when, arrived at Sheikh-Salah, we turn our backs on each other to attain, you Tuat, and I the Niger, all your recommendations, all your orders, will be followed by a subaltern, and, I hope, by a friend as well."

All the time he was talking so openly I delightedly felt my worst recent fears melting away. Nevertheless, I still experienced a mean desire to show him some marks of reserve for having thus disposed of my company at a distance and without consulting me.

"I am very grateful to you, Captain, for your extremely flattering words. When do you wish to leave Wargla?"

He made a gesture of complete detachment.

"Whenever you like. Tomorrow, this evening. I have already delayed you.

Your preparations must have already been made for some time."

My little maneuver had turned against myself. I had not been counting on leaving before the next week.

"Tomorrow then, Captain. But your luggage?"

He smiled delightfully.

"I thought it best to bring as little as possible—light pack and some papers. My brave camel had no difficulty in bringing it along. For the rest I depend on your advice and the resources of Wargla."

I was well caught. I had nothing further to say. And, moreover, such freedom of spirit and manner had already captivated me.

"It seems," said my comrades when the time for aperitifs had brought us all together again, "that this captain of yours is a remarkably charming fellow."

"Remarkably."

"You surely can't have any trouble with him. It is only up to you to see that later on he doesn't get all the glory."

"We aren't working with the same end in view," I answered evasively.

I was thoughtful—only thoughtful, I give you my word. From that moment I harbored no further grudge against Morhange. Yet my silence persuaded him that I was unforgiving. And everyone—do you hear me—everyone—said later on when suspicions became rife:

"He is surely guilty. We saw them go off together. We can affirm it."

I am guilty. But for a low motive of jealousy? How sickening!

After that, there was nothing to do but to flee, flee to the places where there are no more men who think and reason.

Morhange appeared, his arm resting on the major's. He was beaming over this new acquaintanceship.

He presented him enthusiastically:

"Captain Morhange, gentlemen. An officer of the old school, and a man after our own hearts, I give you my word. He wants to leave tomorrow, but we must give him such a reception that he will forget that idea before the time comes. Come, Captain, you have at least eight days to give us."

"I am at the disposition of Lieutenant de Saint- Avit," replied Morhange with a quiet smile.

The conversation became general. The sound of glasses and laughter rang out. I heard my comrades in ecstasies over the stories that the newcomer poured out with never failing humor. And I, never, never have I felt so sad.

The time came to pass into the dining-room.

"At my right, Captain," cried the major, more and more beaming. "And I hope you will keep on giving us these new lines on Paris. We are not up with the times here, you know."

"Yours to command, Major," said Morhange.

"Be seated, gentlemen."

The officers obeyed with a joyous clatter of moving chairs. I had not taken my eyes off Morhange, who was still standing.

"Major, gentlemen, you will allow me," he said.

And before sitting down at that table, where every moment he was the life of the party, in a low voice, with his eyes closed, Captain Morhange recited the *Bénédicité.*

CHAPTER IV

Toward Latitude 25

"Y OU SEE," SAID CAPTAIN MORHANGE TO ME FIFTEEN DAYS LATER, "YOU ARE much better informed about the ancient routes through the Sahara than you have been willing to let me suppose, since you know of the existence of the two Tadekkas. But the one of which you have just spoken is the Tadekka of Ibn-Batuta, located by this historian seventy days from Tuat and placed by Schirmer, very plausibly, in the unexplored territory of the Aouelimmiden. This is the Tadekka by which the Sonrahi caravans passed every year, travelling by Egypt.

"My Tadekka is different, the capital of the veiled people, placed by Ibn-Khaldûn twenty days south of Wargla, which he calls Tadmekka. It is towards this Tadmekka that I am headed. I must establish Tadmekka in the ruins of Es-Souk. The commercial trade route, which in the ninth century bound the Tunis to the bend the Niger makes at Bourroum, passed by Es-Souk. It is to study the possibility of reestablishing this ancient thoroughfare that the ministries gave me this mission, which has given me the pleasure of your companionship."

"You are probably in for a disappointment," I said. "Everything indicates that the commerce there is very slight."

"Well, I shall see," he answered composedly.

This was while we were following the unicolored banks of a salt lake. The great saline stretch shone pale blue under the rising sun. The legs of our five camels cast on it their moving shadows of a darker blue. For a moment the only inhabitant of these solitudes, a bird, a kind of indeterminate heron, rose and hung in the air, as if suspended from a thread, only to sink back to rest as soon as we had passed.

I led the way, selecting the route; Morhange followed. Enveloped in a *burnoose,* his head covered with the straight *chechia* of the Spahis, a great chaplet of alternate red and white beads, ending in a cross, around his neck, he realized perfectly the ideal of Father Lavigerie's White Fathers.

After a two-days' halt at Temassinin we had just left the road followed by Flatters, and taken an oblique course to the south. I have the honor of having antedated Fourcau in demonstrating the importance of Temassinin as a suitable point for the passage of caravans and of selecting the place where Captain Pein has just now constructed a fort. Temassinin, the junction of the roads that lead to Tuat from Fezzan and Tibesti, is the future seat of a marvelous intelligence department. What I had collected there in two days about the disposition of our

Senussi enemies was of importance. I noticed that Morhange let me proceed with my inquiries with complete indifference.

These two days he had passed in conversation with the old Negro guardian of the *turbeh,* which preserves under its plaster dome the remains of the venerated Sidi-Moussa. The confidences they exchanged, I am sorry to say that I have forgotten, but from the Negro's amazed admiration I realized the ignorance in which I stood of the mysteries of the desert and how familiar they were to my companion.

And if you want to get any idea of the extraordinary originality which Morhange introduced into such surroundings, you who, after all, have a certain familiarity with the tropics, listen to this:

It was exactly two hundred kilometers from here in the vicinity of the Great Dune—that horrible stretch of six days without water. We had just enough for the two days we would have to travel before reaching the next well, and you know these wells. As Flatters wrote to his wife, "You have to work for hours before you can clean them out and succeed in watering beasts and men."

By chance we met a caravan which was going east towards Rhadames and which had come too far north. The camels' humps, shrunken and shaking, bespoke the sufferings of the troop. Behind came a little gray ass, a pitiful burro, its hooves "interfering" at every step and lightened of its pack because the merchants knew that it was going to die. Instinctively, with its last strength, it followed, knowing that when it could no longer stagger the end would come and then the flutter of the vultures' wings.

I love animals, which I have solid reasons for preferring to men, but never should I have thought of doing what Morhange did then. I tell you that our water-skins were almost dry and that our own camels, without which one is lost in the empty desert, had not been watered for many hours. Morhange made his camel kneel, uncorked a skin and made the little ass drink. I certainly felt gratification at seeing the poor bare flanks of the miserable beast pant with satisfaction. But the responsibility was mine. Also I had seen Bou-Djema's aghast expression and the disapproval of the thirsty members of the caravan. I remarked on it. How it was received!

"What have I given," replied Morhange, "was my own. We will reach El-Biodh tomorrow evening, about six o'clock. Between here and there I know that I shall not be thirsty."

He spoke in a tone, in which for the first time he allowed the authority of a captain to speak.

"That is easy to say," I thought ill-humoredly. "He knows that when he wants them my water-skin, and Bou-Djema's are at his service."

But I did not yet know Morhange very well and it is true that until the evening of the next day, when we reached El-Biodh, refusing our offers with smiling determination, he drank nothing.

Shades of St. Francis of Assisi! Umbrian hills, so pure under the rising sun! It was in the light of a sunrise, by the border of a pale stream leaping in full cascades from a crescent-shaped niche of the gray rocks of Egele, that Morhange stopped. The unlooked for waters rolled upon the sand, and we saw, in the light which mirrored them, little black fish. Fish in the middle of the Sahara! All three of us were mute before this paradox of nature. One of them had strayed into a little channel of sand. He had to stay there, struggling in vain, his little white belly exposed to the air. Morhange picked him up, looked at him for a moment, and put him back into the little stream. Shades of St. Francis! Umbrian hills— But I have sworn not to break the thread of the story by these untimely digressions.

"You see," Captain Morhange said to me a week later, "that I was right in advising you to go farther south before making for Sheikh-Salah. Something told me that this highland of Egele was not interesting from your point of view. While here you have only to stoop to pick up pebbles which will allow you to establish the volcanic origin of this region much more certainly than Bou-Derba, des Cloizeaux and Doctor Marrés have done."

This was while we were following the western pass of the Tidifest Mountains, about the 25th degree of northern latitude.

"I should indeed be ungrateful not to thank you," I said.

I shall always remember that instant. We had left our camels and were collecting fragments of the most characteristic rocks. Morhange employed himself with a discernment which spoke worlds for his knowledge of geology, a science he had often professed complete ignorance of.

Then I asked him the following question—

"May I prove my gratitude by making you a confession?"

He raised his head and looked at me.

"Well then, I don't see the practical value of this trip you have undertaken."

He smiled.

"Why not? To explore the old caravan route, to demonstrate that a connection has existed from the most ancient times between the Mediterranean world, and the country of the blacks—that seems nothing in your eyes? The hope of settling once for all the secular disputes which have divided so many keen minds—d'Anville, Heeren, Berlioux, Quatremere on the one hand—on the other Gosselin, Walckenaer, Tissit, Vivien, de Saint-Martin—you think that that is devoid of interest? A plague upon you for being hard to please."

"I spoke of practical value," I said. "You won't deny that this controversy is only the affair of cabinet geographers and office explorers."

Morhange kept on smiling.

"Dear friend, don't snub me. Deign to recall that your mission was confided to you by the Ministry of War, while I hold mine on behalf of the Ministry of Public Instruction. A different origin justifies our different aims. It certainly explains, I readily concede that to you, why what I am in search of has no practical value."

"You are also authorized by the Ministry of Commerce," I replied, playing my next card. "By this chief you are instructed to study the possibility of restoring the old trade route of the ninth century. But on this point don't attempt to mislead me; with your knowledge of the history and geography of the Sahara, your mind must have been made up before you left Paris. The road from Djerid to the Niger is dead, stone dead. You knew that no important traffic would pass by this route before you undertook to study the possibility of restoring it."

Morhange looked me full in the face.

"And if that should be so," he said with the most charming attitude, "if, as you say, I had the conviction before leaving, what do you conclude from that?"

"I should prefer to have you tell me."

"Simply, my dear boy, that I had less skill than you in finding the pretext for my voyage, that I furnished less good reasons for the true motives that brought me here."

"A pretext? I don't see—"

"Be sincere in your turn, if you please. I am sure that you have the greatest desire to inform the Arabian Office about the practices of the Senussi. But admit that the information that you will obtain is not the sole and innermost aim of your excursion. You are a geologist, my friend. You have found a chance to gratify your taste in this trip. No one would think of blaming you because you have known how to reconcile what is useful to your country and agreeable to yourself. But, for the love of God, don't deny it! I need no other proof than your presence here on this side of the Tidifest, a very curious place from a mineralogical point of view, but some hundred and fifty kilometers south of your official route."

It would not have been possible to counter me with a better grace. I parried by attacking.

"Am I to conclude from all this that I do not know the real aims of your trip and that they have nothing to do with the official motives?"

I had gone a bit too far. I felt it from the seriousness with which Morhange's reply was delivered.

"No, my dear friend, you must not conclude just that. I should have no taste for a lie which was based on fraud toward the estimable constitutional bodies which have judged me worthy of their confidence and their support. The ends that they have assigned to me I shall do my best to attain. But I have no reason for hiding from you that there is another, quite personal, motive which is far nearer to my heart. Let us say, if you will, to use a terminology that is otherwise deplorable, that this is the end while the others are the means."

"Would there be any indiscretion—"

"None," replied my companion. "Sheikh-Salah is only a few days distant. He whose first steps you have guided with such solicitude in the desert should have nothing hidden from you."

We had halted in the valley of a little dry well where a few sickly plants were growing. A spring nearby was circled by a crown of gray verdure. The camels had been unsaddled for the night and were seeking vainly at every stride to nibble the spiny tufts of had. The black and polished sides of the Tidifest Mountains rose almost vertically, above our heads. Already the blue smoke of the fire on which Bou-Djema was cooking dinner rose through the motionless air.

Not a sound, not a breath. The smoke mounted straight, straight and slowly up the pale steps of the firmament.

"Have you ever heard of *The Atlas of Christianity?*' asked Morhange.

"I think so. Isn't it a geographical work published by the Benedictines under the direction of a certain Dom Granger?"

"Your memory is correct," said Morhange. "Even so let me explain a little more fully some of the things you have not had as much reason as I to interest yourself in. *The Atlas of Christianity* proposes to establish the boundaries of that great tide of Christianity through all the ages, and for all parts of the globe—an undertaking worthy of the Benedictine learning, worthy of such a prodigy of erudition as Dom Granger himself."

"And it is these boundaries that you have come to determine here, no doubt," I murmured.

"Just so," replied my companion.

He was silent, and I respected his silence, prepared by now to be astonished at nothing.

"It is not possible to give confidences by halves without being ridiculous," he continued after several minutes of meditation, speaking gravely in a voice which held no suggestion of that flashing humor which had a month before enchanted the young officers at Wargla. "I have begun on mine. I will tell you everything. Trust my discretion, however, and do not insist upon certain events of my private life.

"If, four years ago, I resolved to enter a monastery, it does not concern you to know my reasons. I can myself marvel that the passing from my life of a being absolutely devoid of interest should have sufficed to change the current of that life. I can marvel that a creature whose sole merit was her beauty should have been permitted by the Creator to swing my destiny to such an unforeseen direction. The monastery at whose doors I knocked had the most valid reasons for doubting the stability of my decision. What the world loses in such fashion it often calls back as readily.

"In short, I cannot blame the abbot for having forbidden me to apply for my army discharge. By his instructions I asked for, and obtained, permission to be placed on the inactive list for three years. He knew that at the end of those three years of consecration it would be seen whether the world was definitely dead to your servant.

"The first day of my arrival at the cloister I was assigned to Dom Granger and by him placed at work on *The Atlas of Christianity*. A brief examination decided him as to what kind of service I was best fitted to render. This is how I came to enter the studio devoted to the cartography of Northern Africa.

"I did not know one word of Arabic, but it happened that in the garrison at Lyon I had taken at the Faculté des Lettres—a course with Berlioux, a very erudite geographer no doubt, but obsessed by one idea—the influence the Greek and Roman civilizations had exercised on Africa. This detail of my life was enough for Dom Granger. He provided me straightway with Berber vocabularies by Venture, by Delaporte and by Brosselard; with *The Grammatical Sketch of the Temahaq* by Stanley Fleeman, and *The Essai de Grammaire de la Langue Temachek* by Major Hanoteau.

"At the end of three months I was able to decipher any inscriptions in Tifinar. You know that Tifinar is the national writing of the Tuareg—the expression of this Terachek language which seems to us the most curious protest of the Targui race against its Mohammedan enemies.

"Dom Granger, in fact, believed that the Tuareg were Christians, dating from a period which it was necessary to ascertain but which coincided no doubt with the splendor of the church of Hippon. Even better than I, you know that the cross is with them the symbol of fate in decoration. Duveyrier has claimed that it figures in their alphabet, on their arms and among the designs of their clothes. The only tattooing that they wear on the forehead or on the back of the hand is a cross with four equal branches. The pommels of their saddles, the handles of their sabers and of their poniards are cross-shaped. And is it necessary to remind you that, although Islam forbids bells as a sign of Christianity, the harnesses of Tuareg camels are trimmed with bells?

"Neither Dom Granger nor I attach an exaggerated importance to such proofs, which resemble too much those which make such a display in *The Genius of Christianity,* but it is indeed impossible to refuse all credence to certain theological arguments. Amanai, the god of the Tuareg, unquestionably the Adonai of the Bible, is unique. They have a hell, *Timsi-tan-elekhaft*—the last fire—where reigns Iblis, our Lucifer. Their Paradise, where they are rewarded for good deeds, is inhabited by *andjelousen*—our angels. Do not urge the resemblance of this theology to the Koran, for I will meet you with historic arguments and remind you that the Tuareg have struggled all through the ages at the cost of partial extermination, to maintain their faith against the encroachments of Mohammedan fanaticism.

"Many times I have studied with Dom Granger that formidable epoch when the aborigines opposed the conquering Arabs. With him I have seen how the army of Sidi-Okba, one of the companions of the Prophet, invaded this desert to reduce the Tuareg tribes and impose on them Musselman rule. These tribes were then rich and prosperous. They were the Ihbggaren, the Imededren, the Ouadelen, the Kel-Gueress, the Kel-Air. But internal quarrels sapped their strength.

"Still, it was not until after a long and cruel war that the Arabians succeeded in getting possession of the capital of the Berbers, which had proved such a redoubtable stronghold. They destroyed it after they had massacred the inhabitants. On the ruins Okba constructed a new city. This city is Es-Souk. The one that Sidi-Okba destroyed was the Berber Tadmekka. What Dom Granger asked of me was precisely that I should try to exhume from the ruins of the

Musselman Es-Souk the ruins of Tadmekka, which was Berber, and perhaps Christian.

"I understand," I murmured.

"So far, so good," said Morhange. "But what you must grasp now is the practical sense of these religious men, my masters. You remember that even after three years of monastic life, they preserved their doubts as to the stability of my vocation. They found at the same time means of testing it once for all and of adapting official facilities to their particular purposes. One morning I was called before the father abbot, and this is what he said to me in the presence of Dom Granger, who expressed silent approval:

"'Your term of inactive service expires in fifteen days. You will return to Paris and apply at the Ministry to be reinstated. With what you have learned here, and the relationships we have been able to maintain at headquarters, you will have no difficulty in being attached to the Geographical Staff of the army. When you reach the rue de Grenelle you will receive our instructions.'

"I was astonished at their confidence in my knowledge. When I was reestablished as captain again in the Geographical Service I understood. At the monastery the daily association with Dom Granger and his pupils had kept me constantly convinced of the inferiority of my knowledge. When I came in contact with my military brethren I realized the superiority of the instruction I had received.

"I did not have to concern myself with the details of my mission. The Ministries invited me to undertake it. My initiative asserted itself on only one occasion. When I learned that you were going to leave Wargla on the present expedition, having reason to distrust my practical qualifications as an explorer, I did my best to retard your departure so that I might join you. I hope that you have forgiven me by now."

The light in the west was fading; the sun had already sunk into a matchless luxury of violet draperies. We were alone in this immensity, at the feet of the rigid black rocks. Nothing but ourselves. Nothing, nothing but ourselves.

I held out my hand to Morhange, and he pressed it. Then he said:

"If they still seem infinitely long to me—the several thousand kilometers which separate me from the instant when, my task accomplished, I shall at last find oblivion in the cloister from the things for which I was not made—let me tell you this: The several hundred kilometers which still separate us from Sheikh-Salah seem to me infinitely short to traverse in your company."

On the pale silvery water of the little pool, motionless and fixed, a star had just been born.

"Sheikh-Salah," I murmured, my heart full of an indefinable sadness. "Patience, we are not there yet."

In truth, we never were to be there.

Chapter V

The Inscription

WITH A BLOW OF THE TIP OF HIS CANE MORHANGE KNOCKED A FRAGMENT OF ROCK from the black flank of the mountain.

"What is it?" he asked, holding it out to me.

"A basaltic peridot," I said.

"It can't be very interesting; you barely glanced at it."

"It is very interesting, on the contrary. But for the moment I admit that I am otherwise preoccupied."

"How?"

"Look this way a bit," I said, showing towards the west to a black spot on the horizon across the white plain.

It was six o'clock in the morning. The sun had risen, but it could not be found in the surprisingly polished air. And not a breath of air, not a breath. Suddenly one of the camels called. An enormous antelope had just come in sight and had stopped in its flight, terrified, facing the wall of rock. It stayed there at a little distance from us, dazed, trembling on its slender legs.

Bou-Djema had rejoined us.

"When the legs of the *mohr* tremble it is because the firmament is shaken," he muttered.

"A storm?"

"Yes, a storm."

"And you find that alarming?"

I did not answer immediately. I was exchanging several brief words with Bou-Djema, who was occupied in soothing the camels, which were giving signs of being restive.

Morhange repeated his question. I shrugged my shoulders.

"Alarming? I don't know. I have never seen a storm on the Hoggar, but I distrust it. And the signs are that this is going to be a big one. See there already."

A slight dust had risen before the cliff. In the still air a few grains of sand had begun to whirl round and round with a speed which increased to dizziness, giving us in advance the spectacle in miniature of what would soon be breaking upon us.

With harsh cries a flock of wild geese appeared, flying low. They came out of the west.

"They are fleeing toward the Sebkha d'Amanghor," said Bou-Djema.
There could be no greater mistake, I thought.
Morhange looked at me curiously.
"What must we do?" he asked.
"Mount our camels immediately before they are completely demoralized and hurry to find shelter in some high places. Take account of our situation: It is easy to follow the bed of a stream, but within a quarter of an hour, perhaps, the storm will have burst. Within a half-hour a perfect torrent will be rushing here. On this soil, which is almost impermeable, rain will roll like a pail of water thrown on a bituminous pavement. Look at this."

And I showed him, a dozen meters high, long hollow gouges, marks of former erosions on the rocky wall.

"In an hour the waters will reach that height. Those are the marks of the last inundation. Let us get started. There is not an instant to lose."

"All right," Morhange replied tranquilly.

We had the greatest difficulty to make the camels kneel and when we had thrown ourselves into the saddle they started off at a pace which their terror rendered more and more disorderly.

Of a sudden the wind rose—a formidable wind—and almost at the same time the light was eclipsed in the ravine. Above our heads the sky had become, in the flash of an eye, darker than the walls of the canyon which we were descending at a breathless pace.

"A path—a stairway in the wall," I screamed against the wind to my companions. "If we don't find one in a minute we are lost."

They did not hear me, but, turning in my saddle, I saw that they had lost no distance, Morhange following me and Bou-Djema in the rear, driving the two baggage camels masterfully before him.

A blinding streak of lightning rent the obscurity. A peal of thunder, re-echoed to infinity by the rocky wall, rang out and immediately great tepid drops began to fall. In an instant, our *burnooses,* which had been blown out behind by the speed with which we were traveling, were stuck tight to our streaming bodies.

"Saved!" I exclaimed suddenly.

Abruptly on our right a crevice opened in the midst of the wall. It was the almost perpendicular bed of a stream, an affluent of the one we had had the unfortunate idea of following that morning. Already a veritable torrent was gushing over it with a fine uproar.

I have never better appreciated the incomparable surefootedness of camels in the most precipitous places. Bracing themselves, stretching out their great legs, balancing themselves among the rocks that were beginning to be swept loose, our camels accomplished at that moment what the mules of the Pyrenees might have failed in.

After several moments of superhuman effort we found ourselves at last out of danger, on a kind of basaltic terrace elevated some fifty meters above the channel of the stream we had just left. Luck was with us; a little grotto opened out behind. Bou-Djema succeeded in sheltering the camels there, and from its threshold we had leisure to contemplate in silence the prodigious spectacle spread out before us.

You have, I believe, been at the camp at Châlons for artillery drills. You have seen, when the shell bursts, how the chalky soil of the Marne effervesces like the ink-wells at school when we used to throw a piece of calcium carbonate into them. Well, it was almost like that, but in the midst of the desert, in the midst of obscurity.

The white waters rushed into the depths of the black hole and rose and rose towards the pedestal on which we stood. And there was the uninterrupted noise of thunder and, still louder, the sound of whole walls of rock, undermined by the flood, collapsing in a heap and dissolving in a few seconds of time in the midst of the rising water which swirled upward.

All the time that this deluge lasted, one hour, perhaps two, Morhange and I stayed bending over this fantastic, foaming vat, anxious to see, to see everything, to see in spite of everything, rejoicing with a kind of ineffable horror when we felt the shelf of basalt on which we had taken refuge swaying beneath us from the battering impact of the water. I believe that never for an instant did we think, so beautiful it was, of wishing for the end of that gigantic nightmare.

Finally a ray of the sun shone through. Only then did we look at each other.

Morhange held out his hand.

"Thank you," he said simply, and added with a smile:

"To be drowned in the very middle of the Sahara would have been pretentious and ridiculous. You have saved us, thanks to your power of decision, from this very paradoxical end."

Ah! If only he had been thrown by a misstep of his camel and rolled to his death in the midst of the flood! Then what followed would never have happened. That is the thought that comes to me in hours of weakness, but I have told you that I pull myself out of it quickly. No, no, I do not regret it. I cannot regret that what happened did happen.

Morhange left me to go into the little grotto where Bou-Djema's camels were now resting comfortably. I stayed alone, watching the torrent which was continuously rising with the impetuous inrush of its unbridled tributaries. It had stopped raining. The sun shone from a sky that had renewed its blueness. I could feel the clothes that had a moment before been drenched, drying upon me with incredible quickness.

A hand was placed on my shoulder. Morhange was again beside me.

"Come here," he said.

Somewhat surprised, I followed him. We went into the grotto.

The opening, which was big enough to admit the camels, made it fairly light. Morhange led me up to the smooth face of rock opposite.

"Look," he said with unconcealed joy.

"What of it?"

"Don't you see?"

"I see that there are several Tuareg inscriptions," I answered, with some disappointment. "But I thought I had told you that I read Tifinar writing very badly. Are these writings more interesting than the others we have come upon before?"

"Look at this one," said Morhange. There was such an accent of triumph in his tone that this time I concentrated my attention.

I looked again.

The characters of the inscription were arranged in the form of a cross. It was designed with great regularity, and the characters were cut deep into the rock. Although I knew so little of rock inscriptions at that time, I had no difficulty in recognizing the antiquity of this one. This is a copy:

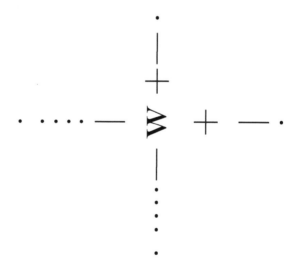

Morhange became more and more radiant as he regarded it.

I looked at him questioningly.

"Well, what have you to say now?" he asked.

"What do you want me to say? I tell you that I can barely read Tifinar."

"Shall I help you?" he suggested.

This course in Berber writing, after the emotions through which we had just passed, seemed to me a little inopportune. But Morhange was so visibly delighted that I could not dash his joy.

"Very well then," began my companion, as much at his ease as if he had been before a blackboard; "what will strike you first about this inscription is its repetition in the form of a cross. That is to say that it contains the same word twice, top to bottom and right to left. The word which it composes has seven letters, so the fourth letter, $\gtrless$, comes naturally in the middle. This arrangement, which is unique in Tifinar writing, is already remarkable enough, but there is better still. Now we will read it."

Getting it wrong three times out of seven I finally succeeded, with Morhange's help, in spelling the word

"Have you got it?" asked Morhange when I had finished my task.

"Less than ever," I answered, a little put out; "a, n, t, i, n, h, a—Antinha, I don't know that word or anything like it in all the Saharan dialects I am familiar with."

Morhange rubbed his hands together. His satisfaction was without bounds.

"You have said it. That is why the discovery is unique."

"Why?"

"There is really nothing, either in Berber or in Arabian, analogous to this word, so far as I know."

"Then?"

"Then, my dear friend, we are in the presence of a foreign word, translated into Tifinar."

"And this word belongs, according to your theory, to what language?"

"You must realize that the letter e does not exist in the Tifinar alphabet. It has here been replaced by the phonetic sign which is nearest to it—h. Restore e to the place which belongs to it in the word and you have—"

"Antinea."

"Antinea, precisely. We find ourselves before a Greek vocable reproduced in Tifinar. And I think that now you will agree with me that my find has a certain interest."

A loud cry, anguished, terrifying, rang out. That day we had no more conferences upon texts.

We rushed out to find a strange spectacle awaiting us.

Although the sky had cleared again, the torrent of yellow water was still foaming and no one could predict when it would fall. In mid-stream, struggling desperately in the current, was an extraordinary mass, gray and soft and swaying.

But what at the first glance overwhelmed us with astonishment was to see Bou-Djema, usually so calm, at this moment apparently beside himself with frenzy, bounding through the gullies and over the rocks of the ledge in full pursuit of the shipwreck.

Of a sudden I seized Morhange by the arm. The grayish thing was alive. A pitiful long neck emerged from it and it uttered the heartrending cry of a beast in despair.

"The fool!" I cried. "He has let one of our beasts get loose and the stream is carrying it away!"

"You are mistaken," said Morhange. "Our camels are all in the cave. The one Bou-Djema is running after is not ours. And the cry of anguish we just heard—that was not Bou-Djema either. Bou-Djema is a brave Chaamba who has at this moment only one idea, to appropriate the intestate capital represented by this camel in the stream."

"Who gave that cry then?"

"Let us try, if you like, to explore up this stream that our guide is descending at such a rate."

And without waiting for my answer he had already set out through the recently washed gullies of the rocky bank.

At that moment it can be truly said that Morhange went to meet his destiny.

I followed him. We had the greatest difficulty in proceeding two or three hundred meters. Finally we saw at our feet a little rushing brook where the water was falling a trifle.

"See there?" said Morhange.

A blackish bundle was balancing on the waves of the creek.

When we had come up even with it we saw that it was a man in the long dark blue robes of the Tuareg.

"Give me your hand," said Morhange, "and brace yourself against a rock—hard!" Morhange was very, very strong. In an instant, as if it were child's play, he had brought the body ashore.

"He is still alive," he pronounced with satisfaction. "Now it is a question of getting him to the grotto. This is no place to resuscitate a drowning man."

He raised the body in his powerful arms.

"It is astonishing how little he weighs for a man of his height."

By the time we had retraced the way to the grotto the man's cotton clothes were almost dry. But the dye had run plentifully, and it was an indigo man that Morhange was trying to recall to life.

When I had made him swallow a few ounces of rum he opened his eyes, looked at the two of us with surprise, then, closing them again, murmured almost unintelligibly a phrase, the sense of which we did not get until some days later—

"Can it be that I have reached the end of my mission?"

"What mission is he talking about?" I said.

"Let him recover himself completely," responded Morhange. "You had better open some preserved food. With fellows of this build you don't have to observe the precautions prescribed for drowning Europeans."

He was indeed a species of giant whose life we had just saved. His face, although very thin, was regular, almost beautiful. He had a clear skin and little beard. His hair, already white, showed him to be a man of about sixty years.

When I placed a tin of corned-beef before him a light of voracious joy came into his eyes. The tin contained an allowance for four persons. It was empty in a flash.

"Behold," said Morhange, "a robust appetite! Now we can put our questions without scruple."

Already the Targa had placed over his forehead and face the blue veil prescribed by the ritual. He must have been completely famished not to have performed this indispensable formality sooner. There was nothing visible now but the eyes watching us with a light that grew steadily more sombre.

"French officers," he murmured at last.

And he took Morhange's hand and, after having placed it against his breast, carried it to his lips.

Suddenly an expression of anxiety passed over his face.

"And my *mehari?*" he asked.

I explained that our guide was then employed in trying to save his beast. He in turn told us how it had stumbled and fallen into the current and how he himself, in trying to save it, had been knocked over. His forehead had struck a rock. He had cried out. After that he remembered nothing more.

"What is your name?" I asked.

"Eg-Anteouen."

"What tribe do you belong to?"

"The tribe of Kel-Tahat."

"The Kel-Tahats are the serfs of the tribe of Kel-Rhela, the great nobles of Hoggar?"

"Yes," he answered, casting a side glance in my direction. It seemed that such precise questions on the affairs of Ahygar were not to his liking.

"The Kel-Tahats, if I am not mistaken, are established on the southwest flank of Atakor.[4] What were you doing when we saved your life, so far from your home territory?"

"I was going, by way of Tit, to In-Saleh," he said.

"What were you going to do at In-Saleh?"

He was about to reply, but we suddenly saw him tremble. His eyes were fixed on a point of the cavern. We looked to see what it was. He had just seen the inscription which had so delighted Morhange an hour before.

"Do you know that?" Morhange asked him with keen curiosity.

The Targa did not speak a word but his eyes had a strange light.

"Do you know that?" insisted Morhange, and he added, "Antinea?"

"Antinea," repeated the man; then he was silent.

"Why don't you answer the captain?" I called out, a strange feeling of rage sweeping over me.

The Targui looked at me. I thought that he was going to speak, but his eyes became suddenly hard. Under the lustrous veil I saw his features stiffening.

Morhange and I turned around.

On the threshold of the cavern, breathless, discomfited, harassed by an hour of vain pursuit, Bou-Djema had returned to us.

---

4   Another name, in the Temahaq language, for Ahaggar. (Note by M. Leroux.)

Chapter VI

The Disaster of the Lettuce

As Eg-Anteouen and Bou-Djema came face to face, I fancied that both the Targa and the Chambaa gave a sudden start which each immediately repressed. It was nothing more than a fleeting impression. Nevertheless it was enough to make me resolve that as soon as I was alone with our guide I would question him closely concerning our new companion.

The beginning of the day had been wearisome enough. We decided, therefore, to spend the rest of it there and even to pass the night in the cave, waiting till the flood had completely subsided.

In the morning, when I was marking our day's march upon the map, Morhange came toward me. I noticed that his manner was somewhat restrained.

"In three days, we shall be at Sheikh-Salah," I said to him. "Perhaps by the evening of the second day, as badly as the camels go."

"Perhaps we shall separate before then," he muttered.

"How so?"

"You see I have changed my itinerary a little. I have given up the idea of going straight to Timissau. First I should like to make a little excursion into the interior of the Ahaggar range."

I frowned.

"What is this new idea?"

As I spoke I looked about for Eg-Anteouen, whom I had seen in conversation with Morhange the previous evening and several minutes before. He was quietly mending one of his sandals with a waxed thread supplied by Bou-Djema. He did not raise his head.

"It is simply," explained Morhange, less and less at his ease, "that this man tells me there are similar inscriptions in several caverns in western Ahaggar. These caves are near the road that he has to take in returning home. He must pass by Tit. Now the journey from Tit, by way of Silet, is hardly two hundred kilometers. It is a quasi-classic route,[5] as short again as the one that I shall have to take alone, after I leave you, from Sheikh-Salah to Timissau. That is in part, you see, the reason which has made me decide to—"

"In part? In very small part," I replied. "But is your mind absolutely made up?"

---

5   The route and the stages from Tit to Timissau were actually plotted out, as early as 1888, by Captain Bissuel. *Les Tuareg de l'Ouest,* itineraries 1 and 10. (Note by M. Leroux.)

"It is," he answered me.

"When do you expect to leave me?"

"Today. The road which Eg-Anteouen proposes to take into Ahaggar crosses this one about four leagues from here. I have a favor to ask of you in this connection."

"Please tell me."

"It is to let me take one of the two baggage-camels, since my Targa has lost his."

"The camel which carries your baggage belongs to you as much as does your own *mehari,*" I answered coldly.

We stood there several minutes without speaking. Morhange maintained an uneasy silence; I was examining my map. All over it in greater or less degree, but particularly towards the south, the unexplored portions of Ahaggar stood out as far too numerous white patches in the tan area of supposed mountains.

I finally said:

"You give me your word that when you have seen these famous grottos, you will make straight for Timissau by Tit and Silet?"

He looked at me uncomprehendingly.

"Why do you ask that?"

"Because if you promise me that—provided, of course, that my company is not unwelcome to you—I will go with you. Either way I shall have two hundred kilometers to go. I shall strike for Sheikh-Salah from the south instead of from the west—that is the only difference."

Morhange looked at me with emotion.

"Why do you do this?" he murmured.

"My dear fellow," I said—it was the first time that I had addressed Morhange in this familiar way—"my dear fellow, I have a sense which becomes marvelously acute in the desert—the sense of danger. I gave you a slight proof of it yesterday morning at the coming of the storm. With all your knowledge of rock inscriptions, you seem to me to have no very exact idea of what kind of place Ahaggar is, nor what may be in store for you there. On that account I should be just as well pleased not to let you run sure risks alone."

"I have a guide," he said with his adorable naiveté.

Eg-Anteouen, in the same squatting position, kept on patching his old slipper.

I took a step toward him.

"You heard what I said to the captain?"

"Yes," the Targa answered calmly.

"I am going with him. We leave you at Tit, to which place you must bring us. Where is the place you proposed to show the Captain?"

"I did not propose to show it to him; it was his own idea," said the Targa coldly. "The grottos with the inscriptions are three-days' march southward in the mountains. At first the road is rather rough, but farther on it turns, and you gain Timissau very easily. There are good wells where the Tuareg Taitoqs, who are friendly to the French, come to water their camels."

"And you know the road well?"

He shrugged his shoulders. His eyes had a scornful smile.

"I have taken it twenty times," he said.

"In that case, let's get started."

We rode for two hours. I did not exchange a word with Morhange. I had a clear intuition of the folly we were committing in risking ourselves so unconcernedly in that least known and most dangerous part of the Sahara. Every blow which had been struck in the last twenty years to undermine the French advance had come from this redoubtable Ahaggar. But what of it? It was of my own will that I had joined in this mad scheme. No need of going over it again. What was the use of spoiling my action by a continual exhibition of disapproval?

I may as well admit, furthermore, that I rather liked the turn that our trip was beginning to take. I had at that instant the sensation of journeying toward something incredible, toward some tremendous adventure. You do not live with impunity for months and years as the guest of the desert. Sooner or later it has its way with you, annihilates the good officer, the timid executive, overthrows his solicitude for his responsibilities. What is there behind those mysterious rocks and those dim solitudes which have held at bay the most illustrious pursuers of mystery? You follow, I tell you, you follow.

"Are you sure at least that this inscription is interesting enough to justify us in our undertaking?" I asked Morhange.

My companion started with pleasure. Ever since we began our journey I had realized his fear that I was coming along half-heartedly. As soon as I offered him a chance to convince me, his scruples vanished and his triumph seemed assured to him.

"Never," he answered in a voice that he tried to control, but through which the enthusiasm rang out, "never has a Greek inscription been found so far south. The farthest points where they have been reported are in the south of Algeria and Cyrene. But in Ahaggar! Think of it! It is true that this one is translated into Tifinar, but this peculiarity does not diminish the interest of the coincidence; it increases it."

"What do you take to be the meaning of this word?"

"Antinea can only be a proper name," said Morhange. "To whom does it refer? I admit I don't know and the reason why at this very moment I am marching toward the south, dragging you along with me, is because I count on learning more about it. Its etymology? It hasn't one definitely, but there are thirty possibilities. Bear in mind that the Tifinar alphabet comes far from tallying with the Greek alphabet; that fact increases the number of hypotheses. Shall I suggest several?"

"I was just about to ask you to."

"To begin with, there is *anti* and *naus—the woman who is placed opposite a vessel*—an explanation which would have been pleasing to Gaffarel and to my venerated master Berlioux. That would apply well enough to the figure-heads of ships. There is a technical term that I cannot recall at this moment.[6]

"Then there is *antinea*, that you must relate to *anti* and *naos*—*she who holds herself before the naos*, the *naos* of the temple—*she who is opposite the sanctuary*—therefore priestess. An interpretation which would enchant Girard and Renan.

"Next we have *antinea*, from *anti* and *neos*, new, which can mean two things: either—*she who is the contrary of young*—which is to say old; or—*she who is the enemy of novelty, or the enemy of youth.*

There is still another sense of *anti*—*in exchange for*—which is capable of complicating all the others I have mentioned; likewise there are four meanings for the verb *nea*, which means in turn—*to go, to flow, to thread or weave, to heap.* There is are more still. And notice, please, that I have not at my disposition on the otherwise commodious hump of this *mehari*, either the great dictionary of Estienne, or the lexicons of Passow, of Pape, or of Liddel and Scott. This is only to show you, my dear friend, that epigraphy is but a relative science, always dependent on the discovery of a new text which contradicts the previous findings, when it is not merely at the mercy of the humors of the epigraphists and their pet conceptions of the universe.[7]

"That was rather my view of it," I said. "But I must admit my astonishment to find that with such a skeptical opinion of the goal you still do not hesitate to take risks which may be quite considerable."

Morhange smiled wanly.

"I do not interpret, my friend; I collect. From what I will take back to him, Dom Granger has the ability to draw conclusions which are beyond my slight knowledge. I was amusing myself a little. Pardon me."

Just then the girth of one of the baggage-camels, evidently not well fastened, came loose. Part of the load slipped and fell to the ground.

Eg-Anteouen descended instantly from his beast and helped Bou-Djema repair the damage.

When they had finished, I made my *mehari* walk beside Bou-Djema's.

"It will be better to resaddle the camels at the next stop. They will have to climb the mountain."

The guide looked at me with amazement. Up to that time I had thought it unnecessary to acquaint him with our new projects, but I supposed Eg-Anteouen would have told him.

"Lieutenant, the road across the white plain to Sheikh-Salah is not mountainous," said the Chaamba.

"We are not keeping to the road across the white plain. We are going south by Ahaggar."

6   It is perhaps worth noting here that *Figures de Proués* is the exact title of a very remarkable collection of poems by Mme. Delarus-Mardrus. (Note by M. Leroux.)

7   Captain Morhange seems to have forgotten in this enumeration, in places fanciful, the etymology of *anthinea*, a Doric dialect form of *anthine*, from *anthos*, a flower, and which would mean—which is in flower. (Note by M. Leroux.)

"By Ahaggar," he murmured. "But—"

"But what?"

"I do not know the road."

"Eg-Anteouen is going to guide us."

"Eg-Anteouen!"

I watched Bou-Djema as he made this suppressed ejaculation. His eyes were fixed on the Targa with a mixture of stupor and fright.

Eg-Anteouen's camel was a dozen yards ahead of us, side by side with Morhange's. The two men were talking. I realized that Morhange must be conversing with Eg-Anteouen about the famous inscriptions. But we were not so far behind that they could not have overheard our words.

Again I looked at my guide. I saw that he was pale.

"What is it, Bou-Djema?" I asked in a low voice.

"Not here, Lieutenant, not here," he muttered.

His teeth chattered. He added in a whisper:

"Not here. This evening, when we stop, when he turns to the east to pray, when the sun goes down—then call me to you. I will tell you. But not here. He is talking but he is listening. Go ahead. Join the captain."

"What next?" I murmured, pressing my camel's neck with my foot so as to make him overtake Morhange.

It was about five o'clock when Eg-Anteouen, who was leading the way, came to a stop.

"Here it is," he said, getting down from his camel.

It was a beautiful and sinister place. To our left a fantastic wall of granite outlined its gray ribs against the sky. This wall was pierced from top to bottom by a winding corridor about a thousand feet high and scarcely wide enough in places to allow three camels to walk abreast.

"Here it is," repeated the Targa.

To the west, straight behind us, the track that we were leaving unrolled like a pale ribbon—the white plain, the road to Sheikh-Salah, the established halts, the well-known wells. And on the other side, this black wall against the mauve sky, this dark passage.

I looked at Morhange.

"We had better stop here," he said simply. "Eg-Anteouen advises us to take as much water here as we can carry."

With one accord we decided to spend the night there before undertaking the mountain.

There was a spring in a dark basin from which fell a little cascade; there were a few shrubs, a few plants.

Already the camels were browsing at the length of their tethers.

Bou-Djema arranged our camp dinner-service of tin cups and plates on a great flat stone. An opened tin of meat lay beside a plate of lettuce which he had just gathered from the moist earth around the spring. I could tell from the distracted manner in which he placed these objects upon the rock how deep was his anxiety.

As he was bending toward me to hand me a plate, he pointed to the gloomy black corridor which we were about to enter.

"Blad-el-Khouf!" he murmured.

"What did he say?" asked Morhange, who had seen the gesture.

"Blad-el-Khouf—*this is the country of fear.* That is what the Arabs call Ahaggar."

Bou-Djema went a little distance off and sat down, leaving us to our dinner. Squatting on his heels, he began to eat a few lettuce leaves that he had kept for his own meal.

Eg-Anteouen was still motionless.

Suddenly the Targa rose. The sun in the west was no larger than a red brand. We saw Eg-Anteouen approach the fountain, spread his blue *burnoose* on the ground and kneel upon it.

"I did not suppose that the Tuareg were so observant of Mussulman tradition," said Morhange.

"Nor I," I replied thoughtfully.

But I had something to do at that moment besides making such speculations.

"Bou-Djema!" I called.

At the same time I looked at Eg-Anteouen. Absorbed in his prayer, bowed toward the west, apparently he was paying no attention to me. As he prostrated himself I called again—

"Bou-Djema, come with me to my *mehari;* I want to get something out of the saddle-bags."

Still kneeling, Eg-Anteouen was mumbling his prayer slowly, composedly. But Bou-Djema had not budged.

His only response was a deep moan.

Morhange and I leaped to our feet and ran to the guide. Eg-Anteouen reached him as soon as we did.

With his eyes closed and his limbs already cold, the Chaamba breathed a death-rattle in Morhange's arms. I had seized one of his hands. Eg-Anteouen took the other. Each in his own way was trying to divine, to understand.

Suddenly Eg-Anteouen leapt to his feet. He had just seen the poor embossed bowl which the Arab had held an instant before between his knees and which now lay overturned upon the ground.

He picked it up, looked quickly at one after another of the leaves of lettuce remaining in it and then gave a hoarse exclamation.

"So," said Morhange, "it's his turn now; he is going to go mad."

Watching Eg-Anteouen closely, I saw him hasten without a word to the rock where our dinner was set; a second later, he was again beside us, holding out the bowl of lettuce which he had not yet touched.

Then he took a thick, long, pale-green leaf from Bou-Djema's bowl and held it beside another leaf he had just taken from our bowl.

"Afahlehle," was all he said.

I shuddered, and so did Morhange. It was the *afahlehla,* the *falestez,* of the Arabs of the Sahara, the terrible plant which had killed a part of the Flatters mission more quickly and surely than Tuareg arms.

Eg-Anteouen stood up. His tall silhouette was outlined blackly against the sky which suddenly had turned pale lilac. He was watching us.

We bent again over the unfortunate guide.

"Afahlehle," the Targa repeated and shook his head.

Bou-Djema died in the middle of the night without having regained consciousness.

Chapter VII
The Country of Fear

"It is curious," said Morhange, "to see how our expedition, uneventful since we left Wargla, is now becoming exciting."

He said this after kneeling for a moment in prayer before the painfully dug grave in which we had lain the guide.

I do not believe in God, but if anything can influence whatever powers there may be, whether of good or of evil, of light or of darkness, it is the prayer of such a man.

For two days we picked our way through a gigantic chaos of black rock in what might have been the country of the moon, so barren was it. No sound was heard save that of stones rolling under the feet of the camels and striking like gunshots at the foot of the precipices.

A strange march indeed. For the first few hours I tried to pick out by compass the route we were following, but my calculations were soon upset—doubtless a mistake due to the swaying motion of the camel. I put the compass back in one of my saddle-bags. From that time on, Eg-Anteouen was our master. We could only trust ourselves to him.

He went first, Morhange followed him and I brought up the rear. We passed at every step most curious specimens of volcanic rock, but I did not examine them. I was no longer interested in such things. Another kind of curiosity had taken possession of me. I had come to share Morhange's madness. If my companion had said to me: "We are doing a very rash thing. Let us go back to the known trails," I should have replied, "You are free to do as you please, but I am going on."

Toward evening of the second day we found ourselves at the foot of a black mountain whose jagged ramparts towered in profile seven thousand feet above our heads. It was an enormous shadowy fortress like the outline of a feudal stronghold silhouetted with incredible sharpness against the orange sky.

There was a well and about it several trees, the first we had seen since cutting into Ahaggar.

A group of men were standing about it. Their camels, tethered close by, were cropping a mouthful here and there.

At seeing us the men drew together, alert and on the defensive.

Eg-Anteouen turned to us and said—

"Eggali Tuareg."

We went toward them.

They were handsome men, those Eggali, the largest Tuareg whom I ever have seen. With unexpected swiftness they drew aside from the well, leaving it to us. Eg-Anteouen spoke a few words to them and they looked at Morhange and me with a curiosity bordering on fear but at any rate with respect.

I drew several little presents from my saddle-bags and was astonished at the reserve of the chief, who refused them. He seemed afraid even of my glance.

When they had gone I expressed my astonishment at this shyness for which my previous experiences with the tribes of the Sahara had not prepared me.

"They spoke with respect, even with fear," I said to Eg-Anteouen, "and yet the tribe of the Eggali is noble. And that of the Kel-Tahats, to which you tell me you belong, is a slave tribe."

A smile lighted the dark eyes of Eg-Anteouen.

"It is true," he said.

"Well then?"

"I told them that we three—the Captain, you and I—were bound for the Mountain of the Evil Spirits."

With a gesture he indicated the black mountain.

"They are afraid. All the Tuareg of Ahaggar are afraid of the Mountain of the Evil Spirits. You saw how they were up and off at the very mention of its name."

"It is to the Mountain of the Evil Spirits that you are taking us?" queried Morhange.

"Yes," replied the Targa; "that is where the inscriptions are that I told you about."

"You did not mention that detail to us."

"Why should I? The Tuareg are afraid of the *ilhinen*—spirits with horns and tails, covered with hair—who make the cattle sicken and die and cast spells over men. But I know well that the Christians are not afraid and even laugh at the fears of the Tuareg."

"And you?" I asked. "You are a Targa and you are not afraid of the *ilhinen?*"

Eg-Anteouen showed a little red leather bag hung about his neck on a chain of white seeds.

"I have my amulet," he replied gravely, "blessed by the venerable Sidi-Moussa himself. And then I am with you. You saved my life. You have desired to see the inscriptions. The will of Allah be done!"

As he finished speaking, he squatted on his heels, drew out his long reed pipe and began to smoke gravely.

"All this is beginning to seem very strange," said Morhange, coming over to me.

"You can say that without exaggeration," I replied. "You remember as well as I the passage in which Barth tells of his expedition to the Idinen, the Mountain of the Evil Spirits of the Azdier Tuareg. The region had so evil a reputation that no Targa would go with him. But he got back."

"Yes, he got back," replied my comrade, "but only after he had been lost. Without water or food he came so near dying of hunger and thirst that he had to open a vein and drink his own blood. The prospect is not particularly attractive."

I shrugged my shoulders. After all it was not my fault that we were there.

Morhange understood my gesture and thought it necessary to make excuses.

"I should be curious," he went on with rather forced gaiety, "to meet these spirits and substantiate the facts of Pomponius Mela, who knew them and locates them, in fact, in the mountain of the Tuareg. He calls them *egipans, blemyens, gamphasantes, satyrs.* 'The *gamphasantes,*' he says, 'are naked. The *blemyens* have no head and their faces are placed on their chests; the *satyrs* have nothing like men except faces. The *egipans* are made as is commonly described.' *Satyrs, egipans*—isn't it very strange to find Greek names given to the barbarian spirits of this region? Believe me, we are on a curious trail. I am sure that Antinea will be our key to remarkable discoveries."

"Listen!" I said, laying a finger on my lips.

Strange sounds rose from about us as the evening advanced with great strides. A kind of crackling followed by long rending shrieks echoed and reechoed to infinity in the neighboring ravines. It seemed to me that the whole black mountain had suddenly begun to moan.

We looked at Eg-Anteouen. He was smoking on, without twitching a muscle.

"The *ilhinen* are waking up," he said simply.

Morhange listened without saying a word. Doubtless he understood as I did—the overheated rocks, the crackling of the stone, a whole series of physical phenomena, the example of the singing statue of Memnon. But for all that, this unexpected concert reacted no less painfully on our overstrained nerves.

The last words of poor Bou-Djema came to my mind.

"The country of fear," I murmured in a low voice.

And Morhange repeated—

"The country of fear."

The strange concert ceased as the first stars appeared in the sky. With deep emotion we watched the tiny bluish flames appear, one after another. At that portentous moment they seemed to span the distance between us—isolated, condemned, lost—and our brothers of higher latitudes, who at that hour were rushing about their poor pleasures with delirious frenzy, in cities where the whiteness of electric lamps came on in a burst.

Chêt-Ahadh essa hetîsenet
Mâteredjrê d'Erredjeâot,
Mâtesekek d-Essekâot,
Mâtelahrlahr d'Ellerhâot,
Ettâs djenen, barâd tit-ennit abâtet.

Eg-Anteouen's voice raised itself in slow guttural tones. It resounded with sad, grave majesty in the silence now complete.

I touched the Targa's arm. With a movement of his head he pointed to a constellation glittering in the firmament.

"The Pleiades," I murmured to Morhange, showing him the seven pale stars, while Eg-Anteouen took up his mournful song in the same monotone:

"The Daughters of the Night are seven:
Mâteredjrê and Erredjeâot
Mâtesekek and Essekâot,
Mâtelahrlahr and Ellerhâot,
The seventh is a boy, one of whose eyes has flown away."

A sudden sickness came over me. I seized the Targa's arm as he was starting to intone his refrain for the third time.

"When will we reach this cave with the inscriptions?" I asked brusquely.

He looked at me and replied with his usual calm—

"We are there."

"We are there! Then why don't you show it to us?"

"You did not ask me," he replied, not without a touch of insolence.

Morhange had jumped to his feet.

"The cave is here?"

"It is here," Eg-Anteouen replied slowly, rising to his feet.

"Take us to it."

"Morhange," I said, suddenly anxious, "night is falling. We will see nothing, and perhaps it is still some way off."

"It is hardly five hundred paces," Eg-Anteouen replied. "The cave is full of dead underbrush. We will set it on fire and the Captain will see as in full daylight."

"Come," my comrade repeated.

"And the camels?" I hazarded.

"They are tethered," said Eg-Anteouen, "and we shall not be gone long."

He had started toward the black mountain. Morhange, trembling with excitement, followed. I followed, too, the victim of profound uneasiness. My pulses throbbed.

"I am not afraid," I kept repeating to myself. "I swear that this is not fear."

And really it was not fear. Yet, what a strange dizziness! There was a mist over my eyes. My ears buzzed. Again I heard Eg-Anteouen's voice, but multiplied, immense, and at the same time, very low.

"The Daughters of the Night are seven—"

It seemed to me that the voice of the mountain, re-echoing, repeated that sinister last line to infinity.

"And the seventh is a boy, one of whose eyes has flown away."

"Here it is," said the Targa.

A black hole in the wall opened up. Bending over, Eg-Anteouen entered. We followed him. The darkness closed around us.

A yellow flame—Eg-Anteouen had struck his flint. He set fire to a pile of brush near the surface. At first we could see nothing. The smoke blinded us.

Eg-Anteouen stayed at one side of the opening of the cave. He was seated and, more inscrutable than ever, had begun again to blow great puffs of gray smoke from his pipe.

The burning brush cast a flickering light. I caught a glimpse of Morhange. He seemed very pale. With both hands braced against the wall, he was working to decipher a mass of signs which I could scarcely distinguish. Nevertheless I thought I could see his hands trembling.

"The devil," I thought, finding it more and more difficult to coordinate my thoughts; "he seems to be as unstrung as I."

I heard him call out to Eg-Anteouen in what seemed to me a loud voice:

"Stand to one side. Let the air in. What a smoke!"

He kept on working at the signs.

Suddenly I heard him again, but with difficulty. It seemed as if even sounds were confused in the smoke.

"Antinea—at last—Antinea. But not cut in the rock—the marks traced in ochre—not ten years old, perhaps not five. Oh!"

He pressed his hands to his head. Again he cried out:

"It is a mystery! A tragic mystery!"

I laughed teasingly.

"Come on, come on. Don't get excited over it."

He took me by the arm and shook me. I saw his eyes big with terror and astonishment.

"Are you mad?" he yelled in my face.

"Not so loud," I replied with the same little laugh.

He looked at me again and sank down, overcome, on a rock opposite me. Eg-Anteouen was still smoking placidly at the mouth of the cave. We could see the red circle of his pipe glowing in the darkness.

"Madman! Madman!" repeated Morhange. His voice seemed to stick in his throat.

Suddenly he bent over the brush which was giving its last darts of flame, high and clear. He picked out a branch which had not yet caught. I saw him examine it carefully, then throw it back in the fire with a loud laugh.

"Ha! Ha! That's good, all right!"

He staggered toward Eg-Anteouen, pointing to the fire.

"It's hemp. Hashish, hashish. Oh, that's a good one, all right."

"Yes, it's a good one," I repeated, bursting into laughter.

Eg-Anteouen quietly smiled approval. The dying fire lit his inscrutable face and flickered in his terrible dark eyes.

A moment passed. Suddenly Morhange seized the Targa's arm. "I want to smoke, too," he said. "Give me a pipe."

The specter gave him one.

"What! A European pipe?"

"A European pipe," I repeated, feeling gayer and gayer.

"With an initial—M. As if made on purpose. M—Captain Morhange."

"Masson," corrected Eg-Anteouen quietly.

"Captain Masson," I repeated in concert with Morhange.

We laughed again.

"Ha! Ha! Ha! Captain Masson—Colonel Flatters—the well of Garama. They killed him to take his pipe—that pipe. It was Cegheir-ben-Cheikh who killed Captain Masson."

"It was Cegheir-ben-Cheikh," repeated the Targa with imperturbable calm.

"Captain Masson and Colonel Flatters had left the convoy to look for the well," said Morhange, laughing.

"It was then that the Tuareg attacked them," I finished, laughing as hard as I could.

"A Targa of Ahaggar seized the bridle of Captain Masson's horse," said Morhange.

"Cegheir-ben-Cheikh had hold of Colonel Flatters' bridle," put in Eg-Anteouen.

"The Colonel puts his foot in the stirrup and receives a cut from Cegheir-ben-Cheikh's saber," I said.

"Captain Masson draws his revolver and fires on Cegheir-ben-Cheikh, shooting off three fingers of his left hand," said Morhange.

"But," finished Eg-Anteouen imperturbably, "but Cegheir-ben-Cheikh, with one blow of his saber, splits Captain Masson's skull."

He gave a silent, satisfied laugh as he spoke. The dying flame lit up his face. We saw the gleaming black stem of his pipe. He held it in his left hand. One finger—no, two fingers only on that hand. Hello! I had not noticed that before.

Morhange also noticed it, for he finished with a loud laugh.

"Then, after splitting his skull, you robbed him. You took his pipe from him. Bravo, Cegheir-ben-Cheikh!"

Cegheir-ben-Cheikh does not reply, but I can see how satisfied with himself he is. He keeps on smoking. I can hardly see his features now. The firelight pales, dies. I have never laughed so much as this evening. I am sure Morhange never has, either. Perhaps he will forget the cloister. And all because Cegheir-ben-Cheikh stole Captain Masson's pipe.

Again that accursed song. "The seventh is a boy, one of whose eyes has flown away." One cannot imagine more senseless words. It is very strange, really. There seem to be four of us in this cave now. Four, I say, five, six, seven, eight. Make yourselves at home, my friends. What! There are no more of you? I am going to find out at last how the spirits of this region are made, the *gamphasantes,* the *blemyens.* Morhange says that the *blemyens* have their faces on the middle of their chests. Surely this one who is seizing me in his arms is not a *blemyen!* Now he is carrying me outside. And Morhange—I do not want them to forget Morhange.

They did not forget him; I see him perched on a camel in front of that one to which I am fastened. They did well to fasten me, for otherwise I surely would tumble off. These spirits certainly are not bad fellows. But what a long way it is! I want to stretch out—to sleep. A while ago we surely were following a long passage; then we were in the open air. Now we are again in an endless stifling corridor. Here are the stars again. Is this ridiculous course going to keep on?

Hello! Lights! Stars, perhaps. No, lights, I say. A stairway, on my word—of rocks, to be sure, but still a stairway. How can the camels— But it is no longer a camel; this is a man carrying me—a man dressed in white, not a *gamphasante* nor a *blemyen.* Morhange must be giving himself airs with his historical reasoning—all false, I repeat, all false.

Good Morhange. I hope his *gamphasante* does not let him fall on this unending stairway. Something glitters on the ceiling. Yes, it is a lamp—a copper lamp, as at Tunis, at Barbouchy's. Good; here again you cannot see anything. But I am making a fool of myself; I am lying down; now I can go to sleep. What a silly day!

Gentlemen, I assure you that it is unnecessary to bind me: I do not want to go down on the boulevards.

Darkness again. Steps of someone going away. Silence.

But only for a moment. There are people talking beside me. What are they saying? No, it is impossible. That metallic ring, that voice. Do you know what it is calling, that voice—do you know what it is calling in the tones of someone used to the phrase? Well, it is calling:

"Play your cards, gentlemen, play your cards. There are ten thousand *louis* in the bank. Play your cards, gentlemen."

In the name of God, am I or am I not at Ahaggar?

Chapter VIII

Awakening At Ahaggar

IT WAS BROAD DAYLIGHT WHEN I OPENED MY EYES. I THOUGHT AT ONCE OF MORHANGE. I could not see him, but I heard him close by, giving little grunts of surprise.

I called to him and he ran to me.

"Then they didn't tie you up?" I asked.

"I beg your pardon. They did. But they did it badly; I managed to get free."

"You might have untied me, too," I remarked crossly.

"What good would it have done? I should only have waked you up. And I thought that your first word would be to call me. There, that's done."

I reeled as I tried to stand on my feet.

Morhange smiled.

"We might have spent the whole night smoking and drinking and not been in a worse state," he said. "Anyhow, that Eg-Anteouen with his hashish is a fine rascal."

"Cegheir-ben-Cheikh," I corrected.

I rubbed my hand over my forehead.

"Where are we?"

"My dear boy," Morhange replied, "since I awakened from the extraordinary nightmare which is mixed up with the smoky cave and the lamp-lit stairway of the Arabian Nights, I have been going from surprise to surprise, from confusion to confusion. Just look around you."

I rubbed my eyes and stared. Then I seized my friend's hand.

"Morhange," I begged, "tell me if we are still dreaming."

We were in a round room, perhaps fifty feet in diameter and of about the same height, lighted by a great window opening on a sky of intense blue.

Swallows flew back and forth outside, giving quick, joyous cries.

The floor, the incurving walls and the ceiling were of a kind of veined marble like porphyry, paneled with a strange metal, paler than gold, darker than silver, clouded just then by the early morning mist that came in through the window in great puffs.

I staggered toward this window, drawn by the freshness of the breeze and the sunlight which was chasing away my dreams, and I leaned my elbows on the balustrade.

I could not restrain a cry of delight.

I was standing on a kind of balcony, cut into the flank of a mountain and overhanging an abyss. Above me, blue sky; below appeared a veritable earthly paradise, hemmed in on all sides by mountains that formed a continuous and impassable wall about it. A garden lay spread out down there. The palm-trees gently swayed their great fronds. At their feet was a tangle of the smaller trees which grow in an oasis under their protection—almonds, lemons, oranges and many others which I could not distinguish from that height. A broad blue stream, fed by a waterfall, emptied into a charming lake, the waters of which had the marvelous transparency which comes in high altitudes. Great birds flew in circles over this green hollow; I could see in the lake the red flash of a flamingo.

The peaks of the mountains which towered on all sides were completely covered with snow.

The blue stream, the green palms, the golden fruit and, above it all, the miraculous snow—all this bathed in that limpid air, gave such an impression of beauty, of purity, that my poor human strength could no longer stand the sight of it. I laid my forehead on the balustrade, which was also covered with that heavenly snow, and began to cry like a baby.

Morhange was also behaving like a child. But he had awakened before I had and doubtless had had time to grasp, one by one, all these details whose fantastic ensemble staggered me.

He laid his hand on my shoulder and gently pulled me back into the room.

"You haven't seen anything yet," he said. "Look! Look!"

"Morhange!"

"Well, old man, what do you want me to do about it? Look!"

I had just realized that the strange room was furnished—God forgive me—in the European fashion. There were indeed, here and there, round leather Tuareg cushions, brightly colored blankets from Gafsa, rugs from Kairouan, and Caramani hangings which at that moment I should have dreaded to draw aside. A half-open panel in the wall showed a bookcase crowded with books. A whole row of photographs of masterpieces of ancient art were hung on the walls. Finally there was a table almost hidden under its heap of papers, pamphlets, books. I thought I should collapse at seeing a recent number of the *Archaeological Review.*

I looked at Morhange. He was looking at me; and suddenly a mad laugh seized us and doubled us up for a good minute.

"I do not know," Morhange finally managed to say, "whether or not we shall someday regret our little excursion into Ahaggar, but admit in the meantime that it promises to be rich in unexpected adventures. That unforgettable guide who puts us to sleep just to distract us from the unpleasantness of caravan life and who lets me experience in the best of good faith the far-famed delights of hashish—that fantastic night ride, and, to cap the climax, this cave of a Nureddin who must have received the education of the Athenian Bersot at the French École Normale—all this is enough, on my word, to upset the wits of the best balanced."

"Seriously, what do you think of it all?"

"What do I think, my poor friend? Why, just what you yourself think. I don't understand it at all, not at all. What you politely call my learning is not worth a cent. And why shouldn't I be all mixed up? This living in caves amazes me. Pliny speaks of the natives living in caves, seven days' march southwest of the country of the Amantes and twelve days to the westward of the great Syrtis. Herodotus says also that the Garaments used to go out in their chariots to hunt the cave-dwelling Ethiopians.

"But here we are in Ahaggar, in the midst of the Targa country, and the best authorities tell us that the Tuareg never have been willing to live in caves. Duveyrier is precise on that point. And what is this, I ask you, but a cave turned into a workroom, with pictures of the Venus de Medici and the Apollo Sauroctonos on the walls? I tell you that it is enough to drive you mad."

And Morhange threw himself on a couch and began to roar with laughter again.

"See," I said, "this is Latin."

I had picked up several scattered papers from the work-table in the middle of the room. Morhange took them from my hands and devoured them greedily. His face expressed unbounded stupefaction.

"Stranger and stranger, my boy. Someone here is composing, with much citation of texts, a dissertation on the Gorgon Islands—*de Gorgonum insulis.* Medusa, according to him, was a Libyan savage who lived near Lake Triton, our present Chott Melhrir, and it is there that Perseus—Ah!"

Morhange's words choked in his throat. A sharp, shrill voice pierced the immense room.

"Gentlemen, I beg you, let my papers alone."

I turned toward the newcomer.

One of the Caramani curtains was drawn aside and the most unexpected of persons came in. Resigned as we were to unexpected events, the improbability of this sight exceeded anything our imaginations could have devised.

On the threshold stood a little bald-headed man with a pointed, sallow face half-hidden by an enormous pair of green spectacles and a pepper-and-salt beard. No shirt was visible, only an impressive broad red cravat. He wore white trousers. Red leather slippers furnished the only Oriental suggestion of his costume.

He wore, not without pride, the rosette of an officer of the Department of Education.

He collected the papers which Morhange had dropped in his amazement, counted them, arranged them and then, casting a peevish glance at us, he struck a copper gong.

The portiére was raised again. A huge white Targa entered. I seemed to recognize him as one of the *genii* of the cave.[8]

---

8   The Negro serfs among the Tuareg are generally called "white Tuareg." While the nobles are clad in blue cotton robes, the serfs wear white robes, hence their name of "white Tuareg." See, in this connection, Duveyrier: *les Tuareg du Nord,* page 292. (Note by M. Leroux.)

"Ferradji," angrily demanded the little officer of the Department of Education, "why were these gentlemen brought into the library?"

The Targa bowed respectfully.

"Cegheir-ben-Cheikh came back sooner than we expected," he replied, "and last night the embalmers had not yet finished. They brought them here in the meantime," and he pointed to us.

"Very well, you may go," snapped the little man.

Ferradji backed toward the door. On the threshold he stopped and spoke again—

"I was to remind you, sir, that dinner is served."

"All right. Go along."

And the little man seated himself at the desk and began to finger the papers feverishly.

I do not know why, but a mad feeling of exasperation seized me. I walked toward him.

"Sir," I said, "my friend and I do not know where we are nor who you are. We can see only that you are French, since you are wearing one of the highest honorary decorations of our country. You may have made the same observation on your part," I added, indicating the slender red ribbon which I wore on my vest.

He looked at me in contemptuous surprise.

"Well, sir?"

"Well, sir," I replied, "the Negro who just went out pronounced the name of Cegheir-ben-Cheikh, the name of a brigand, a bandit, one of the assassins of Colonel Flatters. Are you acquainted with that detail, sir?"

The little man surveyed me coldly and shrugged his shoulders.

"Certainly. But what difference do you suppose that makes to me?"

"What!" I cried, beside myself with rage. "Who are you, anyway?"

"Sir," said the little old man with comical dignity, turning to Morhange, "I call you to witness the strange manners of your companion. I am here in my own house and I do not allow—"

"You must excuse my comrade, sir," said Morhange, stepping forward. "He is not a man of letters as you are. These young lieutenants are hot-headed, you know. And besides you can understand why both of us are not as calm as might be desired."

I was furious and on the point of disavowing these strangely humble words of Morhange, but a glance showed me that there was as much irony as surprise in his expression.

"I know indeed that most officers are brutes," grumbled the little old man. "But that is no reason—"

"I am only an officer myself," Morhange went on in an even humbler tone, "and if ever I have been sensible to the intellectual inferiority of that class, I assure you that it was just now in glancing—I beg your pardon for having taken the liberty to do so—in glancing over the learned pages which you devote to the passionate story of Medusa, according to Proclés of Carthage, cited by Pausanias."

A laughable surprise spread over the features of the little old man. He hastily wiped his spectacles.

"What!" he finally cried.

"It is indeed unfortunate, in this matter," Morhange continued imperturbably, "that we are not in possession of the curious dissertation devoted to this burning question by Statius Sebosus, a work which we know only through Pliny and which—"

"You know Statius Sebosus?"

"And which my master, the geographer Berlioux—"

"You knew Berlioux? You were his pupil?" stammered the little man with the decoration.

"I have had that honor," replied Morhange very coldly.

"But, but, sir, then you have heard mentioned, you are familiar with the question, the problem of Atlantis?"

"Indeed I am not unacquainted with the works of Lagneau, Ploix and Arbois de Jubainville," said Morhange frigidly.

"My God!" The little man was going through extraordinary contortions. "Sir—Captain, how happy I am, how many excuses—"

Just then, the portiére was raised. Ferradji appeared again.

"Sir, they want me to tell you that unless you come they will begin without you."

"I am coming, I am coming. Say, Ferradji, that we will be there in a moment. Why, sir, if I had foreseen— It is extraordinary—to find an officer who knows Proclés of Carthage and Arbois de Jubainville. Again—but I must introduce myself. I am Étienne Le Mesge, Fellow of the University."

"Captain Morhange," said my companion.

I stepped forward in my turn.

"Lieutenant de Saint-Avit. It is a fact, sir, that I am very likely to confuse Proclés of Carthage with Arbois de Jubainville. Later, I shall have to see about filling up those gaps, but just now I should like to know where we are, if we are free and if not, what occult power holds us. You have the appearance, sir, of being sufficiently at home in this house to be able to enlighten us upon this point, which I must confess I weakly consider of the first importance."

M. Le Mesge looked at me. A rather malevolent smile twitched the corners of his mouth. He opened his lips.

A gong sounded impatiently.

"In good time, gentlemen, I will tell you. I will explain everything, but now you see that we must hurry. It is time for lunch and our fellow diners will get tired of waiting."

"Our fellow diners?"

"There are two of them," M. Le Mesge explained. "We three constitute the

European personnel of the house—that is, the fixed personnel," he seemed to feel obliged to add with his disquieting smile. "Two strange fellows, gentlemen, with whom, doubtless, you will care to have as little to do as possible. One is a churchman, narrow-minded, though a Protestant. The other is a man of the world gone astray, an old fool."

"Pardon," I said, "but it must have been he whom I heard last night. He was gambling—with you and the minister, doubtless?"

M. Le Mesge made a gesture of offended dignity.

"The idea! With me, sir? It is with the Tuareg that he plays. He teaches them every game imaginable. There, that is he who is striking the gong to hurry us up. It is half past nine, and the Salle de Trente et Quarante opens at ten o'clock. Let us hurry. I suppose that anyway you will not be averse to a little refreshment."

"Indeed we shall not refuse," Morhange replied.

We followed M. Le Mesge along a long winding corridor with frequent steps. The passage was dark, but at intervals rose-colored night lights and incense-burners were placed in niches cut into the solid rock. Passionate Oriental scents perfumed the darkness and contrasted strangely with the cold air of the snowy peaks.

From time to time a white Targa, mute and expressionless as a phantom, would pass us and we would hear the clatter of his slippers die away behind us.

M. Le Mesge stopped before a heavy door covered with the same pale metal which I had noticed on the walls of the library. He opened it and stood aside to let us pass.

Although the dining room which we entered had little in common with European dining rooms, I have known many which might have envied its comfort. Like the library, it was lighted by a great window, and I noticed that it had an outside exposure, while that of the library overlooked the garden in the center of the crown of mountains.

There was no center table and none of those barbaric pieces of furniture that we call chairs, but a great number of credences of gilded wood, like those of Venice, heavy hangings of dull and subdued colors and Tuareg or Tunisian cushions. In the center was a huge mat on which a feast was placed in finely woven baskets among silver pitchers and copper basins filled with perfumed water. The sight of it filled me with childish satisfaction.

M. Le Mesge stepped forward and introduced us to the two persons who already had taken their places on the mat.

"Mr. Spardek," he said, and by that simple phrase I understood how far our host placed himself above vain human titles.

The Reverend Mr. Spardek of Manchester bowed reservedly and asked our permission to keep on his tall, wide-brimmed hat. He was a dry, cold man, tall and thin. He ate heartily and in pious sadness.

"M. Bielowsky," said M. Le Mesge, introducing us to the second guest.

"Count Casimir Bielowsky, Hetman of Jitomir," the latter corrected with perfect good humor as he stood up to shake hands.

I felt at once a certain liking for the Hetman of Jitomir who was a perfect example of an old beau. His chocolate-coloured hair was parted in the center—later I found out that the Hetman dyed it with a concoction of kohl. He had magnificent whiskers, also chocolate-coloured, in the style of the Emperor Francis Joseph. His nose was undeniably a little red, but very fine and aristocratic. His hands were marvelous.

It took some thought to place the date of the style of the count's costume—bottle green with yellow facings, ornamented with a huge seal of silver and enamel. The recollection of a portrait of the Duke de Morny made me decide on 1860 or 1862, and the further chapters of this story will show that I was not far wrong.

The count made me sit down beside him. One of his first questions was to demand if I ever cut fives—*tirer à cinq,* a card game played only for very high stakes.

"That depends on how I feel," I replied.

"Well said. I have not done so since 1866. I swore off. A row. The devil of a party. One day at Walewski's I cut fives. Naturally I wasn't worrying any. The other had a four. 'Idiot!' cried the little Baron de Chaux Gisseux who was laying staggering sums on my table. I hurled a bottle of champagne at his head. He ducked. It was Marshal Baillant who got the bottle. A scene! The matter was fixed up because we were both members of the same fraternal order. The Emperor made me promise not to cut fives again. I have kept my promise, but there are moments when it is hard."

He added in a voice steeped in melancholy:

"Try a little of this Ahaggar, 1880. Excellent vintage. It is I, Lieutenant, who instructed these people in the uses of the juice of the vine. The vine of the palm-trees is very good when it is properly fermented, but it gets insipid in the long run."

It was powerful, that Ahaggar, 1880. We sipped it from large silver goblets. It was fresh as Rhine wine, dry as the wine of the Hermitage. And then suddenly it brought back recollections of the burning wines of Portugal; it seemed sweet, fruity—an admirable wine, I tell you.

That wine crowned the most perfect of luncheons. There were few meats, to be sure, but those few were remarkably seasoned, and there was a profusion of cakes, pancakes served with honey, fragrant fritters and cheese-cakes of sour milk and dates. And everywhere, in great enamel platters or wicker jars, fruit, masses of fruit—figs, dates, jujubes, pomegranates, apricots, huge bunches of grapes larger than those which bent the shoulders of the Hebrews in the land of Canaan, heavy watermelons cut in two, showing their moist red pulp and their rows of black seeds.

I had scarcely finished one of these beautiful iced fruits when M. Le Mesge rose.

"Gentlemen, if you are ready," he said to Morhange and me.

"Get away from that old dotard as soon as you can," whispered the Hetman of Jitomir to me. "The party of *trente et quarante* will begin soon. You shall see. You shall see. We go it even harder than at Cora Pearl's."

"Gentlemen," repeated M. Le Mesge in his dry tone.

We followed him. When the three of us were back again in the library, he said, addressing me:

"You, sir, asked a little while ago what occult power holds you here. Your manner was threatening and I should have refused to comply had it not been for your friend, whose knowledge enables him to appreciate better than you the value of the revelations I am about to make to you."

He touched a spring in the side of the wall. A cupboard appeared, stuffed with books. He took one.

"You are both of you," continued M. Le Mesge, "in the power of a woman. This woman, the sultaness, the queen, the absolute sovereign of Ahaggar, is called Antinea. Don't start, M. Morhange, you will soon understand."

He opened the book and read this sentence:

"'I must warn you before I take up the subject matter that you must not be surprised to hear me call the barbarians by Greek names.'"

"What is that book?" stammered Morhange, whose pallor terrified me.

"This book," M. Le Mesge replied very slowly, weighing his words with an extraordinary expression of triumph, "is the greatest, the most beautiful, the most secret, of the dialogues of Plato; it is the *Critias of Atlantis.*"

"The *Critias?* But it is unfinished," murmured Morhange.

"It is unfinished in France, in Europe—everywhere else," said M. Le Mesge, "but it is finished here. Look for yourself at this copy."

"But what connection," repeated Morhange while his eyes traveled avidly over the pages, "what connection can there be between this dialogue, complete—yes, it seems to me complete—what connection with this woman, Antinea? Why should it be in her possession?"

"Because," replied the little man imperturbably, "this book is her patent of nobility, her *Almanach de Gotha* in a sense, do you understand? Because it establishes her prodigious genealogy: because she is—"

"Because she is?" repeated Morhange.

"Because she is the granddaughter of Neptune, the last descendant of the Atlantides."

Chapter IX

Atlantis

MR. LE MESGE LOOKED AT MORHANGE TRIUMPHANTLY. IT WAS EVIDENT THAT HE addressed himself exclusively to Morhange, considering him alone worthy of his confidences.

"There have been many, sir," he said, "both French and foreign officers, who have been brought here at the caprice of our sovereign, Antinea. You are the first to be honored by my disclosures. But you were the pupil of Berlioux and I owe so much to the memory of that great man that it seems to me I may do him homage by imparting to one of his disciples the unique results of my private research."

He struck the bell. Ferradji appeared.

"Coffee for these gentlemen," ordered M. Le Mesge.

He handed us a box, gorgeously decorated in the most flaming colors, full of Egyptian cigarettetes.

"I never smoke," he explained. "But Antinea sometimes comes here. These are her cigarettetes. Help yourselves, gentlemen."

I have always had a horror of that pale tobacco which gives a barber of the rue de la Michodière the illusion of oriental voluptuousness, but, in their way, these musk-scented cigarettes were not bad and it had been a long time since I used up my stock of caporal.

"Here are the back numbers of *Le Vie Parisienne,*" said M. Le Mesge to me. "Amuse yourself with them, if you like, while I talk to your friend."

"Sir," I replied brusquely, "it is true that I never studied with Berlioux. Nevertheless you must allow me to listen to your conversation. I shall hope to find something in it to amuse me."

"As you wish," said the little old man.

We settled ourselves comfortably. M. Le Mesge sat down before the desk, shot his cuffs and commenced as follows:

"However much, gentlemen, I prize complete objectivity in matters of erudition, I cannot utterly detach my own history from that of the last descendant of Clito and Neptune.

"I am the creation of my own efforts. From my childhood the prodigious impulse given to the science of history by the nineteenth century has affected me. I saw where my way led. I have followed it, in spite of everything.

"In spite of everything, everything—I mean it literally. With no other resources than my own work and merit, I was received as Fellow of History and Geography at the examination of 1880. A great examination! Among the thirteen who were accepted there were names which have since become illustrious—Julian, Bourgeois, Auerbach.

"I do not envy my colleagues on the summits of their official honors; I read their works with commiseration and the pitiful errors to which they are condemned by the insufficiency of their documents would amply counterbalance my chagrin and fill me with ironic joy, had I not been raised long since above the satisfaction of self-love.

"When I was Professor at the *Lycée du Parc* at Lyons. I knew Berlioux and followed eagerly his works on African history. I had at that time a very original idea for my doctor's thesis. I was going to establish a parallel between the Berber heroine of the seventh century, Kahena, who struggled against the Arab invader, and the French heroine, Joan of Arc, who struggled against the English invader. I proposed to the Faculté des Lettres at Paris this title for my thesis: Joan of Arc and the Tuareg.

"This simple announcement gave rise to a perfect outcry in learned circles, a furor of ridicule. My friends warned me discreetly. I refused to believe them. Finally I was forced to believe when my rector summoned me before him and, after manifesting an astonishing interest in my health, asked whether I should object to taking two years' leave on half pay. I refused indignantly. The rector did not insist, but fifteen days later a ministerial decree, with no other legal procedure, assigned me to one of the most insignificant and remote *lycées* of France, at Mont-de-Marsan.

"Realize my exasperation and you will excuse the excesses to which I delivered myself in that strange country. What is there to do in Landes, if you neither eat nor drink? I did both violently. My pay melted away in *foies gras,* in woodcocks, in fine wines. The result came quickly enough; in less than a year my joints began to crack like the over-oiled axle of a bicycle that has gone a long way upon a dusty track. A sharp attack of gout kept me to my bed. Fortunately, in that blessed country, the cure is in reach of the suffering, so I departed to Dax at vacation time to try the waters.

"I rented a room on the bank of the Adour, overlooking the *Promenade des Baigneur.* A charwoman took care of it for me. She worked also for an old gentleman, a retired examining magistrate, president of the Roger-Ducos Society, which was a vague scientific backwater in which the scholars of the neighborhood applied themselves with prodigious incompetence to the most whimsical subjects.

"One afternoon I stayed in my room on account of a very heavy rain. The good woman was energetically polishing the copper latch of my door. She used a paste called Tripoli, which she spread upon a paper and rubbed and rubbed. The peculiar appearance of the paper made me curious. I glanced at it.

"'Great heavens! Where did you get this paper?' I demanded.

"She was perturbed.

"'At my master's; he has lots of it. I tore this out of a notebook.'

"'Here are ten francs. Go and get me the notebook.'

"A quarter of an hour later, she was back with it. By good luck it lacked only one page, the one with which she had been polishing my door. This manuscript, this notebook, have you any idea what it was ? Merely the *Voyage to Atlantis* of the mythologist Denis de Milet, which is mentioned by Diodorus and the loss of which I had so often heard Berlioux deplore.[9]

"This inestimable document contained numerous quotations from the *Critias*. It gave an abstract of the illustrious dialogue, the sole existing copy of which you held in your hands a little while ago. It established past controversy the location of the stronghold of the Atlantides and demonstrated that this site, which is denied by science, was not submerged by the waves, as is supposed by the rare and timorous defenders of the Atlantide hypothesis. He called it the 'central Mazycian range.' You know there is no longer any doubt as to the identification of the Mazyces of Herodotus with the people of Imoschaoch, the Tuareg. But the manuscript of Denys unquestionably identifies the historical Mazyces with the Atlantides of the supposed legend.

"I learned, therefore, from Denys, not only that the central part of Atlantis, the cradle and home of the dynasty of Neptune, had not sunk in the disaster described by Plato as engulfing the rest of the Atlantide isle, but also that it corresponded to the Tuareg Ahaggar, and that in this Ahaggar, at least in his time, the noble dynasty of Neptune was supposed to be still existent.

"The historians of Atlantis put the date of the cataclysm which destroyed all or part of that famous country at nine thousand years before Christ. If Denis de Milet, who wrote scarcely three thousand years ago, believed that in his time the dynastic issue of Neptune were still ruling its dominion, you will understand that I thought immediately that what has lasted nine thousand years may last eleven thousand. From that instant I had only one aim: To find the possible descendants of the Atlantides, and, since I had many reasons for supposing them to be debased and ignorant of their original splendor, to inform them of their illustrious descent.

"You will easily understand that I imparted none of my intentions to my superiors at the University. To solicit their approval or even their permission, considering the attitude they had taken toward me, would have been almost certainly to invite confinement in a cell. So I raised what I could on my own account and departed without trumpet or drum for Oran. On the first of October I reached In-Salah. Stretched at my ease beneath a palm tree, at the oasis, I took infinite pleasure in considering how, that very day, the principal of Mont-de-Marsan, beside himself, struggling to control twenty horrible urchins howling before the door of an empty class-room, would be telegraphing wildly in all

---

9   How did the *Voyage to Atlantis* arrive at Dax? I have found so far only one credible hy-
     pothesis; it might have been discovered in Africa by the traveller, de Behagle, a member of
     the Roger-Ducos Society, who studied at the college of Dax, and later on several occasions
     visited the town. (Note by M. Leroux.)

directions in search of his lost history professor."

M. Le Mesge stopped and looked at us to mark his satisfaction.

I admit that I forgot my dignity and I forgot the affectation he had steadily assumed of talking only to Morhange.

"You will pardon me, sir, if your discourse interests me more than I had anticipated, but you know very well that I lack the fundamental instruction necessary to understand you. You speak of the dynasty of Neptune. What is this dynasty, from which, I believe, you trace the descent of Antinea? What is her role in the story of Atlantis?"

M. Le Mesge smiled with condescension, meantime winking at Morhange with the eye nearest to him. Morhange was listening without expression, without a word, chin in hand, elbow on knee.

"Plato will answer for me, sir," said the Professor, and he added with an accent of inexpressible pity, "Is it really possible that you have never made the acquaintance of the introduction to the *Critias?*"

He placed on the table the book by which Morhange had been so strangely moved. He adjusted his spectacles and began to read. It seemed as if the magic of Plato vibrated through and transfigured this ridiculous little old man.

"'Having drawn by lot the different parts of the earth, the gods obtained, some a larger, and some a smaller, share. It was thus that Neptune, having received in the division the isle of Atlantis, came to place the children he had had by a mortal in one part of that isle. It was not far from the sea, a plain situated in the midst of the isle, the most beautiful, and, they say, the most fertile of plains.'

"'About fifty stadia from that plain, in the middle of the isle, was a mountain. There dwelt one of those men who, in the very beginning, was born of the Earth, Evenor, with his wife, Leucippe. They had only one daughter, Clito. She was marriageable when her mother and father died and Neptune, being enamored of her, married her. Neptune fortified the mountain where she dwelt by isolating it. He made alternate girdles of sea and land, the one smaller, the others greater, two of earth and three of water, and circled them round the isle in such a manner that they were at all parts equally distant.'"

M. le Mesge broke off his reading.

"Does this arrangement recall nothing to you?" he queried

"Morhange, Morhange!" I stammered "You remember—our route yesterday, our abduction, the two corridors that we had to cross before arriving at this mountain? The girdles of earth and of water? Two tunnels, two enclosures of earth?"

"Ha, ha," chuckled M. Le Mesge.

He smiled as he looked at me. I understood that this smile meant: "Can he be less obtuse than I had supposed?"

As if with a mighty effort, Morhange broke the silence.

"I understand well enough, I understand— The three girdles of water—but then, you are supposing, sir—an explanation the ingeniousness of which I do not contest—you are supposing the exact hypothesis of the Saharan sea!"

"I suppose it and I can prove it," replied the irascible little old chap, banging his fist on the table. "I know well enough what Schirmer and the rest had advanced against it. I know it better than you do. I know all about it, sir. I can present all the proofs for your consideration. And in the meantime, this evening at dinner, you will no doubt enjoy some excellent fish. And you will tell me whether these fish, caught in the lake that you can see from this window, seem to you fresh-water fish.

"You must realize," he continued more calmly, "the mistake of those who, believing in Atlantis, have sought to explain the cataclysm in which they suppose the whole island to have sunk. Without exception, they have thought that it was swallowed up. Actually, there has not been an immersion. There has been an emersion. New lands have emerged from the Atlantic wave. The desert has replaced the sea; the *sebkas,* the salt lakes, the Triton lakes, the sandy Syrtes are the desolate vestiges of the free sea-water over which in former days the fleets swept with a fair wind towards the conquest of Attica.

"Sand swallows up civilization better than water. Today there remains nothing but this chalky mass of the beautiful isle that the sea and winds kept gay and verdant. Nothing has endured in this rocky basin, cut off forever from the living world, but the marvelous oasis that you have at your feet—these red fruits, this cascade, this blue lake, sacred witnesses to the golden age that is gone.

"Last evening, in coming here, you had to cross the five enclosures— the three belts of water, dry forever; the two girdles of earth through which are hollowed the passages you traversed on camel-back, where formerly the triremes floated. The only thing that, in this immense catastrophe has preserved its likeness to its former state, is this mountain, the mountain where Neptune shut up his well-beloved Clito, the daughter of Evenor and Leucippe, the mother of Atlas and the ancestress of Antinea, the sovereign under whose dominion you are about to enter forever."

"Sir," said Morhange with the most exquisite courtesy, "it would be only a natural anxiety which would urge us to inquire the reasons and the end of this dominion. But behold to what extent your revelation interests me; I defer this question of private interest. Of late, in two caverns, it has been my fortune to discover Tifinar inscriptions of this name, Antinea. My comrade is witness that I took it for a Greek name. I understand now, thanks to you and the divine Plato, that I need no longer feel surprised to hear a barbarian called by a Greek name. But I am no less perplexed as to the etymology of the word. Can you enlighten me?"

"I shall certainly not fail you there, sir," said M. Le Mesge. "I may tell you, too, that you are not the first to put to me that question. Most of the explorers that I have seen enter here in the past ten years have been attracted in the same way, intrigued by this Greek work reproduced in Tifinar. I have even arranged a fairly exact catalogue of these inscriptions and the caverns where they are to be met with.

"All, or almost all, are accompanied by this legend: '*Antinea. Here commences her domain.*' I myself have had repainted with ochre such as were beginning to be effaced. But to return to what I was telling you before, none of the Europeans who have followed this epigraphic mystery here have kept their anxiety to solve this etymology, once they found themselves in Antinea's palace. They all become otherwise preoccupied. I might make many disclosures as to the little real importance which purely scientific interests possess even for scholars, and the quickness with which they sacrifice them to the most mundane considerations—their own lives, for instance."

"Let us take that up another time, sir, if it is satisfactory to you," said Morhange, always admirably polite.

"This digression had only one point, sir—to show you that I do not count you among these unworthy scholars. You are really eager to know the origin of this name, *Antinea,* and that before knowing what kind of woman it belongs to and her motives for holding you and this gentleman as her prisoners."

I stared hard at the little old man, but he spoke with profound seriousness.

"So much the better for you, my boy," I thought. "Otherwise it wouldn't have taken me long to send you through the window to air your ironies at your ease. The law of gravity ought not to be topsy-turvy here at Ahaggar."

"You no doubt formulated several hypotheses when you first encountered the name, Antinea," continued M. Le Mesge, imperturbable under my fixed gaze, addressing himself to Morhange. "Would you object to repeating them to me?"

"Not at all, sir," said Morhange.

And very composedly he enumerated the etymological suggestions I have given previously.

The little man with the cherry-colored shirt front rubbed his hands.

"Very good," he admitted with an accent of intense jubilation. "Amazingly good for one with only the modicum of Greek that you possess, but it is all none the less false, absolutely false."

"It is because I suspected as much that I put my question to you," said Morhange blandly.

"I will not keep you longer in suspense," said M. Le Mesge. "The word Antinea is composed as follows: *ti* is nothing but a Tifinar addition to an essentially Greek name. *Ti* is the Berber feminine article. We have several examples of this combination. Take *Tipasa,* the North African town. The name means the whole, from *ti* and from *pan.* So, *tinea* signifies the new, from *ti* and from *nea.*

"And the prefix *an?*" queried Morhange.

"Is it possible, sir, that I have put myself to the trouble of talking to you for a solid hour about the *Critias* with such trifling effect? It is certain that the prefix *an,* alone, has no meaning. You will understand that it has one when I tell you that we have here a very curious case of apocope. You must not read *an;* you must read *atlan. Atl* has been lost by apocope; *an* has survived. To sum up, Antinea is composed in the following manner: Atlantinea, and its meaning, '*the new Atlantis,*' is dazzlingly apparent from this demonstration."

I looked at Morhange. His astonishment was without bounds. The Berber prefix *ti* had literally stunned him.

"Have you had occasion, sir, to verify this very ingenious etymology?" he was finally able to gasp out.

"You have only to glance over these few books," said M. Le Mesge disdainfully.

He opened successively five, ten, twenty cupboards. An enormous library was spread out to our view.

"Everything, everything—it is all here?" murmured Morhange with an astonishing inflection of terror and admiration.

"Everything that is worth consulting, at any rate," said M. Le Mesge. "All the great books whose loss the so-called learned world deplores today."

"And how has it happened?"

"Sir, you distress me. I thought you familiar with certain events. You are forgetting, then, the passage where Pliny the Elder speaks of the library of Carthage and the treasures which were accumulated there? In 146, when that city fell under the blows of the knave Scipio, the incredible collection of illiterates who were the Roman Senate had only the profoundest contempt for these riches. They presented them to the native kings.

"This is how Mantabal received this priceless heritage; it was transmitted to his son and grandsons, Hiempsal, Juba I and Juba II, the husband of the admirable Cleopatra Selene, the daughter of the great Cleopatra and Mark Antony. Cleopatra Selene had a daughter who married an Atlantide king. This is how Antinea, the daughter of Neptune, counts among her ancestors the immortal queen of Egypt. That is how, by following the laws of inheritance, the remains of the library of Carthage, enriched by the remnants of the library of Alexandria, are actually before your eyes.

"Science fled from man. While he was building those monstrous Babels of pseudo-science in Berlin, London and Paris, science was taking refuge in this desert-corner of Ahaggar. They may well forge their hypotheses back there, based on the loss of the mysterious works of antiquity, but these works are not lost. They are here. They are here—the Hebrew, the Chaldean, the Assyrian books. Here, the great Egyptian traditions which inspired Solon, Herodotus and Plato. Here, the Greek mythologists, the magicians of Roman Africa, the Indian mystics—all the treasures, in a word, for the lack of which contemporary dissertations are poor laughable things.

"Believe me he is well avenged, the little universitarian whom they took for a madman, whom they defied. I have lived, I live, I shall live in a perpetual burst of laughter at their false and garbled erudition. And when I shall be dead, error—thanks to the jealous precaution of Neptune, taken to isolate his well-beloved Clito from the rest of the world—error, I say, will continue to reign as sovereign mistress over their pitiful compositions."

"Sir," said Morhange in a grave voice, "you have just affirmed the influence of Egypt on the civilizations of the people here. For reasons which some day perhaps I shall have occasion to explain to you, I would like to have proof of that relationship."

"We need not wait for that, sir," said M. Le Mesge.

Then, in my turn, I advanced.

"Two words, if you please, sir," I said brutally. "I will not hide from you that these historical discussions seem to me absolutely out of place. It is not my fault if you have had trouble with the University and if you are not today at the College of France or elsewhere. For the moment just one thing concerns me: to know just what this lady, Antinea, wants with us. My comrade would like to know her relation with ancient Egypt—very well. For my part, I desire above everything to know her relations with the government of Algeria and the Arabian Bureau."

M. Le Mesge gave a strident laugh.

"I am going to give you an answer that will satisfy you both," he replied. And he added:

"Follow me. It is time that you should learn."

Chapter X

The Red Marble Hall

FOLLOWING M. LE MESGE, WE PASSED THROUGH AN INTERMINABLE SERIES OF STAIRS and corridors.

"You lose all sense of direction in this labyrinth," I muttered to Morhange.

"Worse still, you will lose your head," answered my companion *sotto voce.* "This old fool is certainly very learned, but God knows what he is driving at. However, he has promised that we are soon to know."

M. Le Mesge had stopped before a heavy dark door all incrusted with strange symbols. Turning the lock with difficulty, he opened it.

"Enter, gentlemen, I beg you," he said.

A gust of cold air struck us full in the face. The room we were entering was chill as a vault.

At first, the darkness allowed me to form no idea of its proportions. The lighting, purposely subdued, consisted of twelve enormous copper lamps placed column-like upon the ground and burning with brilliant red flames. As we entered, the wind from the corridor made the flames flicker, momentarily casting about us our own enlarged and misshapen shadows. Then the gust died down and the flames, no longer flurried, again licked up the darkness with their motionless red tongues.

These twelve giant lamps—each one about ten feet high—were arranged in a kind of crown, the diameter of which must have been about fifty feet. In the center of this circle was a dark mass, all streaked with trembling red reflections. When I drew nearer I saw it was a bubbling fountain. It was the freshness of this water which had maintained the temperature of which I have spoken.

Huge seats were cut in the central rock from which gushed the murmuring, shadowy fountain. They were heaped with silky cushions. Twelve incense-burners within the circle of red lamps formed a second crown, half as large in diameter. Their smoke mounted toward the vault, invisible in the darkness, but their perfume, combined with the coolness and sound of the water, banished from the soul all other desire than to remain there forever.

M. Le Mesge made us sit down in the center of the hall, on the Cyclopean seats. He seated himself between us.

"In a few minutes," he said, "your eyes will grow accustomed to the obscurity."

I noticed that he spoke in a hushed voice, as if he were in church.

Little by little our eyes did indeed grow used to the red light. Only the lower part of the great hall was illuminated. The whole vault was drowned in shadow and its height was impossible to estimate. Vaguely I could perceive overhead a great smooth gold chandelier, flecked, like everything else, with sombre red reflections, but there was no means of judging the length of the chain by which it hung from the dark ceiling.

The marble of the pavement was of so high a polish that the great torches were reflected even there.

This room, I repeat, was round—a perfect circle, of which the fountain at our backs was the center.

We sat facing the curving walls. Before long we began to be able to see them. They were of peculiar construction, divided into a series of niches, broken ahead of us by the door which had just opened to give us passage; behind us by a second door, a still darker hole which I divined in the darkness when I turned around. From one door to the other, I counted sixty niches, making in all one hundred and twenty. Each was about ten feet high. Each contained a kind of case, larger above than below, closed only at the lower end. In all these cases, except two just opposite me, I thought I could discern a brilliant shape, a human shape certainly, something like a statue of very pale bronze. In the arc of the circle before me I counted clearly thirty of these strange statues.

What were these statues? I wanted to see. I rose.

M. Le Mesge put his hand on my arm.

"In good time," he murmured in the same low voice; "all in good time."

The professor was watching the door by which we had entered the hall and from behind which we could hear the sound of footsteps becoming more and more distinct.

It opened quietly to admit three Tuareg slaves. Two of them were carrying a long package on their shoulders; the third seemed to be their chief.

At a sign from him they placed the package on the ground and drew out from one of the niches the case which it contained.

"You may approach, gentlemen," said M. Le Mesge.

He motioned the three Tuareg to withdraw several paces.

"You asked me not long since for some proof of the Egyptian influence on this country," said M. Le Mesge. "What do you say to that case, to begin with?"

As he spoke, he pointed to the case that the servants had deposited upon the ground after they took it from its niche.

Morhange uttered a thick cry.

We had before us one of those cases designed for the preservation of mummies. The same shiny wood, the same bright decorations, the only difference being that here Tifinar writing replaced the hieroglyphics. The form, narrow at the base, broader above, ought to have been enough to enlighten us.

I have already said that the lower half of this large case was closed, giving the whole structure the appearance of a rectangular wooden shoe.

˙M. Le Mesge knelt and fastened on the lower part of the case a square of white cardboard, a large label that he had picked up from his desk a few minutes before on leaving the library.

"You may read," he said simply but still in the same low tone.

I knelt also, for the light of the great candelabra was scarcely sufficient to read the label where, none the less, I recognized the professor's handwriting.

It bore these few words in a large round hand:

Number 53. Major Sir Archibald Russell. Born at Richmond July 5, 1860. Died at Ahaggar December 3, 1896.

I leapt to my feet.

"Major Russell!" I exclaimed.

"Not so loud, not so loud," said M. Le Mesge. "No one speaks out loud here."

"The Major Russell," I repeated, obeying his injunction as if in spite of myself, "who left Khartoum last year, to explore Sokoto?"

"The same," replied the Professor.

"And—where is Major Russell?"

"He is there," replied M. Le Mesge.

The professor made a gesture. The Tuareg approached.

A poignant silence reigned in the mysterious hall, broken only by the fresh splashing of the fountain.

The three Negroes were occupied in undoing the package that they had put down near the painted case. Weighed down with wordless horror, Morhange and I stood watching.

Soon a rigid form, a human form, appeared. A red gleam played over it. We had before us, stretched out upon the ground, a statue of pale bronze, wrapped in a kind of white veil, a statue like those all around us, upright in their niches. It seemed to fix us with an impenetrable gaze.

"Sir Archibald Russell," murmured M. Le Mesge slowly.

Morhange approached, speechless, but strong enough to lift up the white veil. For a long, long time he gazed at the sad bronze statue.

"A mummy, a mummy?" he said finally. "You deceive yourself, sir; this is no mummy."

"Accurately speaking, no," replied M. Le Mesge. "This is not a mummy. None the less, you have before you the mortal remains of Sir Archibald Russell. I must point out to you, here, my dear sir, that the processes of embalming used by Antinea differ from the processes employed in ancient Egypt. Here there is no natron, nor bands, nor spices. The industry of Ahaggar in a single effort has achieved a result obtained by European science only after long experiments. Imagine my surprise when I arrived here and found that they were employing a method I supposed known only to the civilized world."

M. Le Mesge struck a light tap with his finger on the forehead of Sir

Archibald Russell. It rang like metal.

"It is bronze," I said. "That is not a human forehead; it is bronze."

M. Le Mesge shrugged his shoulders.

"It is a human forehead," he affirmed curtly, "and not bronze. Bronze is darker, sir. This is the great unknown metal of which Plato speaks in the *Critias* and which is something between gold and silver: it is the special metal of the mountains of the Atlantides. It is *orichalc.*"

Bending again, I satisfied myself that this metal was the same as that with which the walls of the library were overcast

"It is orichalc," continued M. Le Mesge. "You look as if you had no idea how a human body can look like a statue of orichalc. Come, Captain Morhange, you whom I gave credit for a certain amount of knowledge, have you never heard of the method of Dr. Variot, by which a human body can be preserved without embalming? Have you never read the book of that practitioner?[10]

"He explains a method called electro-plating. The skin is coated with a very thin layer of silver salts, to make it a conductor. The body then is placed in a solution of copper sulphate and the polar currents do their work. The body of this estimable English major has been metalized in the same manner, except that a solution of orichalc sulphate, a very rare substance, has been substituted for that of copper sulphate. Thus, instead of the statue of a poor slave, a copper statue, you have before you a statue of metal more precious than silver or gold—in a word, a statue worthy of the granddaughter of Neptune."

M. Le Mesge waved his arm. The black slaves seized the body. In a few seconds, they slid the orichalc ghost into its painted wooden sheath. That was set on end and slid into its niche beside the niche where an exactly similar sheath was labeled "Number 52."

Upon finishing their task they retired without a word. A draft of cold air from the door again made the flames of the copper torches flicker and threw great shadows about us.

Morhange and I remained as motionless as the pale metal specters which surrounded us. Suddenly I pulled myself together and staggered forward to the niche beside that in which they just had laid the remains of the English major. I looked for the label.

Supporting myself against the red marble wall, I read:

Number 52. Captain Laurent Deligne. Born at Paris July 22, 1861. Died at Ahaggar October 30, 1896.

"Captain Deligne!" murmured Morhange. "He left Colomb-Béchar in 1895 for Timmimoun and no more has been heard of him since then."

"Exactly," said M. Le Mesge, with a little nod of approval.

---

10   Variot: *L'anthropologie galvanique.* Paris, 1890. (Note by M. Leroux.)

"'Number 51,'" read Morhange with chattering teeth. "'Colonel von Wittman, born at Jena in 1855. Died at Ahaggar, May 1, 1896.' Colonel Wittman, the explorer of Kanem, who disappeared off Agadès."

"Exactly," said M. Le Mesge again.

"'Number 50,'" I read in my turn, steadying myself against the wall so as not to fall. "'Marquis Alonzo d'Oliveira, born at Cadiz, February 21, 1868. Died at Ahaggar February 1, 1896.' Oliveira, who was going to Araouan."

"Exactly," said M. Le Mesge again. "That Spaniard was one of the best educated. I used to have interesting discussions with him on the exact geographical position of the kingdom of Antée."

"'Number 49,'" said Morhange in a tone scarcely more than a whisper. "'Lieutenant Woodhouse, born at Liverpool, September 16, 1870. Died at Ahaggar, October 4, 1895.'"

"Hardly more than a child," said M. Le Mesge.

"'Number 48,'" I said. "'Lieutenant Louis de Maillefeu, born at Provins the—"

I did not finish. My voice choked.

Louis de Maillefeu, my best friend, the friend of my childhood and of Saint-Cyr. I looked at him and recognized him under the metallic coating. Louis de Maillefeu!

I laid my forehead against the cold wall and with shaking shoulders began to sob.

I heard the muffled voice of Morhange speaking to the Professor:

"Sir, this has lasted long enough. Let us make an end to it."

"He wanted to know," said M. Le Mesge. "What am I to do?"

I went up to him and seized his shoulders.

"What happened to him? What did he die of?"

"Just like the others," the Professor replied, "like Lieutenant Woodhouse, like Captain Deligne, like Major Russell, like Colonel van Wittman, like the forty-seven of yesterday and all those of tomorrow."

"Of what did they die?" Morhange demanded imperatively in his turn.

The Professor looked at Morhange. I saw my comrade grow pale.

"Of what did they die, sir? *They died of love!*"

And he added in a very low, very grave voice:

"Now you know."

Gently and with a tact which we should hardly have suspected in him, M. Le Mesge drew us away from the statues. A moment later Morhange and I found ourselves again seated, or rather sunk, among the cushions in the center of the room. The invisible fountain murmured its plaint at our feet.

Le Mesge sat between us.

"Now you know," he repeated. "You know but you do not yet understand."

Then, very slowly, he said:

"You are, as they have been, the prisoners of Antinea. And vengeance is due Antinea."

"Vengeance?" said Morhange, who had regained his self-possession. "For what, I beg to ask? What have the lieutenant and I done to Atlantis? How have we incurred her hatred?"

"It is an old quarrel, a very old quarrel," the professor replied gravely. "A quarrel which long antedates you, M. Morhange."

"Explain yourself, I beg of you, Professor."

"You are man. She is a woman," said the dreamy voice of M. Le Mesge. "The whole matter lies there."

"Really, sir, I do not see—we do not see."

"You are going to understand. Have you really forgotten to what an extent the beautiful queens of antiquity had just cause to complain of the strangers whom fortune brought to their borders? The poet, Victor Hugo, pictured their detestable acts well enough in his colonial poem called "La Fille d'O-Taiti." Wherever we look we see similar examples of fraud and ingratitude. These gentlemen made free use of the beauty and the riches of the lady. Then, one fine morning they disappeared. She was indeed lucky if her lover, having observed the position carefully, did not return with ships and troops of occupation.

"Your learning charms me," said Morhange. "Continue."

"Do you need examples? Alas, they abound. Think of the cavalier fashion in which Ulysses treated Calypso; Diomedes, Callirrhoë. What should I say of Theseus and Ariadne? Jason treated Medea with inconceivable lightness. The Romans continued the tradition with still greater brutality. Aeneas, who has many characteristics in common with the Reverend Spardek, treated Dido in a most undeserved fashion. Caesar was a laurel-crowned blackguard in his relations with the divine Cleopatra. Titus, that hypocrite Titus, after having lived a whole year in Idummaea at the expense of the plaintive Berenice, took her back to Rome only to make game of her. It is time that the sons of Japheth paid this formidable reckoning of injuries to the daughters of Shem.

"A woman has taken it upon herself to re-establish the great Hegelian law of equilibrium, for the benefit of her sex. Separated from the Aryan world by the formidable precautions of Neptune, she draws the youngest and bravest to her. Her body is condescending, while her spirit is inexorable. She takes what these bold young men can give her. She lends them her body, while her soul dominates them. She is the first sovereign who has never been made the slave of passion, even for a moment. She has never been obliged to regain her self-mastery, for she never has lost it. She is the only woman who has been able to disassociate those two inextricable things, love and voluptuousness."

M. Le Mesge paused a moment and then went on.

"Once every day, she comes to this vault. She stops before the niches; she meditates before the rigid statues; she touches the cold bosoms, so burning when she knew them. Then, after dreaming before the empty niche where the next victim soon will sleep his eternal sleep in a cold case of orichalc, she returns nonchalantly to where he is waiting for her."

The professor stopped speaking. The fountain again made itself heard in the midst of the shadow. My pulses beat, my head seemed on fire. A fever was consuming me.

"And all of them," I cried, regardless of the place, "all of them complied? They submitted? Well, she has only to come and she will see what will happen."

Morhange was silent.

"My dear sir," said M. Le Mesge in a very gentle voice, "you are speaking like a child. You do not know. You have not seen Antinea. Let me tell you one thing: That among those"—and with a sweeping gesture he indicated the silent circle of statues—"there were men as courageous as you and perhaps less excitable. I remember one of them especially well, a phlegmatic Englishman who now is resting under Number 32. When he first appeared before Antinea he was smoking a cigar. And, like all the rest, he bent before the gaze of his sovereign.

"Do not speak until you have seen her. A university training hardly fits one to discourse upon matters of passion and I feel scarcely qualified myself to tell you what Antinea is. I only affirm this, that when you have seen her, you will remember nothing else. Family, country, honor—you will renounce everything for her."

"Everything?" asked Morhange in a calm voice.

"Everything," Le Mesge insisted emphatically. "You will forget all, you will renounce all."

From outside a faint sound came to us.

Le Mesge consulted his watch.

"In any case, you will see."

The door opened. A tall white Targa, the tallest we had yet seen in this remarkable abode, entered and came toward us.

He bowed and touched me lightly on the shoulder.

"Follow him," said M. Le Mesge.

Without a word, I obeyed.

Chapter XI

Antinea

M Y GUIDE AND I PASSED ALONG ANOTHER LONG CORRIDOR. MY EXCITEMENT increased. I was impatient for one thing only, to come face to face with that woman, to tell her. . . . So far as anything else was concerned, I already was done for.

I was mistaken in hoping that the adventure would take an heroic turn at once. In real life these contrasts never are definitely marked out. I should have remembered from many past incidents that the burlesque was regularly mixed with the tragic in my life.

We reached a little transparent door. My guide stood aside to let me pass.

I found myself in the most luxurious of dressing-rooms. A ground glass ceiling diffused a gay, rosy light over the marble floor. The first thing I noticed was a clock, fastened to the wall. In place of the figures for the hours were the signs of the Zodiac. The small hand had not yet reached the sign of Capricorn.

Only three o'clock!

The day seemed to have lasted a century already. And only a little more than half of it was gone.

Another idea came to me and I laughed nervously.

"Antinea wants me to be at my best when I meet her."

A mirror of orichalc formed one whole side of the room. Glancing into it, I realized that in all decency there was nothing exaggerated in the demand.

My untrimmed beard, the frightful layer of dirt which lay about my eyes and furrowed my cheeks, my clothing, spotted by the clay of the Sahara and torn by the thorns of Ahaggar—all this made me appear a pitiable enough suitor.

I lost no time in undressing and plunging into the porphyry bath in the center of the room. A delicious drowsiness came over me in that perfumed water. A thousand little jars, spread on a costly carved wood dressing-table danced before my eyes. They were of all sizes and colors, carved in a very transparent kind of jade. The warm humidity of the atmosphere hastened my relaxation.

I still had strength to think.

"The devil take Atlantis and the vault and Le Mesge."

Then I fell asleep in the bath.

When I opened my eyes again the little hand of the clock had almost reached the sign of Taurus. Before me, his black hands braced on the edge of the bath, stood a huge Negro, bare-faced and bare-armed, his forehead bound with an immense orange turban.

He looked at me and showed his white teeth in a silent laugh.

"Who is this fellow?"

The Negro laughed harder. Without saying a word, he lifted me like a feather out of the perfumed water, now of a color on which I shall not dwell.

In no time at all I was stretched out on an inclined marble table and the Negro began to massage me vigorously.

"More gently there, fellow!"

My masseur did not reply, but laughed and rubbed still harder.

"Where do you come from? Kanem? Torkou? You laugh too much for a Targa."

Unbroken silence. The Negro was as speechless as he was hilarious.

"After all I am making a fool of myself," I said, giving up the case. "Such as he is, he is more agreeable than Le Mesge with his nightmarish erudition. But, on my word, what a recruit he would be for Hamman on the rue des Mathurins!"

"Cigarette, *sidi?*"

Without awaiting my reply he placed a cigarette between my lips, lighted it and resumed his task of polishing every inch of me.

He doesn't talk much, but he is obliging, I thought, and I sent a puff of smoke into his face.

This pleasantry seemed to delight him immensely. He showed his pleasure by giving me great slaps.

When he had dressed me down sufficiently, he took a little jar from the dressing-table and began to rub me with a rose-colored ointment. Weariness seemed to fly away from my rejuvenated muscles.

Suddenly there came a stroke on a copper gong. My masseur disappeared. A stunted old Negress entered, dressed in the most tawdry tinsel. She was talkative as a magpie, but at first I did not understand a word in the interminable string she unwound while she took first my hands, then my feet, and polished the nails with determined grimaces.

Another stroke on the gong followed. The old woman gave place to another Negro, grave this time, and dressed all in white with a knitted skull cap on his oblong head. It was the barber, and a remarkably dexterous one. He quickly trimmed my hair, and, on my word, it was well done. Then without asking me what style I preferred he shaved me clean.

I looked with pleasure at my face, once more visible.

"Antinea must like the American type," I thought. "What an affront to the memory of her worthy grandfather, Neptune!"

The gay Negro entered and placed a package on the divan. The barber disappeared. I was somewhat astonished to observe that the package, which my new valet opened carefully, contained a suit of white flannels exactly like those French officers wear in Algeria in summer.

The wide trousers seemed made to my measure. The tunic fitted without a wrinkle and my astonishment was unbounded at observing that it even had two gilt galons, the insignia of my rank, braided on the cuffs. For shoes there were slippers of red Morocco leather with gold ornaments. The underwear, all of silk, seemed to have come straight from the rue de la Paix.

"Dinner was excellent," I murmured, looking at myself in the mirror with satisfaction. "The apartment is perfectly arranged. Yes, but—"

I could not repress a shudder when I suddenly recalled that room of red marble.

The clock struck half past four.

Someone rapped gently on the door. The tall white Targa who had brought me appeared in the doorway.

He stepped forward, touched me on the arm and signed for me to follow.

Again I followed him.

We passed through interminable corridors. I was disturbed, but the warm water had given me a certain feeling of detachment. And above all, more than I wished to admit, I had a growing sense of lively curiosity. If at that moment someone had offered to lead me back to the route across the white plain near Sheikh-Salah, would I have accepted? Hardly.

I tried to feel ashamed of my curiosity. I thought of Maillefeu.

"He, too, followed this corridor. And now he is down there in the red marble hall."

I had no time to linger over this reminiscence. I was suddenly bowled over, thrown to the ground as if by a sort of meteor. The corridor was dark; I could see nothing. I heard only a mocking growl.

The white Targa had flattened himself back against the wall.

"Good," I mumbled, picking myself up, "the deviltries are beginning."

We continued on our way. A glow, different from that of the rose night lights, soon began to light up the corridor.

We reached a high bronze door on which a strange lacy design had been cut in filigree. A clear gong sounded and the double doors opened part way. The Targa remained in the corridor, closing the doors after me.

I took a few steps forward mechanically, then paused, rooted to the spot, and rubbed my eyes.

I was dazzled by the sight of the sky.

Several hours of shaded light had unaccustomed me to daylight. It poured in through one whole side of the huge room.

The room was in the lower part of this mountain, which was more honeycombed with corridors and passages than an Egyptian pyramid. It was on a level with the garden which I had seen in the morning from the balcony and seemed to be a continuation of it; the carpet extended out under the great palm trees and the birds flew about the forest of pillars in the room.

By contrast the half of the room untouched by direct light from the oasis seemed dark. The sun, sinking behind the mountain, painted the garden paths with rose and flamed with red upon the traditional flamingo which stood with one foot raised at the edge of the sapphire lake.

Suddenly I was bowled over a second time.

I felt a warm, silky touch, a burning breath on my neck. Again the mocking growl which had so disturbed me in the corridor.

With a wrench, I pulled myself free and sent a chance blow at my assailant. The cry, this time of pain and rage, broke out again.

It was echoed by a long peal of laughter. Furious, I turned to look for the insolent onlooker, thinking to speak my mind. And then my glance became fixed.

Antinea was before me.

In the dimmest part of the room, under a kind of arch lit by the mauve rays from a dozen incense-lamps, four women lay on a heap of many-colored cushions and rare white Persian rugs.

I recognized the first three as Tuareg women, of a splendid regular beauty, dressed in magnificent robes of white silk embroidered in gold. The fourth, very dark-skinned, almost negroid, seemed younger. A tunic of red silk enhanced the dusk of her face, her arms and her bare feet. The four were grouped about a sort of throne of white rugs covered with a gigantic lion's skin on which, half raised on one elbow, lay Antinea.

Antinea! Whenever I saw her after that I wondered if I had really looked at her before, so much more beautiful did I find her. More beautiful? Inadequate word. Inadequate language! But is it really the fault of the language or of those who abuse the word?

One could not stand before her without recalling the woman for whom Ephractoeus overcame Atlas, of her for whom Sapor usurped the scepter of Ozymandias, for whom Mamylos subjugated Susa and Tentyris, for whom Antony fled.

O tremblant coeur humain, si jamais tu vibras
C'est dans l'étreinte altière et chaude de ses bras.

An Egyptian *klaft* fell over her abundant blue-black curls. Its two points of heavy, gold-embroidered cloth extended to her slim hips. The golden serpent, emerald-eyed, was clasped about her little, round, determined forehead, darting its double tongue of rubies over her head.

She wore a tunic of black chiffon shot with gold, very light, very full, slightly gathered in by a white muslin scarf embroidered with iris in black pearls.

That was Antinea's costume. But what was she beneath all this? A slim young girl with long green eyes and the slender profile of a hawk. A more intense Adonis. A child-queen of Sheba, but with a look, a smile such as no Oriental ever had. A miracle of irony and freedom.

I did not see her body. Indeed I should not have thought of looking at it had I had the strength. And that perhaps was the most extraordinary thing about that first impression. In that unforgettable moment nothing would have seemed to

me more horribly sacrilegious than to think of the fifty victims in the red marble
hall, of the fifty young men who had held that slender body in their arms.

She was still laughing at me.

"King Hiram!" she called.

I turned and saw my enemy.

On the capital of one of the columns, twenty feet above the floor, a splendid
leopard was crouched. He still looked surly from the blow I had dealt him.

"King Hiram," Antinea repeated. "Come here."

The beast relaxed like a spring released. He fawned at his mistress's feet. I
saw his red tongue licking her bare ankles.

"Ask the gentleman's pardon," she said.

The leopard looked at me spitefully. The yellow skin of his muzzle puckered
about his black moustache.

"Fftt," he grumbled like a great cat.

"Go!" Antinea ordered imperiously.

The beast crawled reluctantly toward me. He laid his head humbly between
his paws and waited.

I stroked his beautiful spotted forehead.

"You must not be vexed," said Antinea. "He is always that way with
strangers."

"Then he must often be in bad humor," I said simply.

Those were my first words. They brought a smile to Antinea's lips.

She gave me a long, quiet look.

"Aguida," she said to one of the Targa women, "you will give twenty-five
pounds in gold to Cegheir-ben-Cheikh."

"You are a lieutenant?" she asked after a pause.

"Yes."

"Where do you come from?"

"From France."

"I might have guessed that," she said ironically; "but from what part of
France?"

"From what we call the Lot-et-Garonne."

"From what town?"

"From Duras."

She reflected a moment.

"Duras! There is a little river there, the Dropt, and a fine old château."

"You know Duras?" I murmured, amazed.

"You go there from Bordeaux by a little branch railway," she went on. "It is
a shut-in road, with vine-covered hills crowned by the feudal ruins. The villages
have beautiful names: Monségur, Sauveterre-de-Guyenne, la Tresne, Créon—
Créon, as in *Antigone.*"

"You have been there?"

She looked at me.

"Don't speak so coldly," she said. "Sooner or later we will be intimate and you may as well lay aside formality now."

This threatening promise suddenly filled me with great happiness. I thought of Le Mesge's words:

"Don't talk until you have seen her. When you have seen her, you will renounce everything for her."

"Have I been in Duras?" she went on with a burst of laughter. "You are joking. Imagine Neptune's granddaughter in the first-class compartment of a local train!"

She pointed to an enormous white rock which towered above the palm-trees of the garden.

"That is my horizon," she said gravely.

She picked up one of several books which lay scattered about her on the lion's skin.

"The time table of the Chemin de Fer de l'Ouest," she said. "Admirable reading for one who never budges. Here it is half-past five in the afternoon. A train, a local, arrived three minutes ago at Surgères in the Charente-Inférieure. It will start on in six minutes. In two hours it will reach La Rochelle. How strange it seems to think of such things here. So far away. So much commotion there. Here, nothing changes."

"You speak French well," I said.

She gave a little nervous laugh.

"I have to—and German, too, and Italian and English and Spanish. My way of living has made me a great polyglot, but I prefer French, even to Tuareg and Arabian. It seems as if I had always known it, and I am not saying that to please you."

There was a pause. I thought of her grandmother, of whom Plutarch said:

"There were few races with which she needed an interpreter. Cleopatra spoke their own language to the Ethiopians, to the Troglodytes, the Hebrews, the Arabs, the Medes and the Persians."

"Do not stand rooted in the middle of the room. You worry me. Come sit here, beside me. Move over, King Hiram."

The leopard obeyed with good temper.

Beside her was an onyx bowl. She took from it a perfectly plain ring of orichalc and slipped it on my left ring-finger. I saw that she wore one like it.

"Tanit-Zerga, give Monsieur de Saint-Avit a rose sherbet."

The dark girl in red silk obeyed.

"My private secretary," said Antinea, introducing her. "Mademoiselle Tanit-Zerga, of Gâo, on the Niger. Her family is almost as ancient as mine."

As she spoke she looked at me. Her green eyes seemed to be appraising me.

"And your comrade, the captain?" she asked in a dreamy tone. "I have not yet seen him. What is he like? Does he resemble you?"

For the first time since I had entered I thought of Morhange. I did not answer.

Antinea smiled.

She stretched herself out full length on the lion skin. Her bare right knee slipped out from under her tunic.

"It is time to go find him," she said languidly. "You will soon receive my orders. Tanit-Zerga, show him the way. First take him to his room. He cannot have seen it."

I rose and lifted her hand to my lips. She struck me with it so sharply as to make my lips bleed, as if to brand me as her possession.

I was in the dark corridor again. The young girl in the red silk tunic walked ahead of me.

"Here is your room," she said. "If you wish, I will take you to the dining-room. The others are about to meet there for dinner."

She spoke an adorable lisping French.

"No, Tanit-Zerga, I would rather stay here this evening. I am not hungry. I am tired."

"You remember my name," she said.

She seemed proud of it. I felt that in her I had an ally in case of need.

"I remember your name, Tanit-Zerga, because it is beautiful."[11] Then I added: "Now, leave me, little one. I want to be alone."

It seemed as if she would never go. I was touched but at the same time vexed. I felt a great need of withdrawing into myself.

"My room is above yours," she said. "There is a copper gong on the table here. You have only to strike if you want anything. A white Targa will answer."

For a second these instructions amused me. I was in a hotel in the midst of the Sahara. I had only to ring for service.

I looked about my room. My room! For how long?

It was fairly large. There were cushions, a couch, an alcove cut into the rock—all lighted by a great window covered by a matting shade.

I went to the window and raised the shade. The light of the setting sun entered.

I leaned my elbows on the rocky sill. Inexpressible emotion filled my heart. The window faced southward. It was about two hundred feet above the ground. The black, polished volcanic wall yawned dizzily below me.

In front of me, perhaps a mile and a half away, was another wall, the first enclosure mentioned in the *Critias,* and beyond it in the distance I saw the limitless red desert.

11   In Berber, *tanit* means a spring; *zerga* is the feminine of the adjective *azreg,* blue. (Note by
       M. Leroux.)

Chapter XII

Morhange Disappears

MY FATIGUE WAS SO GREAT THAT I LAY AS IF UNCONSCIOUS UNTIL THE NEXT DAY. I awoke about three o'clock in the afternoon.

I thought at once of the events of the previous day; they seemed amazing.

"Let me see," I said to myself. "Let us work this out. I must begin by consulting Morhange."

I was ravenously hungry.

The gong which Tanit-Zerga had pointed out lay within arm's reach. I struck it. A white Targa appeared.

"Show me the way to the library," I ordered.

He obeyed. As we wound our way through the labyrinth of stairs and corridors I realized that I could never have found my way without his help.

Morhange was in the library, intently reading a manuscript.

"A lost treatise of Saint Optat," he said. "Oh, if only Dom Granger were here."

I did not reply. My eyes were fixed on an object which lay on the table beside the manuscript. It was an orichalc ring exactly like that which Antinea had given me the previous day and the one which she herself wore.

Morhange smiled.

"Well?" I said.

"Well?"

"You have seen her?"

"I have indeed," Morhange replied.

"She is beautiful, is she not?"

"It would be difficult to dispute that," my comrade answered. "I even believe that I can say that she is as intelligent as she is beautiful."

There was a pause. Morhange was calmly fingering the orichalc ring.

"You know what our fate is to be?"

"I know. Le Mesge explained it to us yesterday in polite mythological terms. This evidently is an extraordinary adventure."

He was silent, then said, looking at me:

"I am very sorry to have dragged you here. The only mitigating feature is that since last evening you seem to have been bearing your lot very easily."

Where had Morhange learned this insight into the human heart? I did not reply, thus giving him the best of proofs that he had judged correctly.

"What do you think of doing?" I finally murmured.

He rolled up the manuscript, leaned back comfortably in his armchair and lit a cigar.

"I have thought it over carefully. With the aid of my conscience I have marked out a line of conduct. The matter is clear and admits no discussion.

"The question is not quite the same for me as for you, because of my semi-religious character, which, I admit, has set out on a rather doubtful adventure. To be sure, I have not taken holy orders, but I admit that I have no taste for the kind of forced servitude for which the excellent Cegheir-ben-Cheikh has so kindly recruited us.

"That granted, the fact remains that my life is not my own with the right to dispose of it as might a private explorer travelling at his own expenses and for his own ends. I have a mission to accomplish, results to obtain. If I could regain my liberty by paying the singular ransom which this country exacts, I should do so. I know the tolerance of the Church and especially that of the order to which I aspire. The end justifies the means.

"But if I give in to the absurd caprices of this woman, that will not keep me from being catalogued down in the red marble hall as Number 54, or as Number 55 if she prefers to take you first. Under those conditions—"

"Under those conditions?"

"Under those conditions it would be unpardonable for me to acquiesce."

"Then what do you intend to do?"

"What do I intend to do?" Morhange leaned back in the armchair and smilingly launched a puff of smoke toward the ceiling.

"Nothing," he said. "And that is all that is necessary."

Then he added with an ironical smile—

"I cannot be forced to accept unless I wish to."

I nodded.

"I tried the most subtle reasoning on Antinea," he continued. "It was breath wasted. 'But,' I said at the end of my arguments, 'why not Le Mesge?' She began to laugh.

"'Why not the Rev. Mr. Spardek?' she replied. 'Le Mesge and Spardek are savants whom I respect. But—

> "'Maudit soit à jamais le rêveur inutile,
>   Qui voulut, le premier, dans sa stupidité,
> S'eprenant d'un problème insoluble et stérile,
>   Aux choses de l'amour mêler l'honnêteté.'

"'Besides,' she added with that really very charming smile of hers, 'probably you have not looked carefully at either of them.'

"There followed several compliments on my figure, to which I found nothing to reply, so completely had she disarmed me by those four lines from Baudelaire.

"She condescended to explain further:

"'Le Mesge is a learned gentleman whom I find useful. He knows Spanish and Italian, keeps my papers in order, and is busy working out my genealogy. The Rev. Spardek knows English and German. Count Bielowsky is thoroughly conversant with the Slavic languages. Besides, I love him like a father. He knew me as a child when I had not dreamed such stupid things as you know of me. They are indispensable to me in my relations with visitors of different races, although I am beginning to get along well enough in the languages which I need.

"'But I am talking a great deal and this is the first time that I have ever explained my conduct. Your friend is not so curious.'

"With that she dismissed me. A strange woman indeed. I think there is a bit of Renan in her, but she is cleverer than that master of sensualism."

"Gentlemen," said Le Mesge, suddenly entering the room, "why are you so late? They are waiting dinner for you."

The little professor was in a particularly good humor that evening. He wore a new violet rosette.

"Well?" he said, in a mocking tone. "You have seen her?"

Neither Morhange nor I replied.

The Rev. Mr. Spardek and the Hetman of Jitomir already had begun eating when we arrived. The setting sun threw raspberry lights on the cream-colored mat.

"Be seated, gentlemen," said Le Mesge noisily. "Lieutenant de Saint-Avit, you were not with us last evening. You are about to taste the cooking of Koukou, our Bambara chef, for the first time. You must give me your opinion of it."

A Negro waiter set before me a superb fish covered with a pimento sauce as red as tomatoes.

I have explained that I was ravenously hungry. The dish was exquisite. The sauce immediately made me thirsty.

"White Ahaggar, 1879," the Hetman of Jitomir breathed in my ear as he filled my goblet with a clear topaz liquid. "I developed it myself. *Rien pour la téte, tout pour les jambes.*"

I emptied the goblet at a gulp. The company began to seem charming.

"Well, Captain Morhange," Le Mesge called out to my comrade, who had taken a mouthful of fish, "what do you say to this acanthopterygian? It was caught today in the lake in the oasis. Do you begin to admit the hypothesis of the Saharan sea?"

"The fish is an argument," my companion replied.

Suddenly he became silent. The door had opened. A white Targa entered. The diners stopped talking.

The veiled man walked slowly toward Morhange and touched his right arm.

"Very well," said Morhange.

He got up and followed the messenger.

The pitcher of Ahaggar, 1879, stood between me and Count Bielowsky. I filled my goblet—a goblet which held a pint—and gulped it down.

The hetman looked at me sympathetically.

"Ha, ha!" laughed Le Mesge, nudging me with his elbow. "Antinea has respect for the hierarchic order."

The Rev. Mr. Spardek smiled modestly.

"Ha, ha!" laughed Le Mesge again.

My glass was empty. For a moment I was tempted to hurl it at the head of the Fellow in History. But what of it? I filled it and emptied it again.

"Morhange will miss this delirious roast of mutton," said the professor, more and more hilarious, as he awarded himself a thick slice of meat.

"He won't regret it," said the hetman crossly. "This is not roast; it is ram's horn. Really Koukou is beginning to make fun of us."

"Blame it on the reverend," the shrill voice of Le Mesge cut in; "I have told him often enough to hunt other proselytes and leave our cook alone."

"Professor," Spardek began with dignity.

"I maintain my contention," cried Le Mesge, who seemed to me to be getting a bit overloaded. "I call the gentleman to witness," he went on, turning to me. "He has just come. He is unbiased. Therefore I ask him. Has one the right to spoil a Bambara cook by addling his head with theological discussions for which he has no predisposition?"

"Alas," the pastor replied sadly, "you are mistaken. He has only too strong a propensity to controversy."

"Koukou is a good-for-nothing who uses Colas' cow as an excuse for doing nothing and letting our scallops burn," declared the hetman. "Long live the Pope!" he cried, filling the glasses all around.

"I assure you that this Bambara worries me," Spardek went on with great dignity. "Do you know what he has come to? He denies transubstantiation. He is within an inch of the heresy of Zwingli and Oecolampades. Koukou denies transubstantiation."

"Sir," said Le Mesge, very much excited, "cooks should be left in peace."

"Exactly so," said the Hetman approvingly.

He was holding a jar between his knees and trying to draw its cork.

"Oh, Côtes Rôties, wine from the Côte-Rôtie," he murmured to me as he finally succeeded. "Touch glasses."

"Koukou denies transubstantiation," the pastor continued, sadly emptying his glass.

"Eh!" said the Hetman of Jitomir in my ear, "let them talk on. Don't you see that they are quite drunk?"

His own voice was thick. He had the greatest difficulty in the world in filling my goblet to the brim. I wanted to push the pitcher away; then a thought came to me:

"At this very moment, Morhange— Whatever he may say—she is so beautiful."

I reached out for the glass and emptied it once more.

Le Mesge and the pastor were now engaged in the most extraordinary religious controversy, throwing at each other's heads the *Book of Common Prayer, The Declaration of the Rights of Man,* and the *Unigenitus.* Little by little the hetman began to show that ascendancy over them, which is the characteristic of a man of the world even when he is thoroughly drunk; the superiority of education over instruction. Count Bielowsky had drunk five times as much as the Professor or the pastor, but he carried his wine ten times better.

"Let us leave these drunken fellows," he said with disgust. "Come on, old man. Our partners are waiting in the gaming-room."

"Ladies and gentlemen," said the hetman as we entered, "permit me to present a new player to you, my friend Lieutenant de Saint-Avit."

"Let it go at that," he murmured in my ear. "They are the servants, but I like to fool myself, you see."

I saw that he was very drunk indeed.

The gaming-room was very long and narrow. A huge table, almost level with the floor and surrounded with cushions on which a dozen natives were lying, was the chief article of furniture. Two engravings on the wall gave evidence of the happiest broad-mindedness in taste; one of da Vinci's "St. John the Baptist," and another of the *"Maison des Dernières Cartouches"* of Alphonse de Neuville. On the table were earthenware goblets. A heavy jar held palm liqueur.

I recognized acquaintances among those present—my masseur, the manicure, the barber and two or three Tuareg who had lowered their veils and were gravely smoking long pipes. While waiting for something better all were plunged in the delights of a card game that looked like rams. Two of Antinea's beautiful ladies in waiting, Aguida and Sydya, were among the number. Their smooth bistre skins gleamed beneath veils shot with silver. I was sorry not to see the red silk tunic of Tanit-Zerga. Again I thought of Morhange, but only for an instant.

"The chips, Koukou," demanded the hetman.

The Zwinglian cook placed a box of many-colored chips in front of him. Count Bielowsky set about counting them and arranging them in little piles with infinite care.

"The white are worth a louis," he explained to me. "The red, a hundred francs. The yellow, five hundred. The green, a thousand. Oh, it's the devil of a game that we play here. You will see."

"I open with ten thousand," said the Zwinglian cook.

"Twelve thousand," said the hetman.

"Thirteen," said Sydya with a slow smile as she began to arrange her chips lovingly in little piles.

"Fourteen," I said.

"Fifteen," said the sharp voice of Rosita, the old manicure.

"Seventeen," proclaimed the hetman.

"Twenty thousand," the cook broke in.

He hammered on the table and, casting a defiant look at us, repeated:

"I take it at twenty thousand."

The hetman made an impatient gesture.

"That devil, Koukou! You can't do anything against the beast. You will have to play carefully, Lieutenant."

Koukou had taken his place at the end of the table. He threw down the cards with an air which abashed me.

"I told you so—the way it was at Anna Deslions'," the hetman murmured proudly.

"Make your bets, gentlemen," yelped the Negro. "Make your bets."

"Wait, you beast!" called Bielowsky. "Don't you see that the glasses are empty? Here, Cacambo!"

The goblets were filled immediately by the jolly masseur.

"Cut," said Koukou, addressing Sydya, the beautiful Targa who sat at his right.

The girl cut, like one who knows superstitions, with her left hand, but it must be said that her right was busy lifting a cup to her lips. I watched the curve of her beautiful throat.

"My deal," said Koukou.

We were thus arranged: At the left, the hetman; Aguida, whose waist he had encircled with the most aristocratic freedom; Cacambo; a Tuareg woman; then two veiled Negroes who were watching the game intently. At the right, Sydya; myself; the old manicure, Rosita; Barouf, the barber; another woman and two white Tuareg, grave and attentive, exactly opposite those on the left.

"Give me one," said the hetman.

Sydya made a negative gesture.

Koukou drew, passed a four-spot to the hetman, gave himself a five.

"Eight," announced Bielowsky.

"Six," said pretty Sydya.

"Seven," broke in Koukou. "One card makes up for another," he added coldly.

"I double," said the hetman.

Cacambo and Aguida followed his example. On our side we were more careful. The manicure, especially, would not risk more than twenty francs at a time.

"I demand that the cards be evened up," said Koukou imperturbably.

"This fellow is unbearable," grumbled the count. "There, are you satisfied?"

Koukou dealt and laid down a nine.

"My country and my honor!" raged Bielowsky. "I had an eight."

I had two kings and so showed no ill temper. Rosita took the cards out of my hands.

I watched Sydya at my right. Her heavy black hair covered her shoulders. She was really very beautiful, though a bit tipsy, as were all that fantastic company. She looked at me, too, but with lowered eyelids, like a timid little wild animal.

Oh, I thought. *She may well be afraid. I am labeled "No trespassing."*

I touched her foot. She drew it back in fright.

"Who wants cards?" Koukou demanded.

"Not I," said the hetman.

"Served," said Sydya.

The cook drew a four.

"Nine," he said.

"That card was meant for me," cursed the count. "And five, I had a five. If only I had never promised his Majesty, the Emperor Napoleon III, never to cut fives! There are times when it is hard, very hard. And look at that beast of a Negro who plays Charlemagne."

It was true. Koukou swept in three-quarters of the chips, rose with dignity, and bowed to the company.

"Till tomorrow, gentlemen."

"Get along, the whole pack of you!" howled the Hetman of Jitomir. "Stay with me, Lieutenant de Saint-Avit."

When we were alone he poured out another huge cupful of liqueur. The ceiling of the room was lost in the gray smoke.

"What time is it?" I asked.

"After midnight. But you are not going to leave me like this, my dear boy? I am heavy-hearted."

He wept bitterly. The tail of his coat spread out on the divan behind him like the apple-green wings of a beetle.

"Isn't Aguida a beauty?" he went on, still weeping. "She makes me think of the Countess de Teruel, though she is a little darker. You know the Countess de Tereul, Mercedes, who went in bathing nude at Biarritz in front of the Rock of the Virgin one day when Prince Bismarck was standing on the foot-bridge? You do not remember her? Mercedes de Teruel."

I shrugged my shoulders.

"I forget; you must have been too young. Two, perhaps three years old. A child. Yes, a child. Oh, my child, to have been of that generation and to be reduced to playing cards with savages. I must tell you—"

I stood up and pushed him off.

"Stay, stay," he implored. "I will tell you everything you want to know, how I came here, things I have never told anyone. Stay, I must unbosom myself to a true friend. I will tell you everything, I repeat. I trust you. You are a Frenchman, a gentleman. I know that you will repeat nothing to her."

"That I will repeat nothing to her? To whom?"

His voice stuck in his throat. I thought I saw a shudder of fear pass over him.

"To her—to Antinea," he murmured.

I sat down again.

Chapter XIII

The Hetman of Jitomir's Story

COUNT CASIMIR HAD REACHED THAT STAGE WHERE DRUNKENNESS TAKES ON A KIND of gravity, of regretfulness.

He thought a little, then began his story. I regret that I cannot reproduce more perfectly its archaic flavor.

"When the grapes begin to color in Antinea's garden, I shall be sixty-eight. It is very sad, my dear boy, to have sowed all your wild oats. It isn't true that life is always beginning over again. How bitter to have known the Tuileries in 1860 and to have reached the point where I am now!

"One evening, just before the war—I remember that Victor Black was still living—some charming women whose names I need not disclose—I read the names of their sons from time to time in the society news of the Gaulois— expressed to me their desire to rub elbows with some real demi-mondaines of the artist quarter. I took them to a ball at the Grande Chaumière.

"There was a crowd of young painters, models, students. In the midst of the uproar several couples danced the cancan till the chandeliers shook with it. We noticed especially a little dark man dressed in a miserable top-coat and checked trousers which assuredly knew the support of no suspenders. He was cross-eyed, with a wretched beard and hair as greasy as could be. He bounded and kicked extravagantly. The ladies called him Leon Gambetta.

"What an annoyance when I realize that I need only to have felled this wretched lawyer with one pistol shot to have guaranteed perfect happiness to myself and to my adopted country; for, my dear fellow, I am French at heart if not by birth.

"I was born in 1829 at Warsaw, of a Polish father and a Russian mother. It is from her that I hold my title of Hetman of Jitomir. It was restored to me by Czar Alexander II on a request made to him on his visit to Paris by my august master, Emperor Napoleon III.

"For political reasons, which I cannot describe without retelling the history of unfortunate Poland, my father, Count Bielowsky, left Warsaw in 1830 and went to live in London. After the death of my mother he began to squander his immense fortune—from sorrow, he said. When, in his time, he died at the period of the Prichard affair, he left me barely a thousand pounds sterling of income, plus two or three systems of gaming, the impracticability of which I learned later.

"I will never be able to think of my nineteenth and twentieth years without emotion, for I then completely liquidated this small inheritance. London was indeed an adorable spot in those days. I had a jolly bachelor's apartment in Piccadilly.

> *"'Piccadilly! Shops, palaces, bustle and breeze,*
> *The whirling of wheels and the murmur of trees.'*

"Fox hunting in a briska, driving a buggy in Hyde Park, the rout, not to mention the delightful little parties with the light Venuses of Drury Lane, these took all my time. All? I am unjust. There was also gaming, and a sentiment of filial piety forced me to verify the systems of the late Count, my father. It was gaming which was the cause of the event I must describe to you, by which my life was to be so strangely changed.

"My friend, Lord Malmesbury, had said to me a hundred times, 'I must take you to see an exquisite creature who lives in Oxford Street, number 277, a Miss Howard.' One evening I went with him. It was the twenty-second of February, 1848. The mistress of the house was really marvelously beautiful and the guests were charming. Besides Malmesbury, I observed several acquaintances: Lord Clebden, Lord Chesterfield, Sir Francis Mountjoye, a major in the Second Life Guards, and Count d'Orsay.

"They played cards and then began to talk politics. Events in France played the main part in the conversation and they discussed endlessly the consequences of the revolt that had broken out in Paris that same morning in consequence of the interdiction of the banquet in the Twelfth Arrondissement, of which word had just been received by telegram. Up to that time I had never bothered myself with public affairs. So I don't know what moved me to affirm with the impetuosity of my nineteen years that the news from France meant the Republic next day and the Empire the day after.

"The company received my sally with a discreet laugh and their looks were centered on a guest who made the fifth at a bouillotte table where they had just stopped playing.

"The guest smiled, too. He rose and came towards me. I observed that he was of middle height, perhaps even shorter, buttoned tightly into a blue frock coat, and that his eye had a far-off, dreamy look.

"All the players watched this scene with delighted amusement.

"'Whom have I the honor of addressing?' he asked in a very gentle voice.

"'Count Bielowsky,' I answered coolly to show him that the difference in our ages was not sufficient to justify the interrogation.

"'Well, my dear Count, may your prediction indeed be realized, and I hope that you will not neglect the Tuileries,' said the guest in the blue coat, with a smile.

"And he added, finally consenting to present himself:

"'Prince Louis-Napoleon Bonaparte.'

I played no active role in the coup d'état and I do not regret it. It is a principle with me that a stranger should not meddle with the internal affairs of a country. The prince understood this discretion and did not forget the young man who had been of such good omen to him.

"I was one of the first whom he called to the *Elysée*. My fortune was definitely established by a defamatory note on 'Napoleon the Little.' The next year I was made Gentleman of the Chamber, and the Emperor was even so kind as to have me marry the daughter of the Marshal Repeto, Duke of Mondovi.

"I have no scruple in announcing that this union was not what it should have been. The Countess, who was ten years older than I, was crabbed and not particularly pretty. Moreover, her family had insisted resolutely on a marriage portion. Now I had nothing at this time except the twenty-five thousand pounds for my appointment as Gentleman of the Chamber—a sad lot for anyone on intimate terms with the Count d'Orsay and the Duke of Gramont-Caderousse! Without the kindness of the Emperor where would I have been?

"One morning in the spring of 1852 I was in my study opening my mail. There was a letter from His Majesty calling me to the Tuileries at four o'clock and a letter from Clémentine informing me that she expected me at five o'clock at her house. Clémentine was the beautiful one for whom just then I was ready to commit any folly. I was so proud of her that one evening at the Maison Dorée I flaunted her before Prince Metternich, who was tremendously taken with her. All the court envied me that conquest and I was morally obliged to continue to assume its expenses. And then Clémentine was so pretty!

"The other letters—good Lord—the other letters were the bills of the dressmakers of that young person, who in spite of my discreet remonstrances insisted on having them sent to my conjugal dwelling.

"There were bills for something over forty thousand francs; gowns and ball dresses from Gagelin-Opigez, 23 rue de Richelieu; hats and bonnets from Madame Alexandrine, 14 rue d'Antin; lingerie and many petticoats from Madame Pauline, 100 rue de Clery; dress trimmings and gloves from the Ville de Lyon, 6 rue de la Chaussée d'Antin; foulards from the Malle des Indes; handkerchiefs from the Compagnie Irlandaise; laces from Ferguson and cosmetics from Candès. This whitening cream of Candès in particular overwhelmed me with stupefaction. The bill showed fifty-one flasks. Six hundred and twenty-seven francs and fifty centimes' worth of whitening cream from Candès. Enough to soften the skin of a squadron of a hundred guards.

"'This can't keep on,' I said, putting the bills in my pocket.

"At ten minutes to four I crossed the wicket by the Carrousel.

"In the salon of the aides-de-camp I happened on Bacciochi.

"'The Emperor has the grippe,' he said to me, 'He is keeping to his room. He has given orders to have you admitted as soon as you arrive. Come.'

"His Majesty, dressed in a braided vest and Cossack trousers, was meditating before a window. The pale green of the Tuileries showed luminously under a gentle warm shower.

"'Ah! Here he is,' said Napoleon. 'Here, have a cigarette. It seems that you had great doings, you and Gramont-Caderousse, last evening, at the Château des Fleurs.'

"I smiled with satisfaction.

"'So Your Majesty knows already—'

"'I know; I know vaguely.'

"'Do you know Gramont-Caderousse's last *mot?*'

"'No, but you are going to tell it to me.'

"'Here goes, then. We were five or six—myself, Viel-Castel, Gramont, Persigny—'

"'Persigny!' said the Emperor. 'He has no right to associate with Gramont after all that Paris says about his wife.'

"'Just so, Sire. Well, Persigny was excited, no doubt, about it. He began telling us how troubled he was because of the Duchess's conduct.'

"'This Fialin isn't over tactful,' murmured the Emperor.

"'Just so, Sire. Then, does Your Majesty know what Gramont hurled at him?'

"'What?'

"'He said to him, 'Monsieur le Duc, I forbid you to speak ill of my mistress before me.'''

"'Gramont goes too far,' said Napoleon with a dreamy smile.

"'That is what we all thought, including Viel-Castel, who was nevertheless delighted.'

"'Apropos of this,' said Napoleon after a silence, 'I have forgotten to ask you for news of the Countess Bielowsky.'

"'She is very well, Sire, I thank Your Majesty.'

"'And Clémentine? Still the same dear child?'

"'Always, Sire. But—'

"'It seems that M. Baroche is madly in love with her.'

"'I am very much honored, Sire. But this honor becomes too burdensome.'

"I had drawn from my pocket that morning's bills and I spread them out under the eyes of the Emperor. He looked at them with his distant smile.

"'Come, come. If that is all, I can fix that, since I have a favor to ask of you.'

"'I am entirely at Your Majesty's service.'

"He struck a gong.

"'Send for M. Mocquard.'

"'I have the grippe,' he said. 'Mocquard will explain the affair to you.'

"The Emperor's private secretary entered.

"'Here is Bielowsky, Mocquard,' said Napoleon. 'You know what I want him to do. Explain it to him.'

"And he began to tap on the window-panes against which the rain was bearing furiously.

"'My dear Count,' said Mocquard, taking a chair, 'it is very simple. You have doubtless heard of a young explorer of promise, M. Henry Duveyrier.'

"I shook my head as a sign of negation, very much surprised at this beginning.

"'M. Duveyrier,' continued Mocquard, 'has returned to Paris after a particularly daring trip to South Africa and the Sahara. M. Vivien de Saint-Martin, whom I have seen recently, has assured me that the Geographical Society intends to confer its great gold medal upon him in recognition of these exploits. In the course of his trip, M. Duvreyrier has entered into negotiations with the chiefs of the people who always have been so rebellious to His Majesty's armies, the Tuareg.'

"I looked at the Emperor. My bewilderment was such that he began to laugh.

"'Listen,' he said.

"'M. Duveyrier,' continued Mocquard, 'was able to arrange to have a delegation of these chiefs come to Paris to present their respects to His Majesty. Very important results may arise from this visit, and His Excellency the Colonial Minister does not despair of obtaining the signature of a treaty of commerce, reserving special advantages to our fellow countrymen. These chiefs, five of them, among them Sheik Otham, Amenokol or Sultan of the Confederation of Adzger, arrive tomorrow morning at the Gare de Lyon. M. Duveyrier will meet them. But the Emperor has thought that besides—'

"'I thought,' said Napoleon III, delighted by my bewilderment, 'I thought that it was correct to have some one of the Gentlemen of my Chamber wait upon the arrival of these Mussulman dignitaries. That is why you are here, my poor Bielowsky.'

"'Don't be frightened,' he added, laughing harder. 'You will have M. Duveyrier with you. You are charged only with a special part of the reception: to accompany these princes to the lunch that I am giving them tomorrow at the Tuileries; then in the evening, discreetly on account of their religious scruples, to succeed in giving them a very high idea of Parisian civilization, with nothing exaggerated. Do not forget that in the Sahara they are very high religious dignitaries. In that respect, I have confidence in your tact and give you carte blanche. Mocquard!'

"'Sire?'

"'You will apportion on the budget—half to foreign affairs, half to the colonies—the funds Count Bielowsky will need for the reception of the Tuareg delegation. It seems to me that a hundred thousand francs, to begin— The Count has only to tell you if he is forced to exceed that figure.'

"Clémentine lived on the rue Boccador, in a little Moorish pavilion that I had bought for her from M. de Lesseps. I found her in bed. When she saw me she burst into tears.

"'Great fools that we are!" she murmured amidst her sobs. 'What have we done?"

"'Clementine, tell me!"

"'What have we done, what have we done!" she repeated, and I felt against me her floods of black hair and her warm cheek which was fragrant with eau de Nanon.

"'What is it? What can it be?'

"'It is—' and she murmured something in my ear.

"'No!' I said, stupefied. 'Are you quite sure?'

"'Am I quite sure!'

"'I was thunderstruck.

"'You don't seem much pleased,' she said sharply.

"'I did not say that. Though really I am very much pleased, I assure you.'

"'Prove it to me. Let us spend the day together tomorrow.'

"'Tomorrow!' I stammered. 'Impossible!'

"'Why?' she demanded suspiciously.

"'Because tomorrow, I have to pilot the Tuareg mission about Paris—the Emperor's orders.'

"'What bluff is this?' asked Clémentine.

"'I admit that nothing so much resembles a lie as the truth.'

"I retold Mocquard's story to Clémentine as well as I could. She listened to me with an expression that said: 'You can't fool me that way.'

"Finally, furious, I burst out:

"'You can see for yourself. I am dining with them tomorrow and I invite you.'

"'I shall be very pleased to come,' said Clémentine with great dignity.

"I admit that I lacked self-control at that minute. But think what a day it had been! Forty thousand francs of bills as soon as I woke up—the ordeal of escorting the savages around Paris all the next day, and quite unexpectedly the announcement of an approaching irregular paternity.

"'After all,' I thought, as I returned to my house, 'these are the Emperor's orders. He has commanded me to give the Tuareg an idea of Parisian civilization. Clémentine comports herself very well in society and just now it would not do to aggravate her. I will engage a room for tomorrow at the Café de Paris, and tell Gramont-Caderousse and Viel-Castel to bring their silly mistresses. It will be very French to enjoy the attitude of these children of the desert in the midst of this little party.'

"The train from Marseilles arrived at ten-twenty. On the platform I found M. Duveyrier, a young man of twenty-three with blue eyes and a little blond beard. The Tuareg fell into his arms as they descended from the train. He had lived with them for two years, in their tents, the devil knows where. He presented me to their chief, Sheik Otham, and to four others, splendid fellows in their blue cotton draperies and their amulets of red leather. Fortunately, they all spoke a kind of sabir[12] which helped things along.

"I only mention in passing the luncheon at the Tuileries, the visits in the

---

12   Dialect spoken in Algeria and the Levant—a mixture of Arabian, French, Italian and Spanish.

evening to the Museum, to the Hôtel de Ville, to the Imperial Printing Press. Each time the Tuareg inscribed their names in the registry of the place they were visiting. It was interminable. To give you an idea, here is the complete name of Sheik Otham alone: Otham-ben-el-Hadj-el-Bekri-ben-el-Hadj-el-Faqqi-ben-Mohammad-Bouya-ben-si-Ahmed-es-Souki-ben-Mahmoud.[13]

"And there were five of them like that!

"I maintained my good humor, however, because on the boulevards, everywhere, our success was colossal. At the Café de Paris at six-thirty it amounted to frenzy. The delegation, a little drunk, embraced me:

"'Bono, Napoléon; bono, Eugénie; bono, Casimir; bono, Christians!'

"Gramont-Caderousse and Viel Castel were already in booth number eight with Anna Grimaldi, of the Folies Dramatiques, and Hortense Schneider, both beautiful enough to strike terror to the heart. But the palm was for my dear Clémentine when she entered.

"I must tell you how she was dressed: A gown of white tulle over China blue tarletan with pleatings and ruffles of tulle over the pleatings. The tulle skirt was caught up on each side by garlands of green leaves mingled with rose clusters. Thus it formed a valence which allowed the tarletan skirt to show in front and on the sides. The garlands were caught up to the belt and in the space between their branches were knots of rose satin with long ends. The pointed bodice was draped with tulle; the billowy bertha of tulle was edged with lace. By way of head-dress she had placed upon her black locks a diadem of the same flowers. Two long leafy tendrils were twined in her hair and fell on her neck. As cloak, she had a kind of scarf of blue cashmere embroidered in gold and lined with blue satin.

"So much beauty and splendor immediately moved the Tuareg and especially Clémentine's right-hand neighbor, El-Hadj-ben-Guemâma, brother of Sheik Otham and Sultan of Ahaggar. By the time the soup arrived, a bouillon of wild game seasoned with Tokay, he was already much smitten. When they served the compote of fruits Martinique à la liqueur de Mme. Amphoux, he showed every indication of illimitable passion. The Cyprian wine de la Commanderie made him quite sure of his sentiments.

"Hortense kicked my foot under the table. Gramont, intending to do the same to Anna, made a mistake and aroused the indignant protests of one of the Tuareg. I can safely say that when the time came to go to Mabille, we were enlightened as to the manner in which our visitors respected the prohibition decreed by the Prophet in respect to wine.

"At Mabille, while Clémentine, Hortense, Anna, Ludovic and the three Tuareg gave themselves over to the wildest galops, Sheik Otham took me aside and confided to me with visible emotion a certain commission with which he had just been charged by his brother, Sheik Ahmed.

"The next day very early I reached Clémentine's house.

---

13   I have succeeded in finding on the registry of the Imperial Printing Press the names of the Taureg chiefs and those who accompanied them on their visit, M. Henry Duveyrier and Count Bielowsky. (Note by M. Leroux.)

"'My dear,' I began after having waked her, not without difficulty, 'listen to me. I want to talk to you seriously.'

"She rubbed her eyes a bit crossly.

"'How did you like that young Arabian gentleman who was so taken with you last night?'

"'Why, well enough,' she said, blushing.

"'Do you know that in his country he is the sovereign prince and reigns over territories five or six times greater than those of our august master, the Emperor Napoleon III?'

"'He murmured something of that kind to me,' she said, becoming interested.

"'Well, would it please you to mount on a throne like our august sovereign, the Empress Eugénie?'

"Clémentine looked startled.

"'His own brother, Sheik Otham, has charged me in his name to make this offer.'

"Clémentine, dumb with amazement, did not reply.

"'I, Empress!' she finally stammered.

"'The decision rests with you. They must have your answer before midday. If it is 'yes,' we lunch together at Voisin's and the bargain is made.'

"I saw that she had already made up her mind, but she thought it well to display a little sentiment.

"'And you, you,' she groaned. 'To leave you thus— Never!'

"'No foolishness, dear child,' I said gently. 'You don't know perhaps that I am ruined. Yes, completely. I don't even know how I am going to pay for your complexion cream!'

"'Ah!' she sighed. She added, however: 'And—the child?'

"'What child?'

"'Our child—our child.'

"'Ah, that is so. Why, you will have to put it down to profit and loss. I am even convinced that Sheik Ahmed will find that it resembles him.'

"'You can turn everything into a joke,' she said between laughing and crying.

"The next morning at the same hour the Marseilles express carried away the five Tuareg and Clémentine. The young woman, radiant, was leaning on the arm of Sheik Ahmed, who was beside himself with joy.

"'Have you many shops in your capital?' she asked him languidly.

"And he, smiling broadly under his veil, replied:

"'Besef, besef, bono, roumis, bono.'

"At the last moment Clémentine had a pang of emotion.

"'Listen, Casimir, you have always been kind to me. I am going to be a queen. If you weary of it here promise me, swear to me—'

"The sheik had understood. He took a ring from his finger and slipped it onto mine.

"'Sidi Casimir, comrade,' he affirmed. 'You come—find us. Take Sidi Ahmed's ring and show it. Everybody at Ahaggar comrades. *Bono Ahaggar, bono.'*

"When I came out of the Gare de Lyon I had the feeling of having perpetrated an excellent joke."

The Hetman of Jitomir was completely drunk. I had had the utmost difficulty in understanding the end of his story because he interjected, every other moment, couplets from Jacques Offenbach's best score.

Dans un bois passait un jeune homme,
   Un jeune homme frais et beau,
Sa main tenait une pomme,
   Vous voyez d'ici le tableau.

"Who was disagreeably surprised by the fall of Sedan? It was Casimir, poor old Casimir! Five thousand louis to pay by the fifth of September and not the first sou, no, not the first sou. I take my hat and my courage and go to the Tuileries. No more Emperor there, no! But the Empress was so kind. I found her alone—ah, people scatter quickly under such circumstances—alone with a senator, M. Merimée, the only literary man I have ever known who was at the same time a man of the world. 'Madame,' he was saying to her, 'you must give up all hope. M. Thiers, whom I just met on the Pont Royal, would listen to nothing.'

"'Madame,' I said in my turn, 'Your Majesty always will know where her true friends are.'

"And I kissed her hand.

"Evohé, que les déesses
   Ont de drôles de facons
Pour enjôler, pour enjôler, pour enjôler les gaâar-cons!

"I returned to my home in the rue de Lille. On the way I encountered the rabble going from the corps législatif to the *Hôtel de Ville.* My mind was made up.

"'Madame,' I said to my wife, 'my pistols.'

"'What is the matter?' she asked, frightened.

"'All is lost. But there is still a chance to preserve my honor. I am going to be killed on the barricades.'

"'Ah! Casimir,' she sobbed, falling into my arms. 'I have misjudged you. Will you forgive me?'

"'I forgive you, Aurélie,' I said with dignified emotion. 'I have not always been right myself.'

"I tore myself away from this mad scene. It was six o'clock. On the rue de Bac I hailed a cab.

"'Twenty francs tip,' I said to the coachman, 'if you get to the Gare de Lyon in time for the Marseilles train six thirty-seven.'"

The Hetman of Jitomir could say no more. He had rolled over on the cushions and slept with clenched fists.

I walked unsteadily to the great window.

The sun was rising, pale yellow, behind the sharp blue mountains.

Chapter XIV

Hours of Waiting

IT WAS AT NIGHT THAT SAINT-AVIT LIKED TO TELL ME A LITTLE OF HIS ENTHRALLING history. He gave it to me in short installments, exact and chronological, never anticipating the episodes of a drama whose tragic outcome I knew already. Not that he wished to obtain more effect that way—I felt that he was far removed from any calculation of that sort. Simply from the extraordinary nervousness into which he was thrown by recalling such memories.

One evening, the mail from France had just arrived. The letters that Chatelain had handed us lay upon the little table, not yet opened. By the light of the lamp, a pale halo in the midst of the great black desert, we were able to recognize the writing of the addresses. Oh, the victorious smile of Saint-Avit when, pushing aside all those letters, I said to him in a trembling voice:

"Go on."

He acquiesced without further words.

Nothing can give you any idea of the fever I was in from the day when the Hetman of Jitomir told me of his adventures to the day when I found myself in the presence of Antinea. The strangest part was that the thought that I was in a way condemned to death did not enter into this fever. On the contrary it was stimulated by my desire for the event which would be the signal of my downfall—the summons from Antinea. But this summons was not speedy in coming, and from this delay arose my unhealthy exasperation.

Did I have any lucid moments in the course of these hours? I do not think so. I do not recall having even said to myself:

"What, aren't you ashamed? Captive in an unheard of situation, you not only make no attempt to escape, but you even bless your servitude and look forward to your ruin."

I did not even color my desire to remain there, to enjoy the next step in the adventure, by the pretext I might have given—unwillingness to escape without Morhange. If I felt a vague uneasiness at not seeing him again, it was not because of a desire to know that he was well and safe.

Well and safe I knew him to be, moreover. The Tuareg slaves of Antinea's household were certainly not very communicative. The women were hardly more loquacious. I heard, it is true, from Sydya and Aguida that my companion liked pomegranates or that he could not endure *cous-cous* or bananas, but if

I asked for a different kind of information they fled in fright down the long corridors. With Tanit-Zerga it was different. This child seemed to have a distaste for mentioning before me anything bearing in any way upon Antinea. Nevertheless I knew that she was devoted to her mistress with a doglike fidelity, but she maintained an obstinate silence if I pronounced her name or, persisting, the name of Morhange.

As for the Europeans, I did not care to question these sinister puppets. Besides, all three were difficult of approach. The Hetman of Jitomir was sinking deeper and deeper into alcohol. What intelligence remained to him seemed to have dissolved that evening when he had invoked his youth for me. I met him from time to time in the corridors that had become all at once too narrow for him, humming in a thick voice a couplet from the music of La Reine Hortense:

> "De ma fille Isabelle
> Sois l'époux à l'instant,
> Car elle est la plus belle
> Et toi, le plus vaillant."

As for Spardek I would cheerfully have killed the old skinflint. And the hideous little man with the decorations, the placid printer of labels for the red marble hall—how could I meet him without wanting to cry out in his face:

"Eh, eh, sir professor, a very curious case of apocope: Atlantinea—suppression of alpha, of tau, of lambda. I would like to direct your attention to another case as curious: Klemantinea (Clémentine)—apocope of kappa, of lamba, of epsilon and of mu. If Morhange were with us he would tell you many charming erudite things about it. But alas, Morhange does not deign to come among us anymore. We never see Morhange."

My fever for information found more relief from Rosita, the old Negress manicure. Never have I had my nails polished so often as during those days of waiting. Now—after six years—she must be dead. I shall not wrong her memory by recording that she was very partial to the bottle. The poor old soul was defenseless against those that I brought her and that I emptied with her through politeness.

Unlike the other slaves, who are brought from the south toward Turkey by the merchants of Rhat, she was born in Constantinople and had been brought into Africa by her master when he became *kaimakam* of Rhadamès.

But don't let me complicate this already wandering history by the incantations of this manicure.

"Antinea," she said to me, "is the daughter of El-Hadj-Ahmed-ben-Guemâma, Sultan of Ahaggar, and sheik of the great and noble tribe of Kel-Rhela. She was born in the year twelve hundred and eighty-one of the Hegira. She has never wished to marry anyone. Her wish has been respected, for the will of women is sovereign in this Ahaggar where she rules today. She is a cousin of Sidi-el-

Senussi and, if she speaks the word, Christian blood will flow from Djerid to Tuat, and from Tchad to Senegal. If she had wished it she might have lived, beautiful and respected, in the land of the Christians, but she prefers to have them come to her."

"Cegheir-ben-Cheikh," I said, "do you know him? He is entirely devoted to her?"

"Nobody here knows Cegheir-ben-Cheikh very well because he is continually traveling. It is true that he is entirely devoted to Antinea. Cegheir-ben-Cheikh is a Senussi and Antinea is the cousin of the chief of the Senussi. Besides, he owes his life to her. He is one of the men who assassinated the great Kébir Flatters. On account of that, Ikenoukhen, Amenokol of the Adzjer Tuareg, fearing French reprisals, wanted to deliver Cegheir-ben-Cheikh to them. When the whole Sahara turned against him, he found asylum with Antinea. Cegheir-ben-Cheikh will never forget it, for he is brave and observes the law of the Prophet. To thank her he led to Antinea, who was then twenty years old, three French officers of the first troops of occupation in Tunis. They are the ones who are numbered, in the red marble hall, 1, 2, and 3."

"And Cegheir-ben-Cheikh has always fulfilled his duties successfully?"

"Cegheir-ben-Cheikh is well trained and he knows the vast Sahara as I know my little room at the top of the mountain. At first he made mistakes. That is how, on his first trips, he brought back old Le Mesge and the *marabout,* Spardek."

"What did Antinea say when she saw them?"

"Antinea? She laughed so hard that she spared them. Cegheir-ben-Cheikh was vexed to see her laugh so. Since then he has never made a mistake."

"He has never made a mistake?"

"No. I have cared for the hands and feet of all that he has brought here. All were young and handsome, but I think that your comrade, whom they brought to me the other day, after you were here, is the handsomest of all."

"Why," I asked, turning the conversation, "why, since she spared them their lives, did she not free the pastor and M. Le Mesge?"

"She has found them useful, it seems," said the old woman. "And then, whoever once enters here can never leave. Otherwise the French would soon be here, and when they saw the hall of red marble they would massacre everybody. Besides, of all those whom Cegheir-ben-Cheikh has brought here only one has wished to escape after seeing Antinea."

"She keeps them a long time?"

"That depends upon them—two months—three months on the average—it depends. Douglas Kaine, an English officer, she kept almost a year."

"And then?"

"And then he died," said the old woman as if astonished at my question.

"Of what did he die?"

She used the same phrase as M. Le Mesge:

"Like all the others—of love.

"Of love," she continued. "They all die of love when they see that their time is ended and that Cegheir-ben-Cheikh has gone to find others. Several have died quietly with tears in their great eyes. They neither ate nor slept any more. A French naval officer went mad. All night he sang a sad song of his native country, a song which echoed through the whole mountain. Another, a Spaniard, was as if maddened—he tried to bite. It was necessary to kill him. Many have died of *kif*, a *kif* that is more violent than opium. When they no longer have Antinea, they smoke, smoke. Most have died that way—the happiest. Little Kaine died differently."

"How did little Kaine die?"

"In a way that pained us all very much. I told you that he stayed longer among us than anyone else. We had become used to him. In Antinea's room, on a little Kairoun table painted in blue and gold, there is a gong with a long silver hammer with an ebony handle, very heavy. Aguida told me about it. When Antinea gave little Kaine his dismissal, smiling as she always does, he stopped in front of her, mute and very pale. She struck the gong for someone to take him away. A Targa slave came, but little Kaine had leapt for the hammer and the Targa lay on the ground with his skull smashed. Antinea smiled all the time.

"They led little Kaine to his room. The same night, eluding guards, he jumped out of his window at a height of two hundred feet. The workmen in the embalming room told me that they had the greatest difficulty with his body, but they succeeded very well. You have only to go see for yourself. He occupies niche number 26 in the red marble hall."

The old woman drowned her emotion in her glass.

"Two days before," she continued, "I had done his nails here, for this was his room. On the wall near the window he had written something in the stone with his knife. See, it is still here."

Was it not fate that on this July midnight—

At any other moment that verse, traced in the stone of the window through which the English officer had hurled himself, would have killed me with overpowering emotion, but just then, another thought was in my heart.

"Tell me," I said, controlling my voice as well as I could, "when Antinea holds one of us in her power, she shuts him up near her, does she not? Nobody sees him anymore?"

The old woman shook her head.

"She is not afraid that he will escape. The mountain is well guarded. Antinea has only to strike her silver gong; he will be brought back to her immediately."

"But my companion. I have not seen him since she sent for him."

The Negress smiled comprehendingly.

"If you have not seen him it is because he prefers to remain near her. Antinea does not force him to. Neither does she prevent him."

I struck my fist violently upon the table.

"Get along with you, old fool, and be quick about it!"

Rosita fled frightened, hardly taking time to collect her little instruments.

Was it not fate that on this July midnight—

I obeyed the Negress' suggestion. Following the corridors, losing my way, set on the right road again by the Rev. Mr. Spardek, I pushed open the door of the red marble hall. I entered.

The freshness of the perfumed crypt did me good. No place can be so sinister that it is not, as it were, purified by the murmur of running water. The cascade, gurgling in the middle of the hall, comforted me. One day before an attack I was lying with my section in deep grass, waiting for the moment, the blast of the bugle, which would demand that we leap forward into the hail of bullets. A stream was at my feet. I listened to its fresh rippling. I admired the play of light and shade in the transparent water, the little black fish, the green grass, the yellow wrinkled sand. The mystery of water always has carried me out of myself.

Here in this magic hall my thoughts were held by the dark cascade. It felt friendly. It kept me from faltering in the midst of these rigid evidences of so many monstrous sacrifices. Number 26. It was he all right. Lieutenant Douglas Kaine, born at Edinburgh September 21, 1862. Died at Ahaggar July 16, 1890. Twenty-eight. He wasn't even twenty-eight!

His face was thin under the coat of orichalc. His mouth was sad and passionate. It was certainly he. Poor youngster! Edinburgh—I knew Edinburgh without ever having been there. From the wall of the castle you can see the Pentland hills. "Look a little lower down," said Stevenson's sweet Miss Flora to Anne of Saint-Yves, "look a little lower down and you will see, in the fold of the hill, a clump of trees and a curl of smoke that rises from among them. That is Swanston cottage where my brother and I live with my aunt. If it really pleases you to see it, I shall be glad." When he left for Darfour, Douglas Kaine must surely have left in Edinburgh a Miss Flora, as blonde perhaps as Saint-Yves' Flora. But what are these slips of girls beside Antinea!

Kaine, however sensible a mortal, however made for this kind of love, had loved otherwise. He was dead. And here was number 27, on account of whom Kaine dashed himself on the rocks of the Sahara and who in his turn is dead also.

"To die, to love."

How naturally the words resounded in the red marble hall. How Antinea seemed to tower above that circle of pale statues. Does love, then, need so much death in order that it may be multiplied? Other women in other parts of the world are doubtless as beautiful as Antinea, more beautiful perhaps. I hold you to witness that I have not said much about her beauty. Why, then, this obsession, this fever, this consumption of all my being? Why am I ready, for the sake of pressing this quivering form within my arms for one instant, to face things that I dare not think of for fear I should tremble before them?

Here is number 53, the last. Morhange will be 54. I shall be 55. In six months, eight, perhaps—what difference anyway?—I shall be hoisted into this niche, an image without eyes, a dead soul, a finished body.

I touched the heights of bliss. What a child I was just now. I lost my temper with a Negro manicurist. I was jealous of Morhange, on my word. Why not, since I was at it, be jealous of those here present; then of the others, the absent, who will come, one by one, to fill the black circle of the still empty niches?

Morhange, I know, is at this moment with Antinea, and it is to me a bitter and splendid joy to think of his joy, but some evening, in three months—four perhaps—the embalmers will come here. Niche 54 will receive its prey. Then a Targa slave will advance toward me. He will touch my arm, and it will be my turn to penetrate into eternity by the bleeding door of love.

When I emerged from my meditation I found myself back in the library where the falling night obscured the shadows of the people who were assembled there.

I recognized M. Le Mesge, the pastor, the hetman, Aguida, two Tuareg slaves and still others, all joining in the most animated conference.

I drew nearer, astonished, even alarmed to see together so many people who ordinarily felt no kind of sympathy for each other.

An unheard of occurrence had thrown all the people of the mountain into uproar.

Two Spanish explorers from Rio de Oro had been seen to the west, in Adhar Ahnet.

As soon as Cegheir-ben-Cheikh was informed he had prepared to go to meet them, but at that instant he had received the order to do nothing.

Henceforth it was impossible to doubt. For the first time Antinea was in love.

Chapter XV
The Lament of Tanit-Zerga

"A RRAOU! ARRAOU!"

I roused myself vaguely from the half-sleep to which I had finally succumbed. I half-opened my eyes. Immediately I flattened back.

"Arraou!"

Two feet from my face was the muzzle of King Hiram, yellow with a tracery of black. The leopard was helping me to wake up; otherwise he took little interest, for he yawned; his dark red jaws with their beautiful gleaming white fangs opened and closed lazily.

At the same moment I heard a burst of laughter.

It was little Tanit-Zerga. She was crouching on a cushion near the divan where I was stretched out, curiously watching my close interview with the leopard.

"King Hiram was bored," she felt obliged to explain to me. "I brought him."

"How nice," I growled. "Only tell me, could he not have gone somewhere else to be amused?"

"He is all alone now," said the girl. "*They* have sent him away. He made too much noise when he played."

These words recalled me to the events of the previous evening.

"If you like, I will make him go away," said Tanit-Zerga.

"No, let him alone."

I looked at the leopard with sympathy. Our common misfortune brought us together.

I even caressed his rounded forehead. King Hiram showed his contentment by stretching out at full length and uncurling his great amber claws.

"Galé is here, too," said the little girl.

"Galé! Who may he be?"

At the same time I saw on Tanit-Zerga's knees a strange animal about the size of a big cat, with flat ears and a long muzzle. Its pale gray fur was rough. It was watching me with queer little pink eyes.

"It is my mongoose," explained Tanit-Zerga.

"Come now," I said sharply, "is that all?"

I must have looked very crabbed and ridiculous for Tanit-Zerga began to laugh. I laughed, too.

"Galé is my friend," she said when she was serious again. "I saved her life. It was when she was quite little. I will tell you about it someday. See how good-natured she is."

So saying, she dropped the mongoose on my knees.

"It is very nice of you, Tanit-Zerga," I said, "to come and pay me a visit." I passed my hand slowly over the animal's back. "What time is it now?"

"A little after nine. See, the sun is already high. Let me draw the shade."

The room was in darkness. Galé's eyes grew redder. King Hiram's became green.

"It is very nice of you," I repeated, pursuing my idea. "I see that you are free today. You never came so early before."

A shade passed over the girl's forehead.

"Yes, I am free," she said, almost bitterly.

I looked at Tanit-Zerga more closely. For the first time I realized that she was beautiful. Her hair, which she wore falling over her shoulders, was not so much curly as it was gently waving. Her features were of remarkable fineness; the nose very straight, a small mouth with delicate lips, a strong chin. She was not black, but copper colored, with a slender, graceful body.

A large circle of copper made a heavy decoration around her forehead and hair. She had four bracelets, still heavier, on her wrists and anklets, and for clothing a green silk tunic, slashed in points, braided with gold—green, bronze, gold.

"You are a Sonrhaï, Tanit-Zerga?" I asked gently.

She replied with almost ferocious pride:

"I am a Sonrhaï."

Strange little thing, I thought.

Evidently this was a subject on which Tanit-Zerga did not intend the conversation to turn. I recalled how, almost painfully, she had pronounced that "they," when she had told me how they had driven away King Hiram.

"I am a Sonrhaï," she repeated. "I was born at Gâo, on the Niger, the ancient Sonrhaï capital. My fathers reigned over the great Mandigue Empire. You need not scorn me because I am here as a slave."

In a ray of sunlight, Galé, seated on his little haunches, washed his shining mustaches with his forepaws, and King Hiram, stretched out on the mat, groaned plaintively in his sleep.

"He is dreaming," said Tanit-Zerga, a finger on her lips.

There was a moment of silence. Then she said—

"You must be hungry, and I do not think that you will want to eat with the others."

I did not answer.

"You must eat," she continued. "If you like I will go get something to eat for you and me. I will bring King Hiram's and Galé's dinner here, too. When you are sad, you should not stay alone."

And the little green and gold fairy vanished, without waiting for my answer.

That was how my friendship with Tanit-Zerga began. Each morning she came to my room with the two beasts. She rarely spoke to me of Antinea and when she did it was always indirectly. The question that she saw ceaselessly hovering on my lips seemed to be unbearable to her and I felt her avoiding all the subjects towards which I myself dared not direct the conversation. To make sure of avoiding them she prattled, prattled, prattled, like a nervous little parakeet.

I was sick and this sister of charity in green and bronze silk tended me with such care as never was before. The two wild beasts, the big and the little, were there, each side of my couch, and during my delirium I saw their mysterious, sad eyes fixed on me.

In her melodious voice Tanit-Zerga told me wonderful stories and among them the one she thought most wonderful, the story of her life.

It was not till much later, very suddenly, that I realized how far this little barbarian had penetrated into my own life. Wherever thou art at this hour, dear little girl, from whatever peaceful shores thou watchest my tragedy, cast a look at thy friend, pardon him for not having accorded thee, from the very first, the gratitude that thou deservedst so richly.

"I remember from my childhood," she said, "the vision of a yellow and rose-colored sun rising through the morning mists over the smooth waves of a great river, 'the river where there is water;' the Niger, it was. But you are not listening to me."

"I am listening to you. I swear it, little Tanit-Zerga."

"You are sure I am not wearying you? You want me to go on?"

"Go on, little Tanit-Zerga, go on."

"Well, with my little companions, of whom I was very fond, I played at the edge of the river where there is water, under the *jujube*-trees, brothers of the *zeg-zeg*, the spines of which pierced the head of your Prophet and which we call 'the tree of Paradise' because our prophet told us that under it would live those chosen of Paradise.[14] It is sometimes so big—so big that a horseman cannot traverse its shade in a century.

"There we wove beautiful garlands with mimosa, the pink flowers of the caper bush and white cockles. Then we threw them in the green water to ward off evil spirits, and we laughed like mad things when a great snorting hippopotamus raised his swollen head, and we bombarded him in glee until he had to plunge back again with a tremendous splash.

"That was in the mornings. Then there fell on Gâo the deathlike lull of the red siesta. When that was finished we came back to the edge of the river to see the enormous crocodiles with bronze goggle-eyes creep along, little by little, among the clouds of mosquitoes and day-flies on the banks, and work their way into the yellow ooze of the mud flats.

"Then we bombarded them, as we had done the hippopotamus in the

14   *The Koran,* Chapter 66, verse 17. (Note by M. Leroux.)

morning. To fête the sun setting behind the black branches of the douldouls we made a circle, stamping our feet, then clapping our hands as we sang the Sonrhaï hymn.

"Such were the ordinary occupations of free little girls; but you must not think that we were only frivolous, and I will tell you, if you like, how I, who am talking to you, saved a French chieftain who must be vastly greater than yourself, to judge by the number of gold ribbons he had on his white sleeves."

"Tell me, little Tanit-Zerga," I said, my eyes elsewhere.

"You have no right to smile," she said, a little aggrieved, "and to pay no attention to me. But never mind; it is for myself that I tell these things, for the sake of recollection.

"Above Gâo the Niger makes a bend. There is a little promontory in the river, thickly covered with large gum-trees. It was an evening in August and the sun was sinking. Not a bird in the forest but had gone to rest, motionless until the morning.

"Suddenly we heard an unfamiliar noise in the west, *boum-boum, boum-boum, boum-baraboum, boum-boum*—growing louder—*boum-boum, boum-baraboum*—and suddenly there was a great flight of water-birds, aigrets, pelicans, wild ducks and teal, which scattered over the gum-trees and were followed by a column of black smoke which was scarcely flurried by the breeze that was springing up.

"It was a gunboat turning the point, sending out a wake that shook the overhanging bushes on each side of the river. One could see that the red, white and blue flag on the stern had drooped till it was dragging in the water, so heavy was the evening.

"She stopped at the little point of land. A small boat was let down, manned by two native soldiers who rowed and three chiefs who soon leapt ashore.

"The oldest, a French *marabout,* with a great white *burnoose,* who knew our language marvelously, asked to speak to Sheik Sonni-Azkia. When my father advanced and told him that it was he, the *marabout* told him that the commandant of the club at Timbuktu was very angry; that a mile from there the gunboat had run on an invisible pile of logs and that she had sprung a leak and that she could not so continue her voyage towards Ansango.

"My father replied that the French, who protected the poor natives against the Tuareg were welcome: that it was not from evil design but for fish that they had built the barrage; and that he put all the resources of Gâo for repairing the gunboat, including the forge, at the disposition of the French chief.

"While they were talking the French chief looked at me and I looked at him. He was already middle-aged, tall, with shoulders a little bent and blue eyes as clear as the stream whose name I bear.

"'Come here, little one,' he said in his gentle voice.

"'I am the daughter of Sheik Sonni-Azkia and I do only what I wish,' I replied, vexed at his informality.

"'You are right,' he answered smiling, 'for you are pretty. Will you give me the flowers that you have around your neck?'

"It was a great necklace of purple hibiscus. I held it out to him. He kissed me. The peace was made.

"Meantime, under the direction of my father, the native soldiers and strong men of the tribe had hauled the gunboat into a pocket of the river.

"'There is work there for all day tomorrow, Colonel,' said the chief mechanic after inspecting the leaks. 'We won't be able to get away before the day after tomorrow. And if we're to do that these lazy soldiers mustn't loaf on the job.'

"'What an awful bore,' groaned my new friend.

"But his ill-humor did not last long, so ardently did my little companions and I seek to distract him. He listened to our most beautiful songs, and, to thank us, made us taste the good things that had been brought from the boat for his dinner. He slept in our great cabin, which my father gave up to him, and for a long time before I went to sleep I looked through the cracks of the cabin where I lay with my mother, and gazed at the lights of the gunboat, trembling in red ripples on the surface of the dark waves.

"That night I had a frightful dream. I saw my friend, the French officer, sleeping in peace, while a great crow hung croaking above his head:

"'Caw—caw—the shade of the gum-trees of Gâo—caw, caw—will avail nothing tomorrow night—caw, caw—to the white chief nor to his escort.'

"Dawn had scarcely come when I went to find the native soldiers. They were stretched out on the bridge of the gunboat, taking advantage of the fact that the whites were still sleeping.

"I approached the eldest and spoke to him with authority:

"'I saw the black crow in a dream last night. He told me that the shade of the gum-trees of Gâo would be fatal to your chief in the coming night!'

"And as they all remained motionless, stretched out, gazing at the sky without even seeming to have heard, I added:

"'And to his escort.'

"It was the hour when the sun was highest. The colonel was eating in the cabin with the other Frenchmen when the chief mechanic entered.

"'I don't know what has come over the natives. They are working like angels. If they keep on this way, Colonel, we shall be able to leave this evening.'

"'Very good,' said the colonel, 'but don't let them spoil the job by too much haste. We don't have to be at Ansango before the end of the week. It will be better to start in the morning.'

"I trembled. Suppliantly I approached and told him the story of my dream. He listened with a smile of astonishment; then at the last he said gravely:

"'It is agreed, little Tanit-Zerga. We will leave this evening if you wish it.'

"And he kissed me.

"The darkness had already fallen when the gunboat, now repaired, left the harbor. My friend stood in the midst of the group of Frenchmen, who waved their caps as long as we could see them. Standing alone on the rickety jetty,

I waited, watching the water flow by, until the last sound of the steam-driven vessel—*boum-baraboum*—had died away into the night.[15]

"That was the last night of Gâo. While I was sleeping and the moon was still high above the forest a dog yelped, but only for an instant. Then came the cry of men, then of women, the kind of cry that *you* can never forget once heard.

"When the sun rose it found me, quite naked, running and stumbling with my little companions toward the north, beside the swiftly moving camels of the Tuareg who escorted us. Behind followed the women of the tribe, my mother among them, two by two, the yoke upon their necks. There were not many men. Almost all lay with their throats cut under the ruins of the thatch of Gâo beside my father, brave Sonni-Azkia. Once again Gâo had been razed by a band of Awellimiden, who had come to massacre the French on their gunboat.

"The Tuareg hurried us, for they were afraid of being pursued. We traveled thus for ten days, and, as the millet and hemp disappeared the march became more frightful. Finally near Isakeryen, in the country of Kidal, the Tuareg sold us to a caravan of Trarzan Moors who were going from Bamrouk to Rhat. At first, because they went more slowly, this seemed good fortune, but before long the desert was an expanse of rough pebbles, and the women began to fall. As for the men, the last of them had died far back under the blows of the stick for having refused to go farther.

"I still had the strength to keep going and even to keep as far in the lead as possible, so as not to hear the cries of my little playmates. Each time one of them fell by the way, unable to rise again, one of the drivers would descend from his camel and drag her into the bushes a little way to cut her throat.

"One day I heard a cry that made me turn around. It was my mother. She was kneeling, holding out her poor arms to me. In an instant I was beside her, but a great Moor dressed in white separated us. A red moroccan case hung around his neck from a black chaplet. He drew a cutlass from it. I can still see the blue steel against the brown skin. Another horrible cry. An instant later, driven by a club, I was trotting ahead, swallowing my little tears, trying to regain my place in the caravan.

"Near the wells of Asiou the Moors were attacked by a party of Tuareg of Kel-Tazeholet, serfs of the great tribe of Kel-Rhela which rules over Ahaggar. The Moors in their turn were massacred to the last man. That is how I was brought here and offered as homage to Antinea, who was pleased with me and ever since has been kind to me. That is why it is no slave who soothes your fever today with stories that you do not even listen to, but the last descendant of the great Sonrhaï emperors, of Sonni-Ali, the destroyer of men and of countries, of Mohammed Azkia, who made the pilgrimage to Mecca, taking with him fifteen hundred cavaliers and three hundred thousand mithkal of gold. That was in the days when our power stretched without rival from Chad to Tuat and to the

---

15   Cf. the records and the *Bulletin de la Société de Géographie de Paris* (1897) for the cruises on the Niger, made by the *commandant* of the Timbuktu region, Colonel Joffre, Lieutenants Baudry and Bluset, and by Father Hacquart of the White Fathers. (Note by M. Leroux.)

Western Sea, and when Gâo raised her cupola, sister of the sky, above the other cities, higher above her rival cupolas than is the tamarisk above the humble sorghum."

Chapter XVI

The Silver Hammer

Je ne m'en défends plus et je ne veux qu'aller
Reconnaître la place où jé dois l'immoler.
— Andromaque

IT WAS THIS SORT OF A NIGHT WHEN WHAT I AM GOING TO TELL YOU NOW, HAPPENED.
Toward five o'clock the sky clouded over and a sense of the coming storm trembled in the stifling air.

I shall always remember it. It was the fifth of January, 1897.

King Hiram and Galé lay on the matting of my room. Leaning on my elbows beside Tanit-Zerga in the rock-hewn window, I spied the advance tremors of lightning.

One by one they rose, streaking the darkness with their bluish stripes, but no burst of thunder followed. The storm did not attain the peaks of Ahaggar. It passed without breaking, leaving us in our gloomy bath of perspiration.

"I am going to bed," said Tanit-Zerga.

I have said that her room was above mine. Its bay window was some thirty feet above that before which I lay.

She took Galé in her arms, but King Hiram would have none of it. Digging his four paws into the matting, he whined in anger and uneasiness.

"Leave him," I finally said to Tanit-Zerga; "for once, he may sleep here."

So it was that this little beast incurred his large share of responsibility in the events which followed.

Left alone, I became lost in my reflections. The night was black. The whole mountain was shrouded in silence.

It took the louder and louder growls of the leopard to rouse me from my meditation.

King Hiram was braced against the door, digging at it with his drawn claws. He, who had refused to follow Tanit-Zerga a while ago, now wanted to go out. He was determined to go out.

"Be still," I said to him. "Enough of that. Lie down!"

I tried to pull him away from the door. I succeeded only in getting a staggering blow from his paw. Then I sat down on the divan.

My quiet was short.

Be honest with yourself. Since Morhange abandoned you, since the day when you saw Antinea, you have had only one idea. What good is it to beguile yourself with the stories of Tanit-Zerga, charming as they are? This leopard is a pretext, perhaps a guide. Oh, you know that mysterious things are going to happen tonight. How have you been able to keep from doing anything as long as this?

Immediately I made a resolve.

If I open the door, I thought, *King Hiram will leap down the corridor and I shall have great difficulty in following him. I must find some other way.*

The shade of the window was worked by means of a small cord. I pulled it down. Then I tied it into a firm leash, which I fastened to the metal collar of the leopard.

I half-opened the door.

"There, now you can go. But quietly, quietly."

I had all the trouble in the world to curb the ardor of King Hiram as he dragged me along the shadowy labyrinth of corridors. It was shortly before nine o'clock and the rose-colored night lights were almost burned out in the niches. Now and then we passed one which was casting its last flickers. What a labyrinth! I realized that from here on I would not recognize the way to her room. I could only follow the leopard.

At first furious, he gradually became used to towing me. He strained ahead, belly to the ground, with snuffs of joy.

Nothing is more like one black corridor than another black corridor. Doubt seized me. Suppose I should suddenly find myself in the baccarat room? But that was unjust to King Hiram. Barred too long from the dear presence, the good beast was taking me exactly where I wanted him to take me.

Suddenly, at a turn, the darkness ahead lifted. A rose window, faintly glimmering red and green, appeared before us.

The leopard stopped with a low growl before the door in which the rose window was cut.

I recognized it as the door through which the white Targa had led me the day after my arrival, when I had been set upon by King Hiram, when I had found myself in the presence of Antinea.

"We are much better friends today," I said, hoping that he would not give a dangerously loud growl.

I tried to open the door. The light, coming through the window, fell upon the floor, green and red. There was a simple latch, which I turned. I shortened the leash to have better control of King Hiram, who was getting nervous.

The great room where I had seen Antinea for the first time was completely dark, but the garden on which it gave shone under a clouded moon in a sky weighted down with the storm which did not break. There was not a breath of air. The lake gleamed like a sheet of pewter.

I seated myself on a cushion, holding the leopard firmly between my knees. He was purring with impatience. I was thinking, not about my goal—for a long time that had been fixed—but about the means.

Then I seemed to hear a distant murmur, a faint sound of voices.

King Hiram growled louder and struggled. I gave him a little more leash. He began to rub along the dark walls on the sides whence the voices seemed to come. I followed him, stumbling as quietly as I could among the scattered cushions.

My eyes, become accustomed to the darkness, could see the pyramid of cushions on which Antinea had first appeared to me.

Suddenly I stumbled. The leopard had stopped. I realized that I had stepped on his tail. Brave beast, he did not make a sound.

Groping along the wall, I felt a second door. Quietly, very quietly, I opened it as I had opened the preceding one. The leopard whimpered feebly.

"King Hiram," I murmured, "be quiet."

I put my arms about his powerful neck. I felt his warm wet tongue on my hands. His flanks quivered. He shook with happiness.

In front of us, lighted in the center, another room opened. In the middle six men were squatting on the matting, playing dice and drinking coffee from tiny copper coffee cups with long stems. They were the white Tuareg.

A lamp, hung from the ceiling, threw a circle of light over them. Everything outside that circle was in deep shadow. The black faces, the copper cups, the white robes, the moving light and shadow, made a strange etching.

They played with a reserved dignity, announcing the throws in raucous voices.

Then, slowly, very slowly, I slipped the leash from the collar of the impatient little beast.

"Go, boy."

He leapt with a sharp yelp, and what I had foreseen happened.

The first bound of King Hiram carried him into the midst of the white Tuareg, sowing confusion in the bodyguard. Another leap carried him into the shadow again. I made out vaguely the shaded opening of another corridor on the side of the room opposite where I was standing.

There! I thought.

The confusion in the room was indescribable, but noiseless. One realized the restraint which nearness to a great presence imposed upon the exasperated guards. The stakes and the dice-boxes had rolled in one direction, the copper cups, in another. Two of the Tuareg, doubled up with pain, were rubbing their ribs.

I need not say that I profited by this silent confusion to glide into the room. I was now flattened against the wall of the second corridor, down which King Hiram had just disappeared

At that moment a clear gong echoed in the silence. The trembling which seized the Tuareg assured me that I had chosen the right way.

One of the six men got up. He passed me in the darkness and I fell in behind him. I was perfectly calm. My least movement was perfectly calculated.

"All that I risk here now," I said to myself, "is being led back politely to my room."

The Targa lifted a curtain. I followed on his heels into the chamber of Antinea.

The room was huge and at the same time well lighted and very dark. While the right half, where Antinea was, gleamed under shaded lamps, the left was dim.

Those who have penetrated into a Mussulman home know what a *guignol* is, a kind of square niche in the wall, four feet from the floor, its opening covered by a curtain. One mounts to it by wooden steps. I noticed such a *guignol* at my left. I crept into it. My pulse was beating furiously, but I was calm, quite calm. There I could see and hear everything.

I was in Antinea's chamber. There was nothing singular about the room except the great luxury of the hangings. The ceiling was in shadow, but multi-colored lanterns cast a vague and gentle light over gleaming stuffs and furs.

Antinea was stretched out on a lion's skin, smoking. A little silver tray and pitcher lay beside her. King Hiram was flattened out at her feet, licking them madly.

The Targa slave stood rigid before her, one hand on his heart, the other on his forehead, saluting.

Antinea spoke in a hard voice without looking at the man.

"Why did you let the leopard pass? I told you that I wanted to be alone."

"He knocked us over, mistress," said the Targa humbly.

"The doors were not closed, then?"

The slave did not answer.

"Shall I take him away?" he asked.

His eyes, fastened upon King Hiram, who stared at him maliciously, expressed well enough his desire for a negative reply.

"Let him stay since he is here," said Antinea.

She tapped nervously on the little silver tray.

"What is the captain doing?" she asked.

"He dined a while ago and seemed to enjoy his food," the Targa answered.

"Has he said nothing?"

"Yes, he asked to see his companion, the other officer."

Antinea tapped the little tray still more rapidly.

"Did he say nothing else?"

"No, mistress," said the man.

A pallor overspread the Atlantide's little forehead.

"Go get him," she said brusquely.

Bowing the Targa left the room.

I listened to this dialogue with great anxiety. Was this Morhange? Had he been faithful to me after all? Had I suspected him unjustly? He had wanted to see me and been unable to.

My eyes never left Antinea's.

She was no longer the haughty, mocking princess of our first interview. She no longer wore the golden circlet on her forehead—not a bracelet, not a ring. She was dressed only in a full-flowing tunic. Her black hair, unbound, lay in masses of ebony over her slight shoulders and her bare arms.

Her beautiful eyes were deep-circled. Her divine mouth drooped. I did not know whether I was glad or sorry to see this new, quivering Cleopatra.

Flattened at her feet, King Hiram gazed submissively at her.

An immense *orichalc* mirror was set into the wall at the right. She raised herself erect before it.

The six incense-burners scattered about the room sent up invisible columns of perfume. The balsam spices of Arabia wore floating webs in which my shameless senses were entangled. And, her back toward me, standing straight as a lily, Antinea smiled into her mirror.

Low steps sounded in the corridor. Antinea immediately fell back into the nonchalant pose in which I had first seen her. One had to see such a transformation to believe it possible.

Morhange entered the room, preceded by a white Targa.

He, too, seemed rather pale, but I was most struck by the expression of serene peace on that face, which I thought I knew so well. I felt that I never had understood what manner of man Morhange was—never.

He stood erect before Antinea without seeming to notice her gesture inviting him to be seated

She smiled at him.

"You are surprised, perhaps," she said finally, "that I should send for you at so late an hour."

Morhange did not move an eyelash.

"Have you considered it well?" she demanded.

Morhange smiled gravely—but did not reply.

I could read in Antinea's face the effort it cost her to continue smiling; I admired the self-control of these two beings.

"I sent for you," she continued. "You do not guess why? Well, it is to tell you something that you do not expect. It will be no surprise to you if I say that I never met a man like you. During your captivity you have expressed only one wish. Do you recall it?"

"I asked your permission to see my friend before I died," said Morhange simply.

I do not know what stirred me more on hearing these words—delight at Morhange's formal tone in speaking to Antinea, or emotion at hearing the one wish he had expressed.

But Antinea continued calmly:

"That is why I sent for you—to tell you that you are going to see him again. And I am going to do something else. You will perhaps scorn me even more when you realize that you had only to oppose me to bend me to your will—I, who have bent all other wills to mine. But, however that may be, it is decided: I give you both your liberty. Tomorrow Cegheir-ben-Cheikh will lead you past the fifth enclosure. Are you satisfied?"

"I am," said Morhange with a mocking smile. "That will give me a chance," he continued, "to make better plans for the next trip I intend to make this way, for you need not doubt that I shall feel bound to return to express my gratitude. Only next time, to render so great a queen the honors due her, I shall ask my government to furnish me with two or three hundred European soldiers and several cannon."

Antinea was standing up, very pale.

"What are you saying?"

"I am saying," said Morhange coldly, "that I foresaw this. First threats, then promises."

Antinea stepped toward him. He had folded his arms. He looked at her with a sort of grave pity.

"I will make you die in the most atrocious agonies," she said finally.

"I am your prisoner," Morhange replied.

"You shall suffer things that you cannot even imagine."

"I am your prisoner," repeated Morhange in the same sad calm.

Antinea paced the room like a beast in a cage. She advanced toward my companion and, no longer mistress of herself, struck him in the face.

He smiled and caught hold of her, drawing her little wrists together with a strange mixture of force and gentleness.

King Hiram growled. I thought he was about to leap, but the cold eyes of Morhange held him fascinated.

"I will have your comrade killed before your eyes," gasped Antinea.

It seemed to me that Morhange paled, but only for a second. I was overcome by the nobility and insight of his reply.

"My companion is brave. He does not fear death. And in any case he would prefer death to life purchased at the price you name."

So saying, he let go Antinea's wrists. Her pallor was terrible. From the expression of her mouth I felt that this would be her last word to him.

"Listen," she said.

How beautiful she was in her scorned majesty, her beauty powerless for the first time.

"Listen," she continued. "Listen for the last time. Remember that I hold the gates of this palace, that I have supreme power over your life. Remember that you breathe only at my pleasure. Remember—"

"I have remembered all that," said Morhange.

"A last time," she repeated.

The serenity of Morhange's face was so powerful that I scarcely noticed his opponent. In that transfigured countenance, no trace of worldliness remained.

"A last time," came Antinea's voice, almost breaking.

Morhange was not even looking at her.

"As you will," she said.

Her gong resounded. She had struck the silver disc. The white Targa appeared.

"Leave the room!"

Morhange, his head held high, went out.

Now Antinea is in my arms. This is no haughty, voluptuous woman whom I am pressing to my heart. It is only an unhappy, scorned little girl.

So great was her trouble that she showed no surprise when I stepped out beside her. Her head is on my shoulder.

Like the crescent moon in the black clouds, I see her clear little bird-like profile amid her mass of hair. Her warm arms hold me convulsively. *O tremblant coeur humain!*

Who could resist such an embrace, amid the soft perfumes, in the languorous night? I feel myself a being without will. Is this my voice, the voice which is murmuring:

"Ask me what you will and I will do it, I will do it."

My senses are sharpened, tenfold keen. My head rests against a soft, nervous little knee. Clouds of odors whirl about me.

Suddenly it seems as if the golden lanterns are waving from the ceiling like giant censers. Is this my voice, the voice repeating in a dream:

"Ask me what you will and I will do it. I will do it."

Antinea's face is almost touching mine. A strange light flickers in her great eyes.

Beyond, I see the gleaming eyes of King Hiram. Beside him, there is a little table of Kairouan, blue and gold. On that table I see the gong with which Antinea summons the slaves.

I see the hammer with which she struck it just now, a hammer with a long ebony handle, a heavy silver head—the hammer with which little Lieutenant Kaine dealt death.

I see nothing more.

Chapter XVII
The Maidens of the Rocks

I AWAKENED IN MY ROOM. THE SUN, ALREADY AT ITS ZENITH, FILLED THE PLACE WITH unbearable light and heat.

The first thing I saw on opening my eyes was the shade, ripped down, lying in the middle of the floor. Then, confusedly, the night's events began to come back to me.

My head felt stupid and heavy. My mind wandered. My memory seemed blocked. I went out with the leopard, that is certain. That red mark on my forefinger shows how he strained at the leash. My knees are still dusty. I remember creeping along the wall in the room where the white Tuareg were playing at dice. That was the minute after King Hiram had leapt past them. After that—oh, Morhange and Antinea. . . . And then?

I recalled nothing more, but something must have happened, something which I could not remember.

I was uneasy. I wanted to go back, yet it seemed as if I were afraid to go. I have never felt anything more painful than those conflicting emotions.

"It is a long way from here to Antinea's apartments. I must have been very sound asleep not to have noticed when they brought me back, for they have brought me back."

I stopped trying to think it out. My head ached too much.

"I must have air," I murmured. "I am roasting here; it will drive me mad."

I had to see someone, no matter whom. Mechanically I walked toward the library.

I found M. Le Mesge in a transport of delirious joy. The professor was engaged in opening an enormous bale, carefully sewed in a brown blanket.

"You come at a good time, sir," he cried, on seeing me enter. "The magazines have just arrived."

He dashed about in feverish haste. Presently a stream of pamphlets and magazines—blue, green, yellow and salmon—was bursting from an opening in the bale.

"Splendid, splendid!" he cried, dancing with joy. "Not too late, either; here are the numbers for October fifteenth. We must give a vote of thanks to good Ameur."

His good spirits were contagious.

"There is a good Turkish merchant who subscribes to all the interesting
133

magazines of the two continents. He sends them on by Rhadames to a destination which he little suspects. Ah, here are the French ones."

M. Le Mesge ran feverishly over the tables of contents.

"Internal politics—articles by Francis Charmes, Anatole Leroy-Beaulieu—d'Haussonville on the Czar's trip to Paris. Look, a study by Avenel of wages in the Middle Ages. And verse, verses of the young poets, Fernand Gregh, Edmond Haraucourt. Ah, the resume of a book by Henry de Castries on Islam. That may be interesting. Take what you please."

Joy makes people amiable and M. Le Mesge was really delirious with it.

A puff of breeze came from the window. I went to the balustrade and, resting my elbows on it, began to run through a number of the *Revue des Deux Mondes*.

I did not read, but flipped over the pages, my eyes now on the lines of swarming little black characters, now on the rocky basin which lay shivering, pale pink, under the declining sun.

Suddenly my attention became fixed. There was a strange coincidence between the text and the landscape.

> In the sky overhead were only light shreds of cloud, like bits of white ash floating up from burnt-out logs. The sun fell over a circle of rocky peaks, silhouetting their severe lines against the azure sky. From on high, a great sadness and gentleness poured down into the lonely enclosure, like a magic drink into a deep cup. . . .[16]

I turned the pages feverishly. My mind seemed to be clearing.

Behind me, M. Le Mesge, deep in an article, voiced his opinions in indignant growls.

I continued reading:

> On all sides a magnificent view spread out before us in the raw light. The chain of rocks, clearly visible in their barren desolation which stretched to the very summit, lay stretched out like some great heap of gigantic, unformed things left by some primordial race of Titans to stupefy human beings. Overturned towers. . . .

"It is shameful, downright shameful," the professor was repeating.

> Overturned towers, crumbling citadels, cupolas fallen in, broken pillars, mutilated colossi, prows of vessels, thighs of monsters, bones of titans—this mass, impassable with its ridges and gullies, seemed the embodiment of everything huge and tragic. So clear were the distances. . . .

16   Gabrielle d'Annunzio: Les Vierges aux Rochers. Cf. *The Revue des Deux Mondes* of October 15, 1896; page 867.

"Downright shameful," M. Le Mesge kept on saying in exasperation, thumping his fist on the table.

> So clear were the distances that I could see, as if I had it under my eyes, infinitely enlarged, every contour of the rock which Violante had shown me through the window with the gesture of a creator...

Trembling, I closed the magazine. At my feet I saw the rock, now red, which Antinea had pointed out to me the day of our first interview, huge, steep, overhanging the reddish brown-garden.

"That is my horizon," she had said.

M. Le Mesge's excitement had passed all bounds.

"It is worse than shameful; it is infamous."

I almost wanted to strangle him into silence. He seized my arm.

"Read that, sir, and, although you don't know a great deal about the subject, you will see that this article on Roman Africa is a miracle of misinformation, a monument of ignorance. And it is signed—do you know by whom it is signed?"

"Leave me alone," I said brutally.

"Well, it is signed by Gaston Boissier. Yes, sir! Gaston Boissier, grand officer of the Legion of Honor, lecturer at the École Normale Supérieure, permanent secretary of the French Academy, member of the Academy of Inscriptions and Literature, one of those who once ruled out the subject of my thesis—one of those—ah, poor University, ah, poor France!"

I was no longer listening. I had begun to read again. My forehead was covered with perspiration, but it seemed as if my head had been cleared like a room when a window is opened; memories were beginning to come back like doves winging their way home to the dovecote.

> At that moment, an irrepressible tremor shook her whole body; her eyes dilated as if some terrible sight had filled them with horror.
>
> "Antonello," she murmured, and for seconds she was unable to say another word.
>
> I looked at her in mute anguish and the suffering which drew her dear lips together seemed also to clutch at my heart. The vision which was in her eyes passed into mine, and I saw again the thin white face of Antonello, and the quick quivering of his eyelids, the waves of agony which seized his long worn body and shook it like a reed.

I threw the magazine upon the table.

"That is it," I said.

To cut the pages I had used the knife with which M. Le Mesge had cut the cords of the bale, a short ebony-handled dagger, one of those daggers that the Tuareg wear in a bracelet-sheath against the upper left arm.

I slipped it into the big pocket of my flannel dolman and walked toward the door.

I was about to cross the threshold when I heard M. Le Mesge call me.

"Monsieur de Saint Avit! Monsieur de Saint Avit! I want to ask you something, please."

"What is it?"

"Nothing important. You know that I have to mark the labels for the red marble hall."

I walked toward the table.

"Well, I forgot to ask M. Morhange at the beginning, the date and place of his birth. After that I had no chance. I did not see him again. So I am forced to turn to you. Perhaps you can tell me."

"I can," I said very calmly.

He took a large white card from a box which contained several, and dipped his pen.

"Number 54. Captain?"

"Captain Jean Marie Francois Morhange."

While I dictated, one hand resting on the table, I noticed on my cuff a stain, a little stain, reddish brown.

"Morhange," repeated M. Le Mesge, finishing the lettering of my friend's name. "Born at?"

"Villefranche."

"Villefranche, Rhône. What date?"

"The fourteenth of October, 1859."

"The fourteenth of October, 1859. Good. Died at Ahaggar, the fifth of January, 1897. There, that is done. A thousand thanks, sir, for your kindness."

"You are welcome."

I left M. Le Mesge.

My mind, thenceforth was well made up, and as I said I was perfectly calm. Nevertheless, when I had taken leave of M. Le Mesge I felt the need of waiting a few minutes before executing my decision.

First, I wandered through the corridors; then, finding myself near my room, I went to it. It was still intolerably hot. I sat down on my divan and began to think.

The dagger in my pocket bothered me. I took it out and laid it on the floor.

It was a good dagger with a diamond-shaped blade and with a collar of orange leather between the blade and the handle. The sight of it recalled the silver hammer. I remembered how easily it fitted into my hand when I struck.

Every detail of the scene came back to me with incomparable vividness, but I did not even shiver. It seemed as if my determination to kill the instigator of the murder permitted me peacefully to evoke its brutal details.

If I reflected over my deed, it was to be surprised at it, not to condemn myself.

"Well," I said to myself, "I have killed this Morhange, who was once a baby, who, like all the others, cost his mother so much trouble with his baby sicknesses. I have put an end to his life. I have reduced to nothingness the monument of love, of tears, of trials overcome and pitfalls escaped, which constitutes a human existence. What an extraordinary adventure!"

That was all. No fear, no remorse, none of that Shakespearean horror after the murder which today, skeptic though I am and blasé and utterly, utterly disillusioned, sets me shuddering whenever I am alone in a dark room.

Come, I thought. *It's time—time to finish it up.*

I picked up the dagger. Before putting it in my pocket I went through the motion of striking. All was well. The dagger fitted into my hand.

I had been through Antinea's apartment only when guided, the first time by the white Targa, the second time by the leopard, yet I found the way again without trouble. Just before coming to the door with the rose window I met a Targa.

"Let me pass," I ordered. "Your mistress has sent for me."

The man obeyed, stepping back.

Soon a dim melody came to my ears. I recognized the sound of a rebaza, the violin with a single string, played by the Tuareg women. It was Aguida playing, squatting as usual at the feet of her mistress. The three other women were also squatted about her. Tanit-Zerga was not there.

Since that was the last time I saw her, let me tell you of Antinea, of how she looked in that supreme moment.

Did she feel the danger hovering over her and did she wish to brave it by her surest artifices? I had in mind the slender, unadorned body, without rings, without jewels, which I had pressed to my heart the night before, and now I started in surprise at seeing before me, adorned like an idol, not a woman but a queen.

The heavy splendor of the Pharaohs weighted down her slender body. On her head was the great gold *pschent* of Egyptian gods and kings; emeralds, the national stone of the Tuareg, were set in it, tracing and retracing her name in Tifinar characters. A red satin *schenti,* embroidered in golden lotus, enveloped her like the casket of a jewel. At her feet lay an ebony scepter, headed with a trident. Her bare arms were encircled by two serpents, whose fangs touched her armpits as if to bury themselves there. From the ear-pieces of the *pschent* streamed a necklace of emeralds; its first strand passed under her determined chin; the others lay in circles against her bare throat.

She smiled as I entered.

"I was expecting you," she said simply.

I advanced till I was four steps from the throne, then stopped before her.

She looked at me ironically.

"What is that?" she asked with perfect calm.

I followed her gesture. The handle of the dagger protruded from my pocket.

I drew it out and held it firmly in my hand, ready to strike.

"The first of you who moves will be sent naked six leagues into the red desert and left there to die," said Antinea coldly to her women, whom my gesture had thrown into a frightened murmuring.

She turned to me.

"That dagger is very ugly and you hold it badly. Shall I send Sydya to my room to get the silver hammer? You are more adroit with it than with the dagger."

"Antinea," I said in a low voice, "I am going to kill you."

"Do not speak so formally. You were more affectionate last night. Are you embarrassed by them?" she said, pointing to the women, whose eyes were wide with terror.

"Kill me?" she went on. "You are hardly reasonable. Kill me at the moment when you can reap the fruits of the murder of—"

"Did—did he suffer?" I asked suddenly, trembling.

"Very little. I told you that you used the hammer as if you had done nothing else all your life."

"Like little Kaine," I murmured.

She smiled in surprise.

"Oh, you know that story. Yes, like little Kaine. But at least Kaine was sensible. You—I do not understand."

"I do not understand myself, very well."

She looked at me with amused curiosity.

"I did what you told me to. May I in turn ask one favor, ask you one question?"

"What is it?"

"It was dark, was it not, in the room where *he* was?"

"Very dark. I had to lead you to the bed where he lay asleep."

"He *was* asleep, you are sure?"

"I said so."

"He—did not die instantly, did he?"

"No. I know exactly when he died—two minutes after you struck him and fled with a shriek."

"Then surely *he* could not have known?"

"Known what?"

"That it was I who—who held the hammer."

"He might not have known it, indeed," said Antinea. "But he did know."

"What!"

"He did know—because I told him," she said, staring straight into my eyes with magnificent audacity.

"And," I murmured, "he—he believed it?"

"With the help of my explanation he recognized your shriek. If he had not realized that you were his murderer, the affair would not have interested me," she finished with a scornful little smile.

Four steps, I said, separated me from Antinea. I sprang forward, but before I reached her I was struck to the floor.

King Hiram had leapt at my throat.

At the same moment I heard the calm, haughty voice of Antinea.

"Call the men," she commanded.

A second later I was released from the leopard's clutch. The six white Tuareg had surrounded me and were trying to bind me.

I am fairly strong and quick. I was on my feet in a second. One of my enemies lay on the floor, ten feet away felled by a well-placed blow on the jaw. Another was gasping under my knee. That was the last time I saw Antinea. She stood erect, both hands resting on her ebony scepter, watching the struggle with a smile of contemptuous interest.

Suddenly I gave a loud cry and loosed the hold I had on my victim. I felt a cracking in my left arm; one of the Tuareg had seized it and twisted until my shoulder was dislocated.

When I completely lost consciousness I was being carried down the corridor by two white phantoms, so bound that I could not move a muscle.

Chapter XVIII
The Fireflies

THROUGH THE GREAT OPEN WINDOW, WAVES OF PALE MOONLIGHT SURGED INTO MY room.

A slender white figure was standing beside the bed where I lay.

"You, Tanit-Zerga!" I murmured. She laid a finger on her lips.

"Sh! Yes, it is I."

I tried to raise myself up on the bed. A terrible pain seized my shoulder. The events of the afternoon came back to my poor harassed mind.

"Oh, little one, if you knew!"

"I know," she said.

I was weaker than a baby. After the overstrain of the day had come a fit of utter nervous depression. A lump rose in my throat, choking me.

"If you knew, if you only knew! Take me away, little one. Get me away from here."

"Not so loud," she whispered. "There is a white Targa on guard at the door."

"Take me away; save me," I repeated.

"That is what I came for," she said simply.

I looked at her. She no longer was wearing her beautiful red silk tunic. A plain white *haik* was wrapped about her and she had drawn one corner of it over her head.

"I want to go away, too," she said in a smothered voice. "For a long time I have wanted to go away. I want to see Gâo, the village on the bank of the river, and the blue gum-trees, and the green water.

"Ever since I came here I have wanted to get away," she repeated, "but I am too little to go alone into the great Sahara. I never dared speak to the others who came here before you. They all thought only of *her*. But you, you wanted to kill her."

I gave a low moan.

"You are suffering," she said. "They broke your arm."

"Dislocated it, anyhow."

"Let me see."

With infinite gentleness, she passed her smooth little hands over my shoulder.

"You tell me that there is a white Targa on guard before my door, Tanit-

Zerga," I said. "Then how did you get in?"

"That way," she said, pointing to the window. A dark perpendicular line halved its blue opening.

"How can we escape?" I asked.

"That way," she repeated, and she pointed again at the window.

I leaned out. My feverish gaze fell upon the shadowy depths, searching for those invisible rocks, the rocks upon which little Kaine had dashed himself.

"That way!" I exclaimed, shuddering. "Why, it is two hundred feet from here to the ground."

"The rope is two hundred and fifty," she replied. "It is a good strong rope which I stole in the oasis; they used it in felling trees. It is quite new."

"Climb down that way, Tanit-Zerga? With my shoulder?"

"I will let you down," she said firmly. "Feel how strong my arms are—not that I shall rest your weight on them. But see, on each side of the window is a marble column. By twisting the rope around one of them I can let you slip down and scarcely feel your weight.

"And look," she continued, "I have made a big knot every ten feet. I can stop the rope with them, every now and then, if I want to rest."

"And you?" I asked.

"When you are down I shall tie the rope to one of the columns and follow. There are the knots on which to rest if the rope cuts my hands too much. But don't be afraid: I am very agile. At Gâo, when I was just a child, I used to climb almost as high as this in the gum-trees to take the little toucans out of their nests. It is even easier to climb down."

"And when we are down how will we get out? Do you know the way through the barriers?"

"No one knows the way through the barriers," she said, "except Cegheir-ben-Cheikh, and perhaps Antinea."

"Then?"

"There are the camels of Cegheir-ben-Cheikh, those which he uses on his forays. I untethered the strongest one and led him out, just below us, and gave him lots of hay so that he will not make a sound and will be well-fed when we start."

"But—" I still protested.

She stamped her foot.

"But what? Stay if you wish, if you are afraid. I am going. I want to see Gâo once again. Gâo with its blue gum-trees and its green water."

I felt myself blushing.

"I will go, Tanit-Zerga. I would rather die of thirst in the midst of the desert than stay here. Let us start."

"Tut!" she said. "Not yet."

She showed me that the dizzy descent was in brilliant moonlight.

"Not yet. We must wait. They would see us. In an hour the moon will have circled behind the mountain. That will be the time."

She sat silent, her *haik* wrapped completely about her dark little figure. Was she praying? Perhaps. Suddenly I no longer saw her. Darkness had crept in the window. The moon had turned.

Tanit-Zerga's hand was on my arm. She drew me toward the abyss. I tried not to tremble.

Everything below us was in shadow. In a low, firm voice, Tanit-Zerga began to speak:

"Everything is ready. I have twisted the rope about the pillar. Here is the slip-knot. Put it under your arms. Take this cushion. Keep it pressed against your hurt shoulder—a leather cushion—it is tightly stuffed. Keep face to the wall. It will protect you against the bumping and scraping."

I was now master of myself, very calm. I sat down on the sill of the window, my feet in the void. A breath of cool air from the peaks refreshed me.

I felt little Tanit-Zerga's hand in my vest pocket.

"Here is a box. I must know when you are down, so I can follow. You will open the box. There are fire-flies in it; I shall see them and follow you."

She held my hand a moment.

"Now go," she murmured.

I went.

I remember only one thing about that descent: I was overcome with vexation when the rope stopped and I found myself, feet dangling, against the perfectly smooth wall.

"What is the little fool waiting for?" I said to myself. "I have been hung here for a quarter of an hour. Ah—at last! Oh, here I am stopped again."

Once or twice I thought I was reaching the ground, but it was only a projection from the rock. I had to give a quick shove with my foot. Then suddenly I found myself seated on the ground. I stretched out my hands. Bushes—a thorn pricked my finger. I was down.

Immediately I began to get nervous again.

I pulled out the cushion and slipped off the noose. With my good hand, I pulled the rope, holding it out five or six feet from the face of the mountain, and put my foot on it. Then I took the little cardboard box from my pocket and opened it.

One after the other, three little luminous circles rose in the inky night. I saw them rise higher and higher against the rocky wall. Their pale rose aureoles gleamed faintly. Then, one by one, they disappeared.

"You are tired, *sidi* Lieutenant. Let me hold the rope."

Cegheir-ben-Cheikh rose up at my side.

I looked at his tall black silhouette. I shuddered, but I did not let go of the rope on which I began to feel distant jerks.

"Give it to me," he repeated with authority, and took it from my hands.

I don't know what possessed me then. I was standing beside that great dark phantom. But what could I, with a dislocated shoulder, do against that man whose agile strength I already knew? What was there *to* do? I saw him buttressed against the wall, holding the rope with both hands, with both feet, with all his body, much better than I had been able to do.

There was a rustling above our heads. A little shadowy form appeared.

"There," said Cegheir-ben-Cheikh, seizing the little shadow in his powerful arms and placing her on the ground, while the rope, let slack, slapped back against the rock.

Tanit-Zerga recognized the Targa and groaned. He put his hand roughly over her mouth.

"Shut up, camel thief, wretched little fly."

He seized her arm; then he turned to me.

"Come!" he said in an imperious tone.

I obeyed. During our short walk I heard Tanit-Zerga's teeth chattering with terror.

We reached a little cave.

"Go in," said the Targa.

He lighted a torch. The red light showed a superb *mehari* peacefully chewing his cud.

"The little one is not stupid," said Cegheir-ben-Cheikh, pointing to the animal. "She knows enough to pick out the best and the strongest, but she is rattle-brained."

He held the torch nearer the camel.

"She is rattle-brained," he continued. "She only saddled him—no water, no food. At this hour, three days from now, all three of you would have been dead on the road—and on what a road!"

Tanit-Zerga's teeth no longer chattered. She was looking at the Targa with a mixture of terror and hope.

"Come here, *sidi* Lieutenant," said Cegheir-ben-Cheikh, "so that I can explain to you."

When I was beside him, he said:

"On each side is a skin of water. Make that water last as long as possible, for you are going to cross a terrible country. It may be that you will not find a well for three hundred miles.

"There," he went on, "in the saddle-bags are cans of preserved meat. Not many, for water is much more precious. Here also is a carbine, your carbine, *sidi.* Try not to use it except to shoot antelopes. And there is this."

He spread out a roll of paper. I saw his inscrutable face bent over it; his eyes were smiling; he looked at me.

"Once out of the enclosures, what way did you plan to go?" he asked.

"Toward Idelès, to retake the route where you met the captain and me," I said.

Cegheir-ben-Cheikh shook his head.

"I thought as much," he murmured.

Then he added coldly:

"Before sunset tomorrow you and the little one would have been caught and massacred."

"Toward the north is Ahaggar," he continued, "and all Ahaggar is under the control of Antinea. You must go south."

"Then we shall go south."

"By what route?"

"Why, by Silet and Timassou."

The Targa again shook his head.

"They will look for you on that road also," he said. "It is a good road, the road with the wells. They know that you are familiar with it. The Tuareg would not fail to wait at the wells."

"Well then?"

"Well," said Cegheir-ben-Cheikh, "you must not rejoin the road from Timassou to Timbuktu until you are four hundred miles from here toward Iferouane or, better still, at the spring of Telemsi. That is the boundary between the Tuareg of Ahaggar and the Awellimiden Tuareg."

The little voice of Tanit-Zerga broke in:

"It was the Awellimiden Tuareg who massacred my people and carried me into slavery. I do not want to pass through the country of the Awellimiden."

"Be still, miserable little fly," said Cegheir-ben-Cheikh.

Then, addressing me, he continued:

"I have said what I have said. The little one is not wrong. The Awellimiden are a savage people, but they are afraid of the French. Many of them trade with the stations north of the Niger. On the other hand they are at war with the people of Ahaggar, who will not follow you into their country.

"What I have said is said. You must rejoin the Timbuktu road near where it enters the borders of the Awellimiden. Their country is wooded and rich in springs. If you reach the springs at Telemsi, you will finish your journey beneath a canopy of blossoming mimosa. On the other hand the road from here to Telemsi is shorter than by way of Timissau. It is quite straight."

"Yes, it is direct," I said, "but, in following it you have to cross the Tanezruft."

Cegheir-ben-Cheikh waved his hand impatiently.

"Cegheir-ben-Cheikh knows that," he said. "He knows what the Tanezruft is. He who has traveled over all the Sahara knows that he would shudder at crossing the Tanezruft and the Tasili from the south. He knows that the camels that wander into that country either die or become wild, for no one will risk his life to go look for them. It is the terror that hangs over that region that may save you, for you have to choose. You must run the risk of dying of thirst on the tracks of the Tanezruft, or having your throat cut along some other route."

"You can stay here," he added.

"My choice is made, Cegheir-ben-Cheikh," I announced.

"Good!" he replied, again opening out the roll of paper. "This trail begins at the second barrier of earth, to which I will lead you. It ends at Iferouane. I have marked the wells, but do not trust to them too much, for many of them are dry. Be careful not to stray from the route. If you lose it, it is death. Now mount the camel with the little one. Two make less noise than four."

We went a long way in silence. Cegheir-ben-Cheikh walked ahead and his camel followed meekly. We crossed, first, a dark passage, then a deep gorge, then another passage. The entrance to each was hidden by a thick tangle of rocks and briars.

Suddenly a burning breath touched our faces. A dull reddish light filtered in through the end of the passage. The desert lay before us.

Cegheir-ben-Cheikh had stopped.

"Get down," he said.

A spring gurgled out of the rock. The Targa went to it and filled a copper cup with the water.

"Drink," he said, holding it out to each of us in turn.

We obeyed.

"Drink again," he ordered. "You will save just so much of the contents of your water skins. Now try not to be thirsty before sunset."

He looked over the saddle-girths.

"That's all right," he murmured. "Now go. In two hours the dawn will be here. You must be out of sight."

I was filled with emotion at this last moment; I went to the Targa and took his hand.

"Cegheir-ben-Cheikh," I asked in a low voice, "why are you doing this?"

He stepped back and I saw his dark eyes gleam.

"Why?" he said.

"Yes, why?"

He replied with dignity:

"The Prophet permits every just man once in his lifetime to let pity take the place of duty. Cegheir-ben-Cheikh is turning this permission to the advantage of one who saved his life."

"And you are not afraid," I asked, "that I will disclose the secret of Antinea if I return among Frenchmen?"

He shook his head.

"I am not afraid of that," he said, and his voice was full of irony. "It is not to your interest that Frenchmen should know how the captain met his death."

I was horrified at this logical reply.

"Perhaps I am doing wrong," the Targa went on, "in not killing the little one, but she loves you. She will not talk. Now go. Day is coming."

I tried to press the hand of this strange rescuer, but he again drew back.

"Do not thank me. What I am doing I do to acquire merit in the eyes of God. You may be sure that I shall never do it again, neither for you nor for anyone else."

And, as I made a gesture to reassure him on that point.

"Do not protest," he said in a tone the mockery of which still sounds in my ears. "Do not protest. What I am doing is of value to me, but not to you."

I looked at him uncomprehendingly.

"Not to you, *sidi* Lieutenant, not to you," his grave voice continued, "for you will come back and when that day comes do not count on the help of Cegheir-ben-Cheikh."

"I will come back?" I asked, shuddering.

"You will come back," the Targa replied.

He was standing erect, a black statue against the wall of gray rock.

"You will come back," he repeated with emphasis. "You are fleeing now, but you are mistaken if you think that you will look at the world with the same eyes as before. Henceforth one idea will follow you everywhere you go, and in one year, five, perhaps ten years, you will pass again through the corridor through which you have just come."

"Be still, Cegheir-ben-Chekih," said the trembling voice of Tanit-Zerga.

"Be still yourself, miserable little fly," said Cegheir-ben-Cheikh.

He sneered.

"The little one is afraid because she knows that I tell the truth. She knows the story of Lieutenant Ghiberti."

"Lieutenant Ghiberti?" I said, the perspiration standing out on my forehead.

"He was an Italian officer whom I met between Rhat and Rhadames eight years ago. He did not believe that love of Antinea could make him forget all else that life contained. He tried to escape and he succeeded. I do not know how, for I did not help him. He went back to his country, but hear what happened. Two years later, to the very day, when I was leaving the lookout, I discovered a miserable tattered creature, half-dead from hunger and fatigue, searching in vain for the entrance to the northern barrier. It was Lieutenant Ghiberti come back. He fills niche number 39 in the red marble hall."

The Targa smiled slightly.

"That is the story of Lieutenant Ghiberti which you wished to hear. But enough of this. Mount your camel."

I obeyed without saying a word. Tanit-Zerga, seated behind me, put her little arms around me. Cegheir-ben-Cheikh was still holding the bridle.

"One word more," he said, pointing to a black spot against the violet sky of the southern horizon. "You see the gour there; that is your way. It is eighteen miles from here. You should reach it by sunrise. Then consult your map. The next point is marked. If you do not stray from the line, you should be at the springs of Telemsi in eight days."

The camel's neck was stretched toward the dark wind coming from the south.

The Targa released the bridle with a sweep of his hand.

"Now, go."

"Thank you," I called to him, turning back in the saddle. "Thank you, Cegheir-ben-Cheikh, and farewell."

I heard his voice replying in the distance—
"Au revoir, Lieutenant de Saint Avit."

Chapter XIX

The Tanezruft

During the first hour of our flight the great *mehari* of Cegheir-ben-Cheikh carried us at a mad pace. We covered at least five leagues. With fixed eyes I guided the beast toward the gour which the Targa had pointed out, its ridge becoming higher and higher against the paling sky.

The speed caused a little breeze to whistle in our ears. Great tufts of retem, like fleshless skeletons, were tossed to right and left.

I heard the voice of Tanit-Zerga whispering—

"Stop the camel."

At first I did not understand.

"Stop him," she repeated.

Her hand pulled sharply at my right arm.

I obeyed. The camel slackened his pace with very bad grace.

"Listen," she said.

At first I heard nothing; then a very slight noise, a dry rustling behind us.

"Stop the camel," Tanit-Zerga commanded. "It is not worthwhile to make him kneel."

A little gray creature bounded on the camel. The *mehari* set out again at his best speed.

"Let him go," said Tanit-Zerga. "Galé has jumped on."

I felt a tuft of bristly hair under my arm. The mongoose had followed our footsteps and rejoined us. I heard the quick panting of the brave little creature becoming gradually slower and slower.

"I am happy," murmured Tanit-Zerga.

Cegheir-ben-Cheikh had not been mistaken. We reached the gour as the sun rose. I looked back. The Atakor was nothing more than a monstrous chaos amid the night mists that trailed the dawn. It was no longer possible to pick out from among the nameless peaks the one on which Antinea was still weaving her passionate plots.

You know what the Tanezruft is—the "plain of plains," abandoned, uninhabitable, the country of hunger and thirst. We were then starting on the part of the desert which Duveyrier calls the Tasili of the south and which figures on the maps of the Minister of Public Works under this attractive tide—

"Rocky plateau, without water, without vegetation, inhospitable for man and beast."

148

Nothing, unless parts of the Kalahari, is more frightful than this rocky desert. Cegheir-ben-Cheikh did not exaggerate in saying that no one would dream of following us into that country.

Great patches of oblivion still refused to clear away. Memories chased each other incoherently about my head. A sentence came back to me textually: "It seemed to Dick that he had never, since the beginning of original darkness, done anything at all save jolt through the air." I gave a little laugh. *In the last few hours,* I thought, *I have been heaping up literary situations. A while ago, a hundred feet above the ground, I was Fabrice of La Chartreuse de Parme beside his Italian dungeon. Now, here on my camel, I am Dick of The Light That Failed, crossing the desert to meet his companions in arms.*

I chuckled again, then shuddered. I thought of the preceding night, of the Orestes of Andromaque who agreed to sacrifice Pyrrhus. A literary situation indeed.

Cegheir-ben-Cheikh had reckoned eight days to get to the wooded country of the Awellimiden, forerunners of the grassy steppes of the Sudan. He well knew the worth of his beast. Tanit-Zerga had suddenly given him a name, El Mellen—the white one—for the magnificent *mehari* had an almost spotless coat. Once he went two days without eating, merely picking up here and there a branch of an acacia tree whose hideous white spines, four inches long, filled me with fear for our friend's esophagus.

The wells marked out by Cegheir-ben-Cheikh were indeed at the indicated spots, but we found nothing in them but a burning yellow mud. It was enough for the camel, enough so that at the end of the fifth day, thanks to prodigious self-control, we had used up only one of our two water skins. Then we believed ourselves safe.

Near one of these muddy puddles I succeeded that day in shooting down a little straight-horned desert gazelle. Tanit-Zerga skinned the beast and we regaled ourselves with a delicious haunch. Meantime little Galé, who never ceased prying about the cracks in the rocks during our mid-day halts in the heat, discovered an *ourane*—a sand crocodile—five feet long, and made short work of breaking his neck. She ate so much she could not budge. It cost us a pint of water to help her digestion. We gave it with good grace, for we were happy.

Tanit-Zerga did not say so, but her joy at knowing that I was thinking no more of the woman in the gold diadem and the emeralds was apparent. And really during those days I hardly thought of her. I thought only of the torrid heat to be avoided; of the water-skins which, if you wished to drink fresh water, had to be left for an hour in a cleft in the rocks; of the intense joy which seized you when you raised to your lips a leather goblet brimming with that life-saving water. I can say this with authority: That passion, spiritual or physical, is a thing for those who have eaten and drunk and rested.

It was five o'clock in the afternoon. The frightful heat was slackening. We had left a kind of rocky crevice where we had had a little nap. Seated on a huge rock, we were watching the reddening west.

I spread out the roll of paper on which Cegheir-ben-Cheikh had marked the stages of our journey as far as the road from the Sudan. I realized again with joy that his itinerary was exact and that I had followed it scrupulously.

"The evening of the day after tomorrow," I said, "we shall be setting out on the stage which will take us, by the next dawn to the waters at Telemsi. Once there, we shall not have to worry any more about water."

Tanit-Zerga's eyes danced in her thin face.

"And Gâo?" she asked.

"We will be only a week from the Niger. And Cegheir-ben-Cheikh said that at Telemsi one reached a road overhung with mimosa."

"I know the mimosa," she said. "They are the little yellow balls that melt in your hand, but I like the caper-flowers better. You will come with me to Gâo. My father, Sonni-Askia, was killed, as I told you, by the Awellimiden, but my people must have rebuilt the villages. They are used to that. You will see how you will be received."

"I will go, Tanit-Zerga, I promise you, but you also, you must promise me—"

"What? Oh, I guess. You must take me for a little fool if you believe me capable of speaking of things which might make trouble for my friend."

She looked at me as she spoke. Privation and great fatigue had chiseled the brown face where her great eyes shone. Since then I have had time to assemble the maps and compasses and to fix forever the spot where, for the first time, I understood the beauty of Tanit-Zerga's eyes.

There was a deep silence between us. It was she who broke it.

"Night is coming. We must eat so as to leave as soon as possible."

She stood up and went toward the rocks.

Almost immediately I heard her calling in an anguished voice that sent a chill through me.

"Come! Oh, come see!"

With a bound, I was at her side.

"The camel," she murmured. "The camel!"

I looked and a deadly shudder seized me.

Stretched out at full length on the other side of the rocks, his pale flanks knotted by convulsive spasms, El Mellen lay in anguish.

I need not say that we rushed to him in feverish haste. Of what El Mellen was dying, I did not know; I never have known. All camels are that way. They are at once the most enduring and the most delicate of beasts. They will travel for six months across the most frightful deserts with little food, without water, and seem only the better for it. Then one day when nothing is the matter they stretch out and give you the slip with disconcerting ease.

When Tanit-Zerga and I saw that there was nothing more to do we stood there without a word, watching his slackening spasms. When he breathed his last we felt that our life as well as his had gone.

It was Tanit-Zerga who spoke first.

"How far are we from the Sudan road?" she asked.

"We are a hundred and twenty miles from the springs of Telemsi," I replied. "We could make thirty miles by going toward Ifrouane, but the wells are not marked on that route."

"Then we must walk toward the springs of Telemsi," she said. "A hundred and twenty miles—that makes seven days?"

"Seven days at the least, Tanit-Zerga."

"How far is it to the first well?"

"Thirty-five miles."

The little girl's face contracted somewhat, but she braced up quickly.

"We must set out at once."

"Set out on foot, Tanit-Zerga?"

She stamped her foot. I marveled to see her so strong.

"We must go!" she repeated. "We are going to eat and drink and make Galé eat and drink, for we cannot carry all the tins and the water-skin is so heavy that we should not get three miles if we tried to carry it. We will put a little water in one of the tins, after emptying it through a little hole. That will be enough for tonight's stage, which will be eighteen miles without water. Tomorrow we will set out for another eighteen miles and we will reach the wells marked on the paper by Cegheir-ben-Cheikh."

"Oh," I murmured sadly, "if my shoulder were only well, I could carry the water-skin."

"It is as it is," said Tanit-Zerga. "You will take your carbine and two tins of meat. I shall take two more and the one filled with water. Come. We must leave in an hour if we wish to cover the eighteen miles. You know that when the sun is up the rocks are so hot we cannot walk."

I leave you to imagine in what sad silence we passed that hour which we had begun so happily and confidently. Without the little girl I believe I should have seated myself upon a rock and waited. Only Galé was happy.

"We must not let her eat too much," said Tanit-Zerga. "She would not be able to follow us, and tomorrow she must work. If she catches another *ourane* it will be for us."

You have walked in the desert. You know how terrible the first hours of the night are. When the moon comes up, huge and yellow, a sharp dust seems to rise in suffocating clouds. You move your jaws mechanically as if to crush the dust that finds its way into your throat like fire. Then usually a kind of lassitude, of drowsiness, follows. You walk without thinking. You forget where you are walking. You remember only when you stumble. Of course you stumble often. But anyway it is bearable.

"The night is ending," you say, "and with it the march. All in all, I am less tired than at the beginning."

The night ends but then comes the most terrible hour of all. You are perishing of thirst and shaking with cold. All the fatigue comes back at once. The horrible breeze that precedes the dawn is no comfort—quite the contrary. Every time you stumble, you say the next misstep will be the last.

That is what people feel and say even when they know that in a few hours they will have a good rest with food and water.

I was suffering terribly. Every step jolted my poor shoulder. At one time I wanted to stop, to sit down. Then I looked at Tanit-Zerga. She was walking ahead with her eyes almost closed. Her expression was an indefinable one of mingled suffering and determination. I closed my own eyes and went on.

Such was the first stage. At dawn we stopped in a hollow in the rocks. Soon the heat forced us to rise to seek a deeper crevice. Tanit-Zerga did not eat. Instead, she swallowed a little of her half-can of water. She lay drowsy all day. Galé ran about our rock, giving plaintive little cries.

I am not going to tell you about the second march. It was more horrible than anything you can imagine. I suffered all that it is humanly possible to suffer in the desert, but already I began to observe with infinite pity that my man's strength was outlasting the nervous force of my little companion. The poor child walked on without saying a word, chewing feebly one corner of her *haik* which she had drawn over her face. Galé followed.

The well toward which we were dragging ourselves was indicated on Cegheir-ben-Cheikh's paper by the one word *tissaririn*. *Tissaririn* is the plural of *tissarirt* and means "two isolated trees."

Day was dawning when finally I saw the two trees—two gum-trees. Hardly a league separated us from them. I gave a cry of joy.

"Courage, Tanit-Zerga, there is the well."

She drew her veil aside and I saw the poor anguished little face.

"So much the better," she murmured, "because otherwise—"

She could not even finish the sentence.

We finished the last half-mile almost at a run.

We already saw the hole, the opening of the well. Finally we reached it.

It was empty.

It is a strange sensation to be dying of thirst. At first the suffering is terrible. Then gradually it becomes less. You become partly unconscious. Ridiculous little things about your life occur to you, fly about in your brain like mosquitoes. I began to remember my history composition for the entrance examination of Saint-Cyr, "The Campaign of Marengo." Obstinately I repeated to myself:

"I have already said that the battery unmasked by Marmont at the moment of Kellerman's charge included eighteen pieces. No, I remember now, it was only twelve pieces. I am sure it was twelve pieces."

I kept on repeating—

"Twelve pieces."

Then I fell into a sort of coma.

I was recalled from it by feeling something like a red-hot iron on my forehead. I opened my eyes. Tanit-Zerga was bending over me. It was her hand which burnt so.

"Get up," she said. "We must go on."

"Go on, Tanit-Zerga! The desert is on fire. The sun is at the zenith. It is noon."

"We must go on," she repeated.

Then I saw that she was delirious.

She was standing erect. Her *haik* had fallen to the ground and little Galé, rolled up in a ball, was asleep on it.

Bareheaded, indifferent to the frightful sunlight, she kept repeating:

"We must go on."

A little sense came back to me.

"Cover your head, Tanit-Zerga. Cover your head."

"Come," she repeated, "let's go. Gâo is over there, not far away. I can feel it. I want to see Gâo again!"

I made her sit down beside me in the shadow of a rock. I realized that all strength had left her. The wave of pity that swept over me brought back my senses.

"Gâo is just over there, isn't it?" she asked.

Her gleaming eyes became imploring.

"Yes, dear little girl, Gâo is there, but you must lie down. The sun is fearful."

"Oh, Gâo, Gâo!" she repeated. "I know very well that I shall see Gâo again."

She sat up. Her fiery little hands gripped mine.

"Listen. I must tell you so you can understand how I know I shall see Gâo again."

"Tanit-Zerga, be quiet, my little girl, be quiet."

"No, I must tell you. A long time ago, on the bank of the river where there is water, at Gâo, where my father was a prince, there was— Well, one day, one feast day, there came from the interior of the country an old magician dressed in skins and feathers with a mask and a pointed head-dress, with castanets, and two serpents in a bag. On the village square, where all our people formed in a circle, he danced the *boussadilla*. I was in the first row and because I had a necklace of pink tourmaline he quickly saw that I was the daughter of a chief, so he spoke to me of the past, of the great Mandingue Empire over which my grandfathers had ruled, of our enemies, the fierce Kountas, of everything, and finally he said:

"'Have no fear, little girl.' Then he said again: 'Do not be afraid. Evil days may be in store for you, but what does that matter? For one day you will see Gâo gleaming on the horizon, no longer a servile Gâo reduced to the rank of a little Negro town, but the splendid Gâo of other days, the great capital of the country of the blacks, Gâo reborn, with its mosque of seven towers and fourteen cupolas of turquoise, with its houses with cool courts, its fountains, its watered gardens, all blooming with great red and white flowers. That will be for you the hour of deliverance and of royalty.'"

Tanit-Zerga was standing up. All about us the sun blazed on the *hamada,* burning it white.

Suddenly the child stretched out her arms. She gave a terrible cry.

"Gâo! There is Gâo!"

I looked at her.

"Gâo!" she repeated. "Oh, I know it well! There are the trees and the fountains, the cupolas and the towers, the palm-trees, the great red and white flowers. Gâo—"

Indeed, along the shimmering horizon rose a fantastic city with mighty buildings that towered, tier on tier, until they formed a rainbow. Wide-eyed, we stood and watched the terrible mirage quiver feverishly before us.

"Gâo!" I cried. "Gâo!"

And almost immediately I uttered another cry, this time of sorrow and of horror. Tanit-Zerga's little hand relaxed in mine. I had just time to catch the child in my arms and hear her murmur as in a whisper:

"And then that will be the day of deliverance—the day of deliverance and of royalty."

Several hours later I took the knife with which we had skinned the desert gazelle and in the sand at the foot of the rock where Tanit-Zerga had given up her spirit I made a little hollow where she was to rest.

When everything was ready, I wanted to look once more at that dear little face. Courage failed me for a moment; then I quickly drew the *haik* over the brown face and laid the body of the child in the hollow.

I had reckoned without Galé. The eyes of the mongoose had not left me during the whole time that I was about my sad duty. When she heard the first handfuls of sand fall on the *haik* she gave a sharp cry. I looked at her and saw her ready to spring, her eyes darting fire.

"Galé!" I implored; and I tried to stroke her.

She bit my hand and then leapt into the grave and began to dig, throwing the sand furiously aside.

I tried three times to chase her away. I felt that I should never finish my task and that even if I did Galé would stay there and disinter the body.

My carbine lay at my feet. A shot drew echoes from the immense empty desert. A moment later Galé also slept her last sleep, curled up, as I so often had seen her, against the neck of her mistress.

When the surface showed nothing more than a little mound of trampled sand I rose staggering and started off aimlessly into the desert toward the south.

Chapter XX

The Circle Is Complete

A T THE FOOT OF THE VALLEY OF THE MIA, AT THE PLACE WHERE THE JACKAL HAD cried the night Saint-Avit told me he had killed Morhange, another jackal, or perhaps the same one, howled again.

Immediately I had a feeling that this night would see the irremediable fulfilled.

We were seated that evening, as before, on the poor veranda improvised outside our dining-room. The floor was of plaster, the balustrade of twisted branches; four posts supported a thatched roof.

I have already said that from the veranda one could look far out over the desert. As he finished speaking, Saint-Avit rose and stood leaning his elbows on the railing. I followed him.

"And then—" I said.

He looked at me.

"And then what? Surely you know what all the newspapers told—how, in the country of the Awellimiden I was found dying of hunger and thirst by an expedition under the command of Captain Aymard and taken to Timbuktu. I was delirious for a month afterward. I have never known what I may have said during those spells of burning fever. You may be sure the officers of the Timbuktu Club did not feel it incumbent upon them to tell me. When I told them of my adventures as they are related in the report of the Morhange-Saint-Avit Expedition I could see well enough from the cold politeness with which they received my explanations that the official version which I gave them differed at certain points from the fragments which had escaped me in my delirium.

"They did not press the matter. It remains understood that Captain Morhange died from a sunstroke and that I buried him on the border of the Tarhit watercourse, three marches from Timissau. Everybody can detect that there are things missing in my story. Doubtless they guess at some mysterious drama, but proofs are another matter. Because of the impossibility of collecting them, they prefer to smother what could only become a silly scandal. Now you know all the details as well as I."

"And—she?" I asked timidly.

He smiled triumphantly. It was triumph at having led me to think no longer of Morhange or of his crime, the triumph of feeling that he had succeeded in imbuing me with his own madness.

"Yes," he said. "She! For six years I have learned nothing more about her, but I see her; I talk with her. I am thinking now how I shall reenter her presence. I shall throw myself at her feet and say simply: 'Forgive me. I rebelled against your law. I did not know. But now I know and you see that, like Lieutenant Ghiberti, I have come back.'

"'Family, honor, country,' said old Le Mesge, 'you will forget all for her.' Old Le Mesge is a stupid man, but he speaks from experience. He knows, he who has seen broken before Antinea the wills of the fifty ghosts in the red marble hall.

"And now will you in your turn ask me: 'What is this woman?' Do I know myself? And besides what difference does it make? What does her past and the mystery of her origin matter to me; what does it matter whether she is the true descendant of the God of the Sea and the sublime Lagides, or the daughter of a Polish drunkard and a harlot of the Marbeuf quarter?

"At the time when I was foolish enough to be jealous of Morhange these questions might have made some difference to the ridiculous self-esteem that civilized people mix up with passion. But I have held Antinea's body in my arms. I no longer wish to know any other, nor to know whether the fields are in blossom, or what will become of the human spirit.

"I do not wish to know. Or rather it is because I have too exact a vision of that future that I pretend to destroy myself in the only destiny that is worthwhile; a nature unfathomed and virgin, a mysterious love.

"*A nature unfathomed and virgin.* I must explain myself. One Winter day in a large city all streaked with the soot that falls from the black chimneys of factories and of those horrible houses in the suburbs, I attended a funeral.

"We followed the hearse in the mud. The church was new, damp and poor. Aside from two or three people, relatives struck down by a dull sorrow, everyone had just one idea: To find some pretext to get away. Those who went as far as the cemetery were those who did not find an excuse. I see the gray walls and the cypresses, those trees of sun and shade, so beautiful in the country of southern France, against the low, purple hills. I see the horrible undertakers in greasy jackets and shiny top hats. I see— No, I'll stop; it's too horrible.

"Near the wall, in a remote plot, a grave had been dug in frightful, yellow, pebbly clay. It was there that they left the dead man whose name I no longer remember.

"While they were lowering the casket I looked at my hands, those hands which in that strangely lighted country had pressed the hands of Antinea. A great pity for my body seized me, a great fear of what threatened it in these cities of mud. So, I said to myself, it may be that this body, this dear body, will come to such an end. No, no, my body, precious above all other treasures, I swear to you that I will spare you that ignominy; you shall not rot under a registered number in the filth of a suburban cemetery. Your brothers in love, the fifty knights of orichalc, await you, mute and grave, in the red marble hall. I shall take you back to them.

"A mysterious love. Shame to him who retails the secrets of his loves. The Sahara lays its impassable barrier about Antinea; that is why the most unreasonable requirements of this woman are, in reality, more modest and chaste than your marriage will be, with its vulgar public show, the bans, the invitations and announcements.

"I think that is all I have to tell you. No, there is still one thing more. I told you a while ago about the red marble hall. South of Cherchell, to the west of the Mazafran river, on a hill which in the early morning emerges from the mists of the Mitidja, there is a mysterious stone pyramid. The natives call it 'The Tomb of the Christian.' That is where the body of Antinea's ancestress, Cleopatra Selene, daughter of Mark Antony and Cleopatra, was laid to rest. Though it is placed in the path of invasions, this tomb has kept its treasure. No one has ever been able to discover the painted room where the beautiful body reposes in a glass casket.

"All that the ancestress has been able to do the descendant will be able to surpass in grim magnificence. In the center of the red marble hall, on the rock whence comes the plaint of the gloomy fountain, a platform is reserved. It is there, on an orichalc throne, with the Egyptian head-dress and the golden serpent on her brow and the trident of Neptune in her hand, that the marvelous woman I have told you about will be ensconced on that day when the hundred and twenty niches hollowed out in a circle around her throne shall each have received its willing prey.

"When I left Ahaggar you remember that it was niche number 55 that was to be mine. Since then, I have never stopped calculating and I conclude that it is in number 80 or 85 that I shall repose. But any calculations based upon so fragile a foundation as a woman's whim may be erroneous. That's why I am getting more and more nervous. I must hurry, I tell myself. I must hurry.

"I must hurry," I repeated, as if I were in a dream.

He raised his head with an indefinable expression of joy. His hand trembled with happiness when he shook mine.

"You will see," he repeated excitedly; "you will see."

Ecstatically, he took me in his arms and held me there a long moment.

An extraordinary happiness swept over both of us while alternately laughing and crying like children we kept repeating:

"We must hurry. We must hurry."

Suddenly there sprang up a slight breeze that made the tufts of thatch in the roof rustle. The sky, pale lilac, grew paler still and suddenly a great yellow rent tore it in the east. Dawn broke over the empty desert. From within the stockade came dull noises, a bugle call, the rattle of chains. The post was waking up.

For several seconds we stood there silent, our eyes fixed on the southern route by which one reaches Temassinin and Ahaggar.

A rap on the dining-room door behind us made us start.

"Come in," said André de Saint-Avit in a voice which had become suddenly hard.

The quartermaster, Chatelain, stood before us.

"What do you want of me at this hour?" Saint-Avit asked brusquely.

The non-com stood at attention.

"Excuse me, Captain, but a native was discovered near the post last night by the patrol. He was not trying to hide. As soon as he had been brought here he asked to be led before the commanding officer. It was midnight and I didn't want to disturb you."

"Who is this native?"

"A Targa, Captain."

"A Targa? Go get him."

Chatelain stepped aside. Escorted by one of our native soldiers, the man stood behind him.

They came out on the terrace.

The new arrival, six feet tall, was indeed a Targa. The light of dawn fell upon his blue-black cotton robes. One could see his great dark eyes flashing.

When he was opposite my companion I saw a tremor, immediately suppressed, run through both men.

They looked at each other for an instant in silence.

Then, bowing, and in a very calm voice, the Targa spoke.

"Peace be with you, Lieutenant de Saint-Avit."

In the same calm voice, Andre answered him—

"Peace be with you, Cegheir-ben-Cheikh."

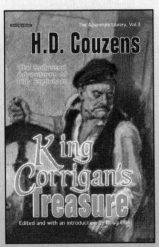

Need A Little Adventure?

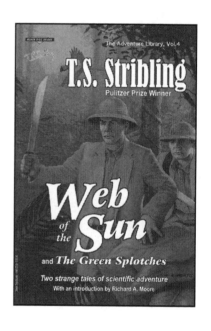
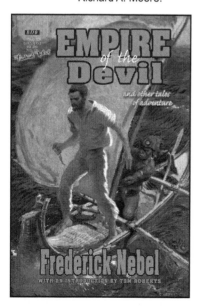

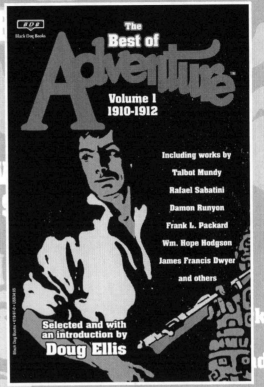

More adventure
from Black Dog Books

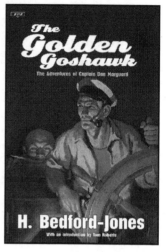
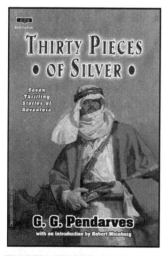

More Mysteries
from Black Dog Books

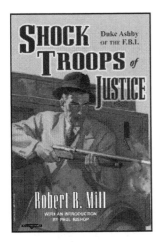
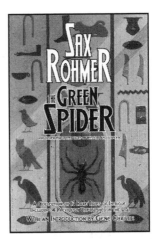

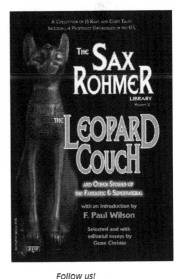

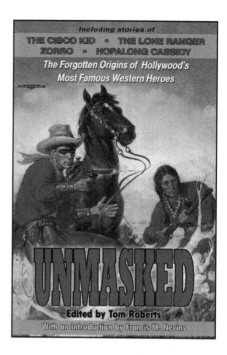

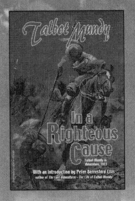
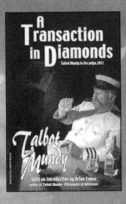
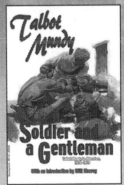

LESTER DENT LIBRARY

Before he began to chronicle the exploits of Doc Savage, Lester Dent produced scores of novels, shorter fiction and articles spanning the range of pulp fiction genres—tales of two-fisted action, mysteries, aviation adventures, war stories, romances and Westerns. Unavailable for decades, these works have been collected and are now available for the first time in book form!

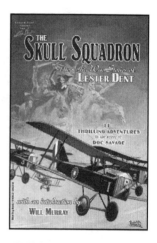

DEAD MEN'S BONES
Trade paperback
239 pages / $24.95
Eight thrilling air-adventure stories.

THE SKULL SQUADRON
Trade paperback
227 pages / $24.95
Eleven thrilling tales set against
the backdrop of World War I.

HELL'S HOOFPRINTS
Trade paperback
237 pages / $24.95
Eighteen wild West tales!
"A GOLD MINE in reading!"—**Amazon**

FIST OF FURY
Trade paperback
278 pages / $27.95
Four novel-length adventures
of two-fisted Curt Flagg.

Order these and other titles through our website:
www.blackdogbooks.net

The Samovar Girl
Frederick F. Moore

According to the Evidence
Hugh Pendexter

Order these and other titles from our website.

www.blackdogbooks.net | info@blackdogbooks.net.
Twitter.com/blackdogbooks1
Facebook.com/blackdogbooks1

Order these and other titles from our website.

www.blackdogbooks.net | info@blackdogbooks.net.
Twitter.com/blackdogbooks1
Facebook.com/blackdogbooks1